Christmas Hotel Reunion

Beauty for Ashes

WELL OF LIFE
PUBLISHING

Christmas Hotel Reunion

Christmas Hotel Series
Book Six

by

Saundra Staats McLemore

Christmas Hotel Series

Book Six

Christmas Hotel Reunion
Beauty for Ashes
By
Saundra Staats McLemore

First published by
Desert Breeze Publishing 2017
© Saundra Staats McLemore 2017
This new and revised edition 2019

Paperback ISBN: 978-1-7336122-4-1
Also available as an eBook
eBook ISBN: 978-1-7336122-3-4

Content Editor: Chris Wright
Cover Artist: Gwen Phifer

Published by

Well of Life Publishing
Ohio
United States of America

http://www.saundrastaatsmclemore.com

Other Books by Saundra Staats McLemore

The Staats Family Chronicles Series

Abraham and Anna – Book One of Staats Family Chronicles Series – Available now
Joy out of Ashes – Book Two of Staats Family Chronicles Series – Available now

Christmas Hotel Series

Book One: Christmas Hotel
(New Edition) Available now
Book Two: Christmas for Lucy
(New Edition) Available now
Book Three: Christmas Redemption
(New Edition) Available now
Book Four: Christmas Pact (New Edition)
Paperback available now
eBook available October 11, 2019
Book Five: Christmas Love and Mercy
(New Edition)
Paperback available now
EBook available November 01, 2019
Book Six: Christmas Hotel Reunion
(New Edition)
Paperback available now
eBook Available November 15, 2019

Dedication and Acknowledgment

Christmas Hotel Reunion is dedicated in memory of my father William Warren Staats. He died from complications suffered with Alzheimer's disease on July 21, 1997.

Also, I dedicate *Christmas Hotel Reunion* to Bertha Staats, the best step-Mother a woman could have. My father William Warren Staats chose well. Bertha was my father's soul-mate. God bless Bertha Staats and all the caregivers of this world.

Acknowledgements

I thank Franklin, Kentucky, historian Denise Shoulders for information regarding businesses around the Franklin, Kentucky square in 1998. She graciously answered my questions, and much of the information I was able to use for the accuracy of pertinent information.

I would like to offer a special thank you to Sid and Jill Broderson for granting me permission to have my characters Christopher and Jerilyn Wright and their children, throughout the Christmas Hotel series, reside in their historical home at 210 South College Street in Franklin, Kentucky. This beautiful home is known in Franklin as the *Montague House* or the *Malone House*. The Italianate structure was built around 1860 by William Clement Montague.

Another special thank you to Barbara Beasley Smith Swearingen for allowing me to have her father Dr. L. F. Beasley "visit" the story.

I offer a special appreciation to my loyal readers. You have sent me letters of love for the Christmas

Hotel series and have recommended the story of Christopher and Jerilyn Wright and their children and friends to your friends and family. An author cannot have a greater approval of his or her work than by the word-of-mouth from readers. Without you, my readers, I would never have completed these six books. Thank you and God bless you.

I also thank my friends and family members who contributed stories about those they have known in the grips of the horrendous disease: Alzheimer's. Many of your stories I was able to incorporate into this story for Jerilyn and Christopher.

I thank our Lord and Savior Jesus Christ for the inspiration He provides for every story I write.

"I have been young, and now am old; yet have I not seen the righteous forsaken, nor his seed begging bread. He is ever merciful, and lendeth; and his seed is blessed."

Psalm 37: 25-26

To love a person is to learn the song that is in their heart, and to sing it to them when they have forgotten.

Arne Garborg

1851-1924

"Never be afraid to trust an unknown future to a known God."
Corrie ten Boom
1892-1983

"Where Does She Go"...
Poem by John E. Moss
Jamestown, Kentucky

In the early morning hours,
I weep for my Sweetheart,
Her mind is going to a far away place,
Where I cannot follow.
In silence she sits,
Without me...
Even though I am beside her...

I weep for my Sweetheart,
And cannot realize the horror,
The frustration,
Of losing the sense,
Of one's own self...
Where does she go when she sits,
In silence...

There is no laughter,
Or soft spoken word,
Anymore,
Where she treads with small steps,
Here or there,
Or stands in silence,
Just beyond the doorway.

Oh my love,
You do not hear my words,
Or see my tears,
But I am beside you,
Despite the hour day or night.
Rest this evening and do not stir,
I am here... only a breath away.

Permission granted to Saundra Staats McLemore by John E. Moss of Jamestown, Kentucky. "Where Does She Go" was published in the February, 2016 issue of *Kentucky Monthly Magazine*.

Chapters

Chapter One

Decisions

"Remember ye not the former things, neither consider the things of old. Behold, I will do a new thing; now it shall spring forth; shall ye not know it? I will even make a way in the wilderness, and rivers in the desert."
Isaiah 43:18-19

Monday Morning
June 01, 1998
Chris peeked in on his mother. She sat in her home office, staring at the screen on the Brother Word Processor. At times, such as these, he wished he could see into her mind and know her thoughts. She had not completed a manuscript in two years. Her days as an author had ended, and the words on the pages were now jumbled ideas and full of typos. Chris quietly pulled the door closed leaving his mom to her thoughts. He needed to see his dad.

Retracing his steps, he walked back into the homey living room and looked around. A conglomeration of family pictures sat on the mantel, lined the walls, and were strewn haphazardly across the baby grand piano. He could mentally picture his dad and sisters Lily, Carrie Emeline, and Lydia Grace playing the piano and singing. He and his brother Ken would harmonize with them, as the two brothers did not play any musical instruments. The gift of playing musical instruments was passed down from his grandmother to only his dad and three sisters.

His parents' dog, Bobby, lifted his head from his extra-large doggy bed. Bobby struggled to his feet and wagged his tail in greeting. The poor old dog was now afflicted with arthritis but never missed a chance to greet Chris. He was the only remaining pup from a litter born a decade ago.

"How ya doing, ol' boy?" He petted the dog and scratched him behind the ears. "You go lie back down." Bobby hobbled back to his bed and flopped down, expelling a loud groan.

Chris figured his dad was in the workshop, so he headed out back. The screen door wobbled and creaked when he opened it. *I need to fix this door for Dad.* He found his dad in the workshop, but not working on a project, as Chris was accustomed. Dad sat on the edge of the workbench, feet braced on a sawhorse, chin in hands, elbows propped on his knees, and looking out one of the open windows. It was a pleasant day, so Dad had the shop's AC turned off and the windows wide open. A slight breeze crossed the shed, and all three overhead fans turned. The radio played music from the forties, and Chris heard one of his parents' favorite songs, "I Know Why (and So Do You)" playing.

Dad turned when the squeaky old door opened, and Chris watched him discreetly wipe the tear off his cheek. "Good morning, son," he greeted in a croaky voice. Clearing his throat, he asked, "What brings you here today?"

Dad slid from the workbench, and the two men hugged. They sat on one of the wood benches his dad had constructed. Woodworking, once a hobby, and now a small business, was at times too much for Dad. His main requests and specialties were in his intricate birdhouses and decorative outdoor benches. Today, his hands were empty. Chris's father worried about the health of his cherished wife. This wasn't the first time he'd found his dad lost in prayer or thought. "Dad, I hope I'm not interrupting."

"Chris, a visit from you is never an interruption."

"Are you worried about the trip to Carrie Emeline's, and the cruise to Alaska? If you don't think Mom is up to the trip this year, we'll all understand. When all of us kids gave you those tickets for the Alaskan cruise on your anniversary,

Mom was better. Now she doesn't always know everyone or her environment. We won't have hurt feelings if you don't think you should go."

Dad raked his fingers through his hair – one of the habits Chris had acquired from his father when he was anxious or nervous. "I don't know, Chris. I'd like to try and make the trip. We'll fly to Carrie Emeline's first, and then I can decide whether we should board the ship or not. I can always give the tickets to Carrie Emeline and Marcus. They'd appreciate the vacation to Alaska, so the tickets won't go to waste."

Chris ran his own fingers through his hair and exhaled. "Lori Anna and I have been discussing you and Mom. Maybe Lori Anna and the children and I should move in here. I think you could use some help."

With one eyebrow raised, Dad grinned. "Do you think I'm an old man and no longer capable of taking care of the house and your mother?"

Chris felt the heat rise in his face. He didn't intend to embarrass his dad. "No, but I worry about you overdoing things. You *are* the youngest eighty-five-year-old I know. However, the doctor told you to take it easy after your heart attack. I know it was mild, and it's been two years, but I have yet to see you slow down. Lori Anna and I conferred, and we agree it's best. We want you to *want* our help.

Would you be okay with us moving in with you and Mom?"

Dad blew out his breath. "I've considered this, too. Yes, I'm okay with it, son. I had always hoped one of you five children would take over the family home. When would you want to move here?"

"We can be packed over the next two weeks, and move in before you leave on the trip."

"What about your farm? You have horses, cattle, barnyard animals, and crops. You added on two bedrooms when you adopted Abigail and Michael, and Olivia was raised on the farm. Your three children are attached to their home. Would you sell everything?"

"No, we wouldn't. I've been in contact with Lydia Grace and Jacob. Lydia Grace has always been fond of my home, even before I was born. She and Jacob have agreed to move here from New York and take over the farm, freeing up Lori Anna and me to move here and help with Mom. Olivia is nearly ten, and she'll be a big help with Mom. She's very mature and wants to be a registered nurse or a photographer someday." He chuckled. "What a wide range of career choices."

Dad shifted on his seat and nodded his head periodically. Although his dad was now elderly, he was still handsome and still very tall with a straight back. His once dark brown, wavy hair was now gray and cut short.

"Yes, Chris, Olivia is a very perceptive child and whatever career she chooses, she will excel. I agree that Olivia will be a great helper for her grandmother, and I also realize your sister has loved your farm even longer than you have. Your mother and I will enjoy having Lydia Grace, Jacob, and Anthony close by."

"I thought you'd like that part, Dad. In reality, the children will adjust just fine. Olivia loves the visits with the patients at Vanderbilt Hospital, and she helps when Lori Anna photographs the patients for social reasons, as you know, rather than medical. Abigail at seven and Michael at five are mature for their ages, too. They enjoy helping on the farm, and they can continue to do so after school and in the summers, if they want."

"What about you, son? Will you adjust? You've poured your heart and soul into your pastoral duties, Christmas Hotel, your family, *and* your farm. You've done an admirable job. I must warn you, taking care of your mother is heartbreaking. I never know when she'll be coherent. She's *usually* fine until the evening, but not always. They call it sundowning, but you know about the term."

Chris looked around the workshop where he had spent many years working beside his dad. He smiled. All his dad's tools were laid out in precise order and cleaned to perfection, as always. Breathing deeply, he inhaled the pleasant smell of the clean air and the wood shavings on the floor. He recalled a conversation he and his dad had with their dear friend, the retired Dr. Beasley. As Dr. Beasley explained in layman language, "Sundowning is a term coined due to the timing of the patient's confusion. A multitude of behavioral problems begin to occur when the sun sets. Sundowning generally occurs in the patient's middle stage of Alzheimer's, and patients understand this is not normal. Jerilyn does realize when she begins to fade away, as she calls it. Sometimes the confusion is like a curtain coming down from one moment to the next."

His dad continued, "However, Chris, it doesn't mean her mornings and afternoons are *always* lucid. She has her good days and bad days. The hardest part is keeping her away from the oven and the range top. She still wants to cook. I thank God I discovered the pot of beans on the stove when I did last month. All the liquid had boiled away, and the pot burned and had just caught fire. I was able to put out the flames before the kitchen burned. Now, I keep a baby monitor in whatever room I leave her, and I have the extension with me at all times." He pointed to the workbench where the monitor sat.

"Dad, it's because of situations, as you just

described, Lori Anna and I want to be here. We'll be able to take some of the pressure off you, so you can relax as much as possible. We want you to enjoy your time with Mom. It will also give you more time to spend with at least three of your grandchildren."

"That alone will give me great pleasure, Chris. I appreciate you and Lori Anna wanting to do this. It's going to be a sacrifice on the part of your family."

"Not nearly as much of a sacrifice as you and Mom have done for me through the years, and you know Lori Anna loves our family home. She's always said it's the prettiest home in Franklin, and I agree. However, I'm also a bit prejudiced."

"I agree, too, Chris."

"Is it a deal, Dad?"

They shook hands. "It's a deal, son."

"Thanks, Dad. I think this is a good plan for all of us."

Chapter Two

New Beginnings

*"Thou wilt shew me the path of life: in thy
presence is fulness of joy; at thy right hand
there are pleasures for evermore."*
Psalm 16:11

Monday
June 15, 1998
Lydia Grace arrived at Chris's farm along with the
moving van. She jumped from her car as soon as
she pulled up beside the van, ran to her brother,
and gave him a big hug and planted a kiss on his
cheek.

"Chris, I'm so happy you were able to convince
Dad you should move into our homeplace. Of
course, if you hadn't been successful, I would have
been here to talk to him with you. This is the best
scenario for Mom and Dad. I'm a bit selfish,
though. I get to live on the farm I've adored since I
was eight. *And* because you've increased the size

9

from three bedrooms to five and from two bathrooms to three, I have plenty of room for Anthony when he's home from Juilliard, as well as his friends, Jacob's, and my guests from New York."

"Whoa. Slow down, sis. How much coffee did you drink?" He smiled, widened his eyes, and shook his head.

"Well, it was a long drive from the city." She looked at him and pouted. "I've been driving for seventeen hours with only four stops."

"Just teasing. I've missed you. You must be exhausted." He kissed the top of her head. "I can't believe we'll practically be neighbors. New York City was such a long way off. Now I can see you whenever I want, without having to wait until Christmas."

"I've missed you, too." She and Chris walked around the rooms of the house and directed the movers where to place furniture. The boxes were marked for the various rooms to deposit. "It appears you've already moved your things out, Chris."

"Pretty much so. Lori Anna and I wanted you and Jacob to have as much room as possible for your belongings. We've emptied the house, stored some things in the barn, and been living at Mom and Dad's for the past two days." The movers brought Lydia Grace and Jacob's bed into the master bedroom. "At home, Lori Anna and I have set up our bedroom, and the children's bedrooms upstairs, and we've set up our living room furniture in the added-on room behind Mom's office so we have plenty of privacy when needed."

Lydia Grace held the headboard stable, then the footboard, while Chris snapped the rails in place. They moved the bed frame between two windows, laid the wooden slats across the rails, and set the box spring and the mattress on the rails. "Since all five bedrooms upstairs are in use, we lost the guest bedroom, but Lori Anna thought it important each child maintains his or her privacy."

"You have nothing to worry about, little brother. Whenever you need a guest room, I will have two for you! Jacob and I will have our bedroom, and Anthony will have his own when he's home from college. Jacob and I'll share one of the bedrooms for an office, so we'll have two spare bedrooms. I think this'll work out perfectly. I feel complete peace in moving here. I believe this is the new path the Lord has set upon our family. Jacob and I will be very happy here on the farm."

"I hope so, sis. I really want Mom and Dad to enjoy their last days together, no matter how many days it'll be." In the living room, they set up the television and connected the VCR. "When's Jacob arriving?"

"He's still sorting things in his office and working with the piano movers. He and our piano will be arriving in two days, along with Anthony. The piano is a special move and must be handled by trained piano transporters."

"It'll be good to see Jacob and Anthony. The whole family only gets together at Thanksgiving and/or Christmas. We've been so spread out around the country."

They finished in the living room and moved into the kitchen. They each grabbed one of the boxes marked "kitchen" and unloaded them on the large bare oak table in the center of the room.

Lydia Grace glanced around the bare kitchen. "I'll need to stop at the *Piggly Wiggly* and stock the icebox and pantry."

"You'll find some things already stocked, sis. There's canned items provided courtesy of the chefs at Christmas Hotel in the pantry." Chris opened the pantry door to show her. "Voila, sis. I also made certain you had a block of ice in the icebox. I still pick up the ice block each morning at the *Woodburn General Store*. I'm sure you remember the place, and Mr. Gentry still runs it."

"Really? Why, Mr. Gentry must be at least ninety."

"He is, and his wife still bakes pies ... *and* his

oldest son is still doctoring in Franklin! If you'll remember, Dr. Gentry delivered Olivia."

Lydia Grace smiled. "It's nice to know some things never change."

"I agree. Oh, there's also a load of wood stacked beside the stove." Chris pointed in the direction. "In fact, I have seasoned wood for the stove and the fireplace pre-cut for at least three years stacked out back by the stock barn." He cocked his head and looked at her. "By the way, do you plan on leaving the kitchen old-fashioned with an icebox and a wood-burning cook stove, *and* the hall bathroom with the porcelain claw-footed tub and the pull chain toilet?"

She chuckled. "Chris, I'm not changing a thing. I love the old-fashioned bathroom. It reminds me of the century–and-a-half-old water closets at Christmas Hotel. As far as the ice box, remember you have the Cadillac of ice boxes: four doors!" She winked and smiled at him. "Regarding the wood stove, I plan to hold classes teaching ladies and any interested men and children, how to cook on the wood-burning cook stove – and also hearth cooking in the fireplace in the living room. I think there'll be many people in Simpson County fascinated by the art of cooking like our ancestors did over a hundred years ago." She examined the wood stove closer. "Do you still rub the surface down with lard?"

"Yes, ma'am. The only way to treat this heirloom."

"Where do you get lard in this day and age?"

"Where else, but at the *Woodburn General Store*. Many of the farmers in Simpson County still butcher their own hogs, and Mr. Gentry has the only business around where items from yesteryear can be purchased. He still has the old pickle barrel, *and* filled with pickles near the entrance! Go visit the store."

"I will, Chris."

The movers finished unloading, and Lydia Grace paid and thanked them before they left. She wiped her forehead with a hand towel and flopped down on the sofa with Chris. "Whew, I'm glad this part's over. After the long drive and placing the items in the proper rooms here, I'm exhausted." She looked at her brother and smiled. "I couldn't have done this without you, Chris. Thank you."

"Don't mention it, sis. I was glad to help." He looked at her with his brows knit together. "So, I'm curious. Will you retire from playing the concert circuit? I can't imagine you and Jacob leaving those exciting, and lucrative I might add, world tours behind."

"No, not completely. However, I will slow down. At fifty-two, the toll of hopping planes, moving from city to city, living in different hotels and out of a suitcase is beginning to wear me down. It's not nearly as exciting as it was twenty-five years ago or even ten years ago. I'm happy being home in Franklin, Kentucky and living at a slower pace. I also plan to teach piano to young students, as Dad's mom did back in the twenties."

"Sounds like you have your time on the farm planned out, but what about Jacob? Does he feel the same?"

"Completely. He's ready for a slower pace, too. He's excited about living in a small southern town. He's lived his whole life in New York City, and in the luxury apartment building at 640 Park Avenue. I don't think I ever told you, but his grandfather first moved there when the building opened in nineteen fourteen. Jacob's parents took the apartment over during World War II when Jacob was born in '42. I dare say I was impressed living there with him. New York is exciting, and we'll keep the apartment to use when we're in the city. However, I'm ready to return home. There really is 'no place like home,' Chris."

He chuckled. "You sound like Dorothy from *The Wizard of Oz*." He patted her hand. "All kidding aside, I'm really glad to have you home, sis. I've missed you." He squeezed her hand. "You're the sibling closest to my age. Oh, I almost forgot." He reached into his pocket. "Here are two sets of house keys: main doors and storm doors. If you need more keys, Mr. Gentry can make them." He stood. "I'm going to head home now. You have the main rooms all set up, and Lori Anna should be home soon. It still feels strange calling 210 South College Street home again." Chris thought again about leaving his farm home. He'd lived there for the past two decades. He glanced around the living room. *This place has been my little baby.*

Lydia Grace stood, patted his hand, and smiled. "I promise to take good care of your home, little brother. Of course, you're welcome here anytime. You'll need to teach Jacob and me how to care for the animals."

"I'll come back after supper tonight to feed the animals and bed them down for the night. I'll take care of them until you and Jacob are ready to handle everything. By the way, when you get a chance, we do need to discuss Dad and Mom's anniversary vacation. Lori Anna is visiting Vanderbilt Hospital today with Olivia, but they'll be home in time for supper. Abigail and Michael are helping Dad." He laughed. "I wonder how much help they're providing. You're going to want supper later, so why not stop by home and have dinner with us. I know you want to see Mom and Dad."

"Sounds like a plan, little brother. I wouldn't miss it. I just need to take a quick shower and I'll be there." She stood on tiptoes and kissed Chris's cheek. "Thanks, again."

Chapter Three

Vacation Peace

"Those things, which ye have both learned, and received, and heard, and seen in me, do: and the God of peace shall be with you."
Philippians 4:9

Monday Morning
June 22, 1998
Christopher tossed and turned all night. He still was unsure of this trip to Bellingham, Washington to visit Carrie Emeline and Marcus and then onto the Alaskan cruise. Although he and Jerilyn had visited their daughter and her family every summer since Carrie Emeline moved there back in '75, it was different now. Jerilyn's Alzheimer's had progressed in the last year. Jerilyn had always wanted to take the cruise to Alaska. Had he waited too long?

At first light, Christopher kneeled beside their bed to pray. *Dear Heavenly Father, I want to take Jerilyn on this trip, at least to visit Carrie Emeline and Marcus and our five grandchildren in Bellingham. I think she'll have a good time.*

However, if Thou doesn't think it's wise for us to take the ship up to Alaska, let me know. My desire is for Jerilyn to have a memorable time and not be scared. I love her so much, Lord. Please help me protect her. Thou knowest how I worry she'll outlive me. I don't want her separated from me, although I know our children will care for her if I die first. I realize none of us knows what tomorrow holds, but we know Thou holds our hand. I understand I'm not supposed to worry and fret, but it's hard not to, Lord. I vowed to love and protect her more than fifty-six years ago. Please go ahead of us, Lord, and please direct my path. In the name of Thy Son Jesus I pray, Amen.

Christopher leaned heavily on the bed to rise from the floor. Although he was in good physical shape, his eighty-five-year-old bones creaked, and the arthritis didn't help. He suspected knee and hip replacements were in the not too distant future. Jerilyn slept soundly. *I'm glad she's able to sleep.*

He entered the bathroom and scrutinized his face in the mirror. Lines etched his forehead, and the bags under his eyes appeared larger than normal. *I'm tired, Lord. Give me strength for myself, and for Jerilyn too.* He showered, shaved, dressed, and headed downstairs to start a pot of coffee, while Jerilyn slept. He glanced toward the front door where their luggage was neatly stacked and ready to be loaded into Chris's pick-up. Chris and Lori Anna would be driving them to the airport in Nashville, and Lydia Grace would be here in an hour to pick up Olivia, Abigail, and Michael to take them to the farm for the day.

Christopher walked into the kitchen, and Lori Anna was already bustling around. He inhaled the pleasant aroma of fresh perked coffee and sausage patties frying in the old iron skillet. The wonderful familiar smells permeated the air.

"Good morning, Dad." She placed her hand on his arm, tiptoed, and kissed him on the cheek. "I hope you slept well."

He ran his fingers through his still damp hair. "Sufficient, I suppose."

He saw her frown before she turned down the burner under the sausage, poured each of them a steaming mug of coffee, and sat beside him at the table. She placed her hand over his. "Are you okay, Dad?"

Lori Anna's concern touched him. Christopher and Jerilyn loved her like another daughter. She was a wonderful wife to Chris and mother to their three children. Chris chose well, like he had with Jerilyn. He patted her hand. "Nothing the Lord can't help me with, dear." He sighed, took a sip of the coffee, and looked into her big brown, anxious eyes. "I'll be fine. I think I need to trust more in

Him." He pointed upward, and she smiled.

"We all need to trust Him more often, Dad." She rose and turned the burner back up on the sausage patties and poured the usual fourteen already beaten eggs from the bowl and into the skillet to scramble. The timer went off on the oven; she grabbed two pot holders, pulled the biscuits from the oven, and sat the baking sheet on a towel on the counter top.

Chris walked in the back door and kissed Lori Anna. He was sweating from his morning run. Lori Anna smiled. "You have time for a shower, Chris, but you'd better hurry. Breakfast will be on the table within fifteen minutes. I just need to make the sausage gravy, scramble the eggs, and set the table."

"Morning, Dad." Chris squeezed his dad's shoulder and hurried up the stairs.

Christopher scooted his chair back from the table. "I'd better go upstairs and see about Jerilyn."

"Please wake the kids, ask them to dress, and come to breakfast, Dad. Their clothes are lying on their chairs." She returned to setting the table for the seven of them.

Jerilyn sat at her vanity, brushing her hair, still wrapped in a towel, fresh from her shower. Powder residue remained on her shoulders. Christopher stood for a moment watching his wife. This morning, she appeared to be herself. He looked up to the ceiling. *I Thank Thee, Lord.* Walking straight to Jerilyn, he kissed her on the cheek, placed his hand on her shoulder rubbed the remainder of the powder into her soft skin, and inhaled deeply. She smelled fresh and as always, she was still very beautiful to him. A few lines in her face, silver streaked her shoulder-length wavy brown hair, but he saw the twenty-year-old woman he fell in love with. Although she had carried and birthed four of their five children, she was still slender. Age had not diminished her beauty inside and out. "Is there anything I can help you with, Jerilyn? Lori Anna is putting breakfast on the table."

"I'm fine, Christopher. Go help her, and I'll be down in ten minutes. I just need to dress."

"Your traveling clothes are laid out on the chair. Remember we're flying to visit Carrie Emeline today."

"We are? Wonderful! I *do* miss her." She smiled up at him. "I feel great this morning," she added and patted his arm. "Now go help Lori Anna."

She didn't remember.

Jerilyn, Chris, and the three children arrived in the kitchen at the same time.

"Who wants orange juice?" Christopher sat a mug of coffee in front of Jerilyn, relieved. *She's wearing the correct clothes. Is this my message from You, Lord? We'll be okay on this trip?*

Olivia, Abigail, and Michael simultaneously shouted, "Me!"

He poured their juice and set out the preferred butter and strawberry preserves for Olivia and Abigail's biscuits. They did not care for gravy on their biscuits.

The family held hands, and Christopher asked the blessing. Throughout breakfast he watched Jerilyn. She didn't talk much, concentrating on eating. However, it was morning, and she was at her best in the morning ... at least for now. He looked across the table at Lori Anna who was watching him. She smiled, nodded, winked, and discreetly showed one thumb up. At 5:30 Lydia Grace arrived. Following hugs and kisses, she turned to her nieces and nephew. "Are you ready to head to the farm?"

"Yes, Aunt Lydia Grace," answered Olivia for all of them.

"Will we get to ride our ponies?"

"Oh, Michael, I think arrangements can be made." Lydia Grace tousled his hair. "However, we first need to muck out their stalls and feed them. Your Uncle Jacob and cousin Anthony are milking the cows as we speak." She glanced at Michael's feet. "You'd better put on your farm boots. Those shoes look new."

Lori Anna looked down at her son's feet. "They *are* new. Michael, didn't I tell you to wear boots today?"

The little boy looked down and shuffled his feet. "I'm sorry, Mommy. I like my new shoes."

Lori Anna knelt and hugged her son. "I know you do, sweetie, but we want them to look nice for church and school. After all, you get to go to Kindergarten in September." She kissed Michael and his face brightened. "Go hurry and change, so you can go with Aunt Lydia Grace."

The little boy raced from the kitchen, and they heard his feet running up the steps. Lydia Grace placed her arm around her mother. "Mom, are you excited to visit Carrie Emeline on Bellingham Bay?"

Jerilyn's eyebrows knit together. "Bellingham Bay? I thought Carrie Emeline was teaching school in Louisville."

Christopher winced.

Lydia Grace continued. "She did, Mom, but now she's in Bellingham, Washington. You and Dad get to travel there today. I think it's exciting."

Christopher kissed Jerilyn. "If you'll remember, dear, Carrie Emeline left Louisville to move with her husband, Marcus, and their children to Bellingham twenty-four years ago." The experts said long-term memory can be recalled much easier than short-term, and she still recalled minute details from her childhood. But he suspected most of her memories were fading.

Jerilyn looked up at Christopher. "Oh, I forgot for a moment. Yes, you're right."

Chris broke some of the tension. "I'm going to load the suitcases into my pick-up. We need to head to the Nashville Airport in the next thirty minutes. Due to morning traffic, I'm allowing an hour and a half for the drive. By the time you get checked in, you'll still have about an hour before your nine-thirty flight. You'll have plenty of time to get to your gate." He turned to his dad. "I'm glad you were able to find a flight straight to Seattle. You won't have to go through the hassle of changing planes."

"I'm relieved, too, Chris. I didn't relish the idea of moving your mom around too much. She's going to reread *Gone with the Wind* again on this trip. Right, Jerilyn?" He turned to his wife and smiled. "You were fifteen when the book was published back in '36. How many times have you read it, dear?"

"I'm not sure, but a lot. It never gets old for me. I know the story so well." She chuckled. "When the movie came out three years later, I went to see it five times with my best girlfriend, Emma, and once with my boyfriend."

Lori Anna laughed, too. "Last year, when *Titanic* hit the box office, teenage girls did the same. I suppose no matter what the era, 'girls will be girls.'

Christopher and Jerilyn hugged their grandchildren, and Christopher thanked Chris and Lori Anna again for moving into their family home. "You were right, son. You and Lori Anna are a Godsend to your mother and me."

When they walked down the front steps, Christopher turned around to look back. He stared at the plaque above the 210 for the address on South College Street. He read the plaque aloud. "The Wright Family." He paused and pointed at it. "That plaque has been there since my parents hung it around nineteen ten. I wasn't born then."

Placing his arm around Jerilyn, he added in a hoarse voice, "There's a lot of wonderful memories here, from *my* childhood, marrying you, Jerilyn, and raising our children." He kissed Jerilyn. "I wouldn't trade my years with you in this magnificent old home for anything." He turned back to Chris, whose eyes glistened. "Take care of everything, son," he shook Chris's hand.

"I will, Dad. You have nothing to worry about. I just want you and Mom to have a wonderful vacation."

Chapter Four

Patience and Love

*"The LORD hath appeared of old unto me, saying,
Yea, I have loved thee with an everlasting love:
therefore with lovingkindness have I drawn thee."*
Jeremiah 31:3

Monday Afternoon
June 22, 1998

The five-hour flight went well. Jerilyn read her book for about thirty minutes, and they both slept for nearly the remainder of the flight.

Christopher was thankful he had upgraded their tickets to first class, because he could ask the attendants to let them sleep, and to awaken him if Jerilyn awakened. He didn't want Jerilyn to have any qualms about the flight. He gave her the aisle seat. He thought it best if she was unable to look out the window.

Christopher awakened to the voice of the pilot. "We are now descending into the Seattle airport, and the temperature is a balmy 75 degrees. I hope you enjoyed your flight, and I thank you for flying with TWA."

Christopher waited until the other first-class passengers disembarked before walking Jerilyn down the Jetway. He didn't have to look far for his family. Carrie Emeline, Marcus, and their sixteen-year-old twins Elise and Erica were waving at them. The four of them ran to hug Christopher and Jerilyn. The twins were talking a mile a minute, bubbling over about the cute guys they met who were working throughout the airport. Jerilyn bit her lip, hung tightly to Christopher's arm, her eyes darting to all the people in the terminal.

Christopher handed Marcus the baggage claim tickets. "Marcus, if you don't mind, would you and the girls claim the luggage, and Carrie Emeline, please take your mom and me to your truck. I need to get her out of this crowd."

Carrie Emeline looked from her mom to her dad. "I understand, Dad."

Marcus took the baggage claim tickets and whisked his daughters away with him.

Jerilyn calmed down once she was settled in the vehicle. Carrie Emeline waited with them in the backseat. "It's so good to see you both. I've been looking forward to this visit." She looked to her dad. "I hope you'll be able to make the cruise up to

Alaska. I hear it's amazing, and the Alaskan scenery is breathtaking."

Christopher placed his arm around Jerilyn, pulling her close to him. She rested her head on his shoulder and closed her eyes. "I hope so, too, Carrie Emeline. However, as you saw in the airport, your mom doesn't bode well with crowds. I don't know how to avoid such situations on the ship."

"You can always retreat to your room if Mom becomes anxious. I hope you don't think we're intruding on your vacation, but Marcus and I will be there on the cruise to help. We talked to Chris and Lydia Grace. We know you're apprehensive about taking Mom on the cruise. We secured a last-minute stateroom close to yours. We'll stay out of your way when you two want to be alone, but we'll be there if you need us."

Christopher sighed in relief. "Thank you, Carrie Emeline. You've just lifted a great weight from my shoulders." He squeezed his daughter's shoulder with his one free hand. Jerilyn remained silent and stared off into some unforeseen world. *Where did she go? Did she understand anything about the conversation? Is she listening at all, or tuning us out?*

They all turned at the thump-thump-thump-thump of four suitcases being loaded into the back of the sport utility vehicle. Marcus spoke to Elise and Erica. "Why don't you two ride back here in the third seat to give your grandparents some privacy?"

The girls climbed into the seat facing the back exit, and Marcus closed the rear door. Carrie Emeline joined Marcus in the front seats, and Christopher strapped Jerilyn in before strapping his own seat belt and shoulder harness.

They entered the interstate, and it took just under two hours to reach Bellingham and the Taylor family residence. Elise and Erica were quick to point out deer, hawks, and even a bear to their grandparents, but Jerilyn slept almost all the way. Marcus and Carrie Emeline cautioned the twins to speak in hushed tones.

Marcus pulled up in front of the home where he lived with Carrie Emeline, his parents, and Elise and Erica. Drew, their only son and oldest child, entered the United States Army right after high school graduation in nineteen eighty-eight. He had now been part of the elite United States Army Rangers for the past eight years, and was married with three children.

Carrie Emeline and Marcus's oldest daughter Angela, now twenty-six, was married with two little boys and living on a productive twenty-two-hundred-acre cattle ranch in Wyoming. Heather, their second oldest daughter, now twenty-three had just received her Bachelor's degree from Wharton

School of the University of Pennsylvania and was working on her Master's Degree in business management. Drew, Angela, and Heather had each called and expressed their sadness at not being able to see their grandparents this summer, but promised to visit them at Christmas Hotel in December.

Marcus parked his truck, and Carrie Emeline and the girls hopped out. Marcus turned around to Christopher. "Dad, what can I do to help?"

"If you could just bring in the luggage, I'll walk Jerilyn to the house."

Jerilyn stirred, glanced at Christopher, then turned sharply to look out the window, and back to Christopher, "Where are we?"

"We're at Carrie Emeline and Marcus's home in Bellingham." He pointed to the house. "We've been coming here every summer for twenty-four years."

She looked at the house. Christopher didn't see recognition on her face, but the traveling had tired her.

Christopher gazed upon his son-in-law's beautiful, historic family home. The wood-frame house, painted a creamy yellow with white trim and moss green shutters, displayed ten steps leading up to the porch encompassing the home on three sides. Two long rectangular sidelight windows with beveled glass and an overhead transom enclosed the heavy brown wooden front door. Above the front door, a walk-out balcony with a wraparound porch adorned the second floor, with another smaller balcony leading out from the third floor.

The front porch held five white rockers on each side of the door. Flower pots filled with brilliant colors of pink, maroon and blue pansies, yellow and white daisies, lavender, multi-colored peonies, and white baby's breath hung above the rocking chairs and along the railing of the porch. Wooden swings painted a deep moss green hung from the ceiling of each of the side porches.

At the top of the steps, Jerilyn pointed at the rockers and turned to Christopher. "I've sat in those rockers on this porch, Christopher."

Christopher smiled at his wife. His heart beat faster whenever she recognized something. Those precious moments appeared to be fewer and farther between. "Jerilyn, yes you have. Would you like to sit on the porch?"

She didn't hesitate. "Yes, I would."

Marcus's parents, Harold and Mildred Taylor joined them on the porch carrying a tray with a pitcher of lemonade and eight glasses. They greeted Christopher and Jerilyn, welcoming them to their home. Carrie Emeline's Cocker Spaniel, Zoey, followed them. The happy little dog wagged its stubby tail and waited for Christopher or Jerilyn to acknowledge her. Jerilyn sat forward on her rocker to pet the dog. "What's her name?"

She and Christopher had been told about this pup when Carrie Emeline first brought her home several months ago. Christopher had owned a Cocker Spaniel named Daisy a few years before he met Jerilyn. Over thirty years later, Christopher and Jerilyn gave Carrie Emeline one of Daisy's descendants whom she named Sophie. This puppy was Sophie's great-great-granddaughter.

Mr. Taylor responded in a soft voice to Jerilyn, while his wife poured and served the lemonade. The Taylors had been informed of Jerilyn's progressive dementia. "This is Zoey. She's now five months old and enjoys being the center of attention. I do believe she thinks all our guests are her very own company."

"We have a dog," Jerilyn continued to pet Zoey. "He's a big dog. His name is Bobby, but he's getting old."

Harold and Mildred knew about Bobby and had even met the dog on their three trips to Christmas Hotel in the past ten years. Christopher mouthed his thanks to Harold and Mildred for their patience and love shown toward Jerilyn.

Carrie Emeline, Marcus, and the girls joined them on the porch. They each poured a glass of lemonade. Zoey ran to Carrie Emeline to sit at her feet. Two hummingbirds flitted around a large pot of peonies, sipped some nectar, and took off as quickly as they arrived.

Christopher held Jerilyn's hand. "It's pleasant out here, isn't it, Jerilyn?"

She nodded her head to him. "Yes, it is. Thank you for bringing me, Christopher."

"You're welcome." Christopher glanced back at his daughter and noted the tears pooling in her eyes.

*****

The next morning, it was time to drive to Vancouver. They planned to spend the night at the cruise line's recommended hotel, Vancouver Hotel and Spa, and board the ship's shuttle the next morning in front of the hotel. Christopher felt this would be best for Jerilyn, rather than driving to Vancouver and boarding all on the same day.

They would board a flight to return to Vancouver following the seven-day cruise. The hotel limo would pick them up at the airport; they'd spend another night at the hotel, and drive back to Bellingham the next morning. Their vehicle would be parked all week in the hotel's garage. Christopher prayed everything went according to plan, for he knew it was all a great deal to coordinate and come together without a hitch.

Jerilyn did very well on the drive up to

Vancouver. Interstate-5 changed to BC-99 as they crossed over the Canadian border. It was a pleasant, sunny day; however, traffic was backed up along the interstate. The air conditioner was not cooling properly. Carrie Emeline rolled down the windows. "This won't be too much air on you and Mom, will it?"

Christopher looked at Jerilyn who was sleeping. "No, we're fine, honey." He checked the clock on the dashboard. The drive time should have been about two hours, but due to the traffic, it would take them much longer.

When the two couples entered the Vancouver Hotel and Spa lobby, all eyes focused on the waterfall centered on the opposite wall of the entrance, perpendicular to the check-in desk. Cascading ferns adorned either side of the waterfall flowing into a winding river trough holding freshwater Koi and Goldfish. Palm Trees interspersed among the groupings of matching brown leather chairs and sofa seating areas. Christopher smiled when Jerilyn walked up to the one wall holding a giant aquarium of exotic saltwater fish. His knowledge of aquatic fish was limited, but he did pick out the Anemones, Clownfish, Angelfish, and Lionfish.

Carrie Emeline placed her arm around her mom and stood by her mother's side, while the men stepped up to the check-in desk. Christopher and Marcus were greeted by a smiling lady whose nametag read Janet. They handed her the papers showing their reservations.

Janet examined the papers and addressed the men. "Good morning, Misters Wright and Taylor. I welcome you to the Vancouver Hotel and Spa."

Christopher smiled. "Good morning to you too, Janet."

"I see the ladies are enjoying the beauty of our lobby. I suggest they take a stroll out in our gardens, and I'll check you in. The door to the courtyard is right here behind me." Janet pointed in the direction.

Christopher nodded. "Thank you, Janet. I'll tell my wife and daughter."

Marcus touched Christopher's arm. "Dad, I'll take care of the check-in and the luggage, and you can join Mom and Carem in the gardens."

"Thanks, Marcus. I'll do just that."

Christopher opened the door, and the three of them meandered out to the enclosed garden.

The women stopped, looked at each other, and said "Wow" at the same time. The gardens, reminiscent of the New Orleans courtyards, were colorful and manicured to perfection. An abundance of flowers cascaded on trellises throughout the garden. Dark purple geraniums nestled between lush green perennials and shrub borders lined either side of the main walkway and gravel and pine needle paths. Wisteria and ivy decorated archways and gazebos. The sound of birds and insects and the smells of earth and plants filled the air.

Three pergolas on the premises supported climbing roses of red, yellow and white, threaded through the slats. "Look, Mom, there's a Violet-Green Swallow." Carrie Emeline pointed, and the bird spread his green and purple wings before flying into the trees above.

As they strolled through the gardens, Jerilyn and Carrie Emeline guessed at the different varieties before getting close enough to read the signs revealing the names of the flowers, trees, and shrubs. "Mom, look at those three trees. I think the Big Leaf Maple is native to British Columbia. Let's read the sign and see if I'm correct."

They drew closer, and Carrie Emeline read the sign aloud. "'Big Leaf Maple.' I was correct." She continued reading. "'Big Leaf Maples are native to British Columbia. They can grow to 160 feet. They provide food and shelter to many of British Columbia's animals such as, deer, elk, squirrels, mice, and beavers.' Amazing! Let's guess at other flowers." She pointed at the flowers from two window boxes. "You're better at identifying flowers,

Mom. What variety are those flowers in the window boxes?"

Jerilyn fixed her eyes on the window boxes. "I see the vibrant colors of daisies, irises, pansies, columbine, and so many flowers too numerous to name."

"Mom, look at the hummingbirds hovering by the spirea and wisteria bushes."

"I see them, honey. Oh, look at the butterflies and bees on the azalea bushes!" Colorful songbirds flitted about the garden. She laughed and smiled for the first time in weeks when a hummingbird flew close, checking her out.

Wrought iron benches were set in the many different garden spaces. Mother and daughter took a seat on a bench by the rhododendron and brilliant blue poppy space and inhaled the mix of floral scents. Christopher leaned against a tree and sighed with contentment in his love for his wife, as she enjoyed the garden with Carrie Emeline.

Jerilyn pointed, and Carrie Emeline followed the direction. A huge fountain, attached to a sculpture of a mid-twentieth century couple holding hands, graced the middle of the outdoor space.

Carrie Emeline swept her hand toward the marble fountain and statue and around the entire courtyard. "We need Dad to take pictures of the statue and gardens. Some of this could be done on a smaller scale in the Christmas Hotel courtyard."

Christopher, who stood several yards away, took his cue. With camera in hand, he walked around the area snapping pictures.

Jerilyn squeezed her daughter's hand. "It's beautiful, Carrie Emeline. Thank you for walking through the gardens with me."

Carrie Emeline smiled at her mother. "You're welcome, Mom. I love you."

"I love you too, honey."

Jerilyn spied her husband snapping the pictures. "Christopher! Isn't the garden stunning?"

He walked toward them, and Carrie Emeline rose. "Sit with Mom, Dad. I'll take the bench across the path."

He kissed his daughter's cheek before sitting beside Jerilyn. Jerilyn took his hand, and with the other she pointed toward the fountain. "The couple in the fountain remind me of us when we met. You would have worn a similar suit. I would have worn a similar dress. Her hairstyle is akin to mine from back then. Do you remember, Christopher?"

Christopher stared at the fountain. The marble couple held hands, smiled at each other, and had the new-love look about their faces. Oh, how he remembered. It was December, 1941. It didn't take him long to fall for the twenty-year-old beauty. He remembered the first day he met Jerilyn when she arrived at Christmas Hotel, a new war-widow, penniless, pregnant, and despondent. However, he had seen in the tortured soul a beautiful spirit. She worked through her depression, accepted his love, and the love of his five-year-old daughter Lily.

They were married on New Year's Eve, 1941 and were deeded Christmas Hotel as a wedding gift from the old and now childless couple, Captain and Mrs. Bazell. He thought about Jerilyn's question. Oh, how beautiful Jerilyn was inside and out. Always immaculately dressed, with her shoulder length, wavy brown hair and her beautiful suits and dresses she wore from the forties era all those years ago. She turned his head the day he met her, but he knew he needed to wait until she was ready to accept his love. She was still mourning her husband, killed at Pearl Harbor.

He turned back to the woman he'd loved for almost fifty-seven years and stared into her lovely but now faded blue eyes. "I remember, Jerilyn." He placed his free hand on her cheek and kissed her on the lips. "I remember it like it was yesterday. I'm still in love with you after all these years." His eyes teared.

"I love you too, Christopher." She frowned and her eyes glistened. "I know there's something wrong with my mind. I don't know what's wrong with me, but I've been reading articles in magazines and the newspaper. I think I know what's wrong. I have dementia, but it may be even worse. It could be Alzheimer's. When I get tired I try to focus, but I know it overpowers me." Her tears spilled down her cheeks. "Please don't stop loving me, Christopher." Her chin quivered.

He wiped her tears with his thumbs. "Never, darling," he said in a hoarse voice and kissed her again. He heard the sniff on the bench across from them. He'd forgotten about Carrie Emeline. He waved her over, and she knelt in front of them.

"I love you, too, Mom, no matter what."

Christopher wrapped them both in his arms.

Chapter Five

Bon Voyage

"Thus saith the LORD, which maketh a way in the sea, and a path in the mighty waters;"
Isaiah 43:16

June 24-29, 1998
Embarkation was easily handled, with continued thanks to Marcus and Carrie Emeline. Their stateroom was only four doors from Christopher and Jerilyn. Marcus and Carrie Emeline also paid extra to upgrade all their embarkation status to VIP. Paying the extra fee allowed them to board ahead of the long line, and it was well worth it. Christopher and Marcus also arranged for the earlier dining slot at 4:00 for the duration of the cruise, when Jerilyn would not be so tired.

Christopher wouldn't have to worry about sundowning, because at this time of year in Alaska it would be past 11 pm before the sun set. Jerilyn would be asleep long before then. Christopher and Marcus had also paid extra and booked their shore excursions well in advance to get them in the morning.

The goal was to create an enjoyable experience for Jerilyn. This would probably be the last vacation he'd take with his wife, and he wanted to capture as many moments on film as possible. Christopher's hobby was photography, and his collection of cameras was extensive, beginning in 1920 when he was seven years old. He still had every camera he ever owned. For this trip, he brought the Pentax MZ-5 he'd purchased two years prior.

He hoped to get some impressive pictures he could develop in Christmas Hotel's basement darkroom. Capturing Jerilyn in her most expressive moments was his goal, pictures of Jerilyn enjoying the Alaskan experience and anything to trigger her memories in the months to come. He yearned to create as many memories with her as possible – before time ran out.

Late in the morning, Christopher seized an opportunity when a school of Northern right whale dolphins swam not too far off the ship's starboard side. In the excitement, Jerilyn threw her head back, laughed, and clapped her hands. A slight breeze blew her hair around her head.

Carrie Emeline stood beside her mother and slid her arm around Jerilyn's waist. Christopher captured the tender moment between mother and daughter.

Marcus viewed the dolphins through binoculars and shifted his focus on the shore. "Dad, look," Marcus pointed to a mama bear and two baby black bears. "It looks as though the mama bear is teaching her offspring how to fish. She just caught a fish in her paw."

Christopher turned his camera in the direction and captured the scene.

*****

Over the next several days, they spent most mornings on shore excursions. Ketchikan was home to some amazing wildlife: bald eagles, black bears and salmon, to name a few. At Juneau, they had several choices, but Christopher thought the aerial tram ride above Juneau would be best for Jerilyn, where there would be less people around them than in a crowded nature exhibit. Christopher chose the Goldbelt Mount Roberts Tramway, because it was less vertical than other aerial trams as advertised in brochures.

The view at Mount Roberts was captivating and still snowcapped even in June. Christopher read from his brochure. "Did you know Mount Roberts is 3,819 feet tall?"

Jerilyn pointed. "Oh look, Christopher ... a bald eagle. Isn't it majestic?"

Christopher snapped a picture.

Carrie Emeline pointed out the river below. "Look down at the winding river, Mom. It says in our brochure it's the Taku River."

"I see it, Carrie Emeline, and are those deer or elk drinking in the river? I never could tell them apart."

Marcus picked up his binoculars, and Christopher zoomed in for a picture. "I think they're elk, Mom. Our brochure says the elk male weighs around 700 pounds with a shaggy coat and rounded nose. The male deer is about half that size. From what I can determine, they're definitely elk."

By the time they reached the top of the mountain, they were ready for lunch. The Timberline Bar & Grill was the only choice, but offered a panoramic view at 1,800 feet above Juneau. Christopher led Jerilyn to the window seat. He worried she might be afraid of the heights from the tramway and atop the mountain, but his fears were abated. She loved the views. "Look, Christopher, on that ridge, a moose and her calf!"

"I see them." Christopher snapped a picture.

Carrie Emeline picked up the notecard on their table. "Mom, according to this notecard," she paused and pointed, "in that direction, you can see the rain forest."

Marcus picked up some Q&A notecards. "Want to play a little trivia?"

"Yes." Carrie Emeline turned to her parents. "Do you remember when we played Trivial Pursuit at home in the early eighties?"

Christopher grinned. "After that game came out, I think we played it when we all got together every Thanksgiving and Christmas for several years. Those are good family memories, Carrie Emeline. In several of the family albums, I have pictures of all of us around the dining room table enjoying out family nights."

"Yes, they are good memories, Dad."

Christopher looked at Jerilyn and then turned to Marcus. "Ask us a question, Marcus."

"How long is the Taku River? Twenty-four miles, fifty-four miles, or seventy miles?" Marcus flipped the card over for the answer.

Carrie Emeline answered. "I think I read fifty-four miles in one of the brochures."

"Right you are!" They clinked water glasses.

Carrie Emeline grabbed a card. "How wide is the average bald eagle's nest? Three feet, five feet, or nine feet?"

Christopher widened his eyes. "It's certainly not a Cardinal's nest."

Marcus chuckled. "I guess three feet."

She flipped the card over and first read to herself. "Wow, this is amazing. It says bald eagles build their nests in large trees near rivers or coasts. A typical nest is around five feet in diameter. Eagles often use the same nest year after year. Over the years, some nests become enormous, as much as nine feet in diameter, weighing two tons!"

Christopher dropped his jaw and shook his head. "I never dreamed the nest was so large."

The waiter arrived with their Alaskan Crab legs. The family held hands and bowed their heads. "Dear Heavenly Father ..."

Following the prayer, Christopher relaxed and breathed a sigh of relief. *Thank Thee Lord for this wonderful experience and the memories Thou art providing, especially for Carrie Emeline. I want her to remember her mother like this ... and I want to remember Jerilyn as the wife who enjoys her family. I love her so very much, Lord.*

*****

On day five of the cruise, Christopher received an invitation to dine at the Captain's table with his family. It turned out Captain Rawlings, his wife, and their children stayed at Christmas Hotel back in 1985 for two weeks in December. Mrs. Rawlings had been strolling around the ship early one morning, when Christopher and Jerilyn turned to her at the same time Mrs. Rawlings recognized them.

"Why it's Mr. and Mrs. Wright from Christmas Hotel," she acknowledged, when she approached them bearing a huge smile along with a hug for Jerilyn.

Christopher watched the hug and how it would be received by Jerilyn, but she appeared fine. "Mrs. Rawlings," Christopher said in return, "we knew your husband was the captain on this cruise, but we had no idea you'd be here, too."

"I join him several times each season on these cruises. The scenery on the inside passage voyage is so beautiful. In fact, Captain Rawlings only takes the Alaskan cruise assignments now, so he's always off work in the winter months. We've been thinking about a return trip to Christmas Hotel. Because of you two, your family, and Christmas Hotel itself, we experienced one of our most memorable vacations."

"Why, thank you, Mrs. Rawlings," responded Jerilyn with a genuine smile. "We always try to make the visits pleasurable for our guests."

"Well, you do, Mrs. Wright."

"Please, call me Jerilyn, and my husband Christopher."

"Well, you must call me Carolyn." She cocked her head. "If you're available, Captain Rawlings and I would love for you to dine at our table tonight. I remember you two inviting us to join you at your table at Christmas Hotel. I'd be honored to return the invitation."

Christopher turned to Jerilyn for her reaction. "We'd love to. Right, Christopher?" She looked up at her husband.

"Carolyn, we do have one of our daughters and her husband with us on this cruise."

"Not a problem. We have seating for up to fourteen at our table. We're on the early dining schedule at four o'clock, except tonight, since it's formal night. Dining times are later at six and nine."

Christopher nodded. "We're on the early dining schedule, too, Carolyn. The four of us will see you and Captain Rawlings at dinner tonight at six o'clock."

"I'll see if I can get the orchestra to play some forties music in your honor," added Carolyn with a smile.

At 5:30, they finished dressing for dinner. Jerilyn wore a long white silk evening gown they had brought specially for formal night, along with a white lace shawl. She handed Christopher the diamond and pearl necklace he had given her for their forty-fifth anniversary, and he clasped it around her neck. He kissed the nape of her neck and turned her around. "You look mighty fetching,

Mrs. Wright."

She smiled and straightened his bow tie. "You look mighty fetching yourself, Mr. Wright, in your tuxedo."

Along with Carrie Emeline and Marcus, four other couples joined Christopher and Jerilyn at Captain and Mrs. Rawlings' private table. All around the dining room, the guests were dressed in their finery, and the tables were decorated with centerpieces of fresh cut yellow or red roses and baby's breath. Dimmed wall sconces surrounded the dining room, and at least twenty cut-glass chandeliers adorned the ceiling. Several couples who arrived late descended the elegant horse shoe-shaped Brazilian Mahogany staircase.

The dinner arrived. Carrie Emeline closed her eyes and inhaled the aroma. "Yum, grilled Moroccan chicken! It's one of my favorite chicken dishes, and I haven't had it in years." She turned to Marcus. "We need to add this to our restaurant menu at home." Marcus and his sister inherited the restaurant in Bellingham, Washington his parents founded years ago.

The fifteen-piece house band tuned up for the evening as the dinner dishes were cleared. Carolyn Rawlings smiled at Christopher and Jerilyn. "As I promised, I requested a forties music night in honor of you two. I hope the songs bring back wonderful memories."

Christopher nodded. "Thank you, Carolyn. We appreciate your thoughtfulness."

Couples headed out to the dance floor. Upon hearing the first line of the song "I Know Why (and So Do You)," recognition lit up Jerilyn's face, and she presented him with a radiant smile. "They're playing our song, Christopher."

"May I have this dance, Jerilyn?"

Christopher's heart melted when Jerilyn's eyes widened and twinkled. She was still his girl, the Jerilyn he remembered. The years fell away, and he saw the lovely twenty-year-old Jerilyn. "Oh yes, Christopher. I'd love to dance with you."

He took her hand, and they rose together. He caught the smile and the sparkle in Carrie Emeline's eyes. He twirled Jerilyn and escorted her the short distance to the now crowded dance floor. Jerilyn smiled up at him and rested her head on his shoulder. While they danced, he held her close, as they listened to the lyrics.

Why do robins sing in December,
Long before the springtime is due?
And even though it's snowing,
Violets are growing,
I know why and so do you.

Why do breezes sigh ev'ry evening,
Whispering your name as they do?
And why have I the feeling
Stars are on my ceiling?
I know why and so do you.

Before the last stanza, she looked at him with tears in her eyes. "Do you remember, Christopher?"

"Yes, darling, I remember all the times we danced to this song. I remember when the Glen Miller Band came to the Andrew Jackson Hotel in Nashville. We drove there and spent the night. It was an unforgettable evening."

"Yes, it was, Christopher." She looked away for a moment. "I sometimes wish we could go back and live our lives again. I hate not being able to remember some things. I hope you'll love me through whatever is wrong with me. If I've asked this before, please forgive me." She had an expectant look on her face.

She had now brought up her fears twice on this trip. He stroked her hair and kissed her on the lips. "Jerilyn, I will love you forever." She relaxed in his arms.

"I think the ship's orchestra plays our song very well, and the woman singing is a close vocal comparison to Paula Kelly, don't you think?"

"Yes, I do."

"It's a wonderful memory for us, Jerilyn."

"It *is* a wonderful memory, darling. Thank you for helping me keep alive these old memories. I love you, Christopher."

"I love you, too, Jerilyn, and with all my heart."

He held her close as they swayed to the music, and the lyrics took him back to a long ago decade.

When you smile at me,
I hear gypsy violins;
When you dance with me,
I'm in heaven when the music begins.

I can see the sun when it's raining,
Hiding ev'ry cloud from my view;
And why do I see rainbows
When you're in my arms?
I know why and so do you.

Christopher glanced over to their table when he saw the camera flash. Marcus photographed them as they danced, while Carrie Emeline wiped the tears streaming down her face. Christopher held his wife. *Thank you, God, for another memorable moment with Jerilyn.*

Chapter Six

A Troublesome Night

"And call upon me in the day of trouble: I will deliver thee, and thou shalt glorify me."
Psalm 50:15

June 30, 1998

Each day on the ship had presented new experiences and challenges. Jerilyn had done quite well – until the evening of day six and the morning of day seven. At dinner on their final evening aboard the ship, Jerilyn had become tired and agitated. She'd stare at people, at other tables, saying nothing, her face holding a blank expression. She'd glance at Christopher and watch him without saying a word. *Does she know me? Does she know where we are?*

Christopher grew terrified for Jerilyn, and he was unsure of what she was inclined to do or how he could help her. She shook her foot under the table and rung her hands. Perspiration erupted on her forehead. The waiters and guests sang Happy

Birthday at one of the tables and applause broke out.

Jerilyn jerked her head toward the laughing people at the table and gaped, with wide-eyed fear. The waiters brought their table's food and Jerilyn still said nothing. She stared in response when one waiter asked her if she needed anything else. Christopher placed his hand over Jerilyn's and spoke softly to calm her. "We're fine, thank you."

Christopher watched while she pushed her dinner around her plate with her fork, taking no bites, with furtive glances toward her table mates. Out of the blue, Jerilyn stood and spoke in a loud voice. "Where am I? Who *are* you people?" She looked from face to face, wild-eyed. "Someone take me home. I want my husband." She picked up her napkin and flung it down, spilling and breaking her water glass.

Christopher stood beside her, placed his arm around her waist, and said in a composed and gentle voice, "I'm here, Jerilyn. It's okay. We're at dinner on the ship. We'll go home tomorrow."

She jerked his arm off her, pulling away, and he watched her lovely face contort and turn red in anger. She gritted her teeth, backed away from him, and knocked over her chair. "I don't know you," she shouted. "You're *not* my husband." Tears spilled down her cheeks. "I want my husband!"

By now, the surrounding tables had picked up on the scene. Carrie Emeline stood and took her mom's hand. She spoke in a soothing voice, "Come with me, Mom. I'll take you to your room."

Jerilyn stared blankly at her daughter, blinked a few times, but followed Carrie Emeline like an obedient child – with Christopher close behind. Christopher paused, leaned over and whispered to Marcus, "Please offer our apologies and provide a brief explanation."

Marcus nodded to his father-in-law.

In the room, Jerilyn sat on the edge of the bed and then stood and paced the room, resembling a caged animal. "I want my husband," she cried over and over. She pointed at Christopher. "Get *him* out of here!"

Marcus entered the room, and Christopher asked him to go for the ship's doctor. He ran his fingers through his hair. "Carrie Emeline, I'll wait in the bathroom."

When Marcus returned with the doctor, Jerilyn was lying on the bed, curled in the fetal position, still crying, and her face red and bloated.

Christopher walked softly from the bathroom, and Marcus introduced Dr. Mallory to Christopher. "I have a sedative for your wife. It will calm her nerves and allow her to sleep. I need a glass of water for her to take the pills."

Carrie Emeline returned with the water. She sat on the edge of the bed and placed her arm around her mother "Mom, the doctor is here with some medicine for you. Can you sit up, please?"

Jerilyn stared at her daughter, blinked twice, and sat up. The doctor handed the pills to Carrie Emeline. "Open your mouth, Mom, and I'll put the pills on your tongue."

Like a submissive child, Jerilyn did as her daughter asked. She drank the water and swallowed the pills.

"She should sleep through the night," Dr. Mallory explained to Christopher. "However, if she awakens, please don't hesitate to call me." The doctor shook his head, and at the door, in a very emotional voice, added, "My dad had this dreadful disease. God bless you. I'll just see myself out."

Christopher removed Jerilyn's nightgown from the drawer. "Carrie Emeline, your mother seems to respond to you better than me at the moment. Please see if you can remove her dress and put her gown on her. Marcus and I will wait in the hallway."

Christopher closed the door and succumbed to the pressure. With his back against the wall, he slowly slid to the floor. Tucking his knees up against his chest, he broke down, crying, and covering his face with his hands. He felt Marcus's arms surround him, and the two men cried together.

When they broke apart, Christopher pulled out his handkerchief, sniffed, and wiped his eyes. He inhaled and slowly blew out his breath. Looking directly at Marcus, he spoke in a hoarse voice. "It's hard, Marcus. It's so ... painful to watch a vibrant, loving, energetic woman change before your eyes. The woman we saw tonight ... was ... was not my wife. My heart breaks for Jerilyn, my family ... and selfishly ... me. I love her. I vowed to protect her, but I can't fight this disease destroying her brain. I feel so helpless."

"I know, Dad. Carrie Emeline and I hurt the same for Mom, but mostly for you. You're not selfish. We love Mom, but we understand how much harder her condition is for you."

"I'm thankful you and Carrie Emeline came with us, Marcus. I don't know how I could have handled the incident tonight without your help."

"I'm glad we did, too. We love you and Mom. We'll be here for you, Dad."

"Thank you, Marcus."

Carrie Emeline opened the door, and the men quickly stood. "Mom's asleep, Dad. I washed her face, she's in her gown, and I also removed her hearing aids. They're on the nightstand. Do you want me to stay tonight?"

"No, honey. Go back to your room with Marcus. I'll call if I need you. Your mom will probably be fine in the morning and not remember what happened."

Carrie Emeline hugged him and planted a kiss on his cheek. "I'll pray Mom's okay in the morning. Try to get some sleep, Dad."

"I will, honey." Christopher walked into the room, quietly closed the door, and stared at his sleeping wife. He picked up his old worn Bible on the end table and sat in the reclining chair with the Bible open on his lap. He watched Jerilyn. Her now relaxed face held a peaceful expression. Her wavy hair framed her face. *Carrie Emeline must have brushed it.*

He blinked back tears and sniffed. In a whisper, he spoke to his sleeping wife. "Jerilyn, I love you. You are just as beautiful to me as when I met you." He wiped a tear and continued. "The Lord could not have given me a better wife. You have a kind and sweet spirit. Our five children could not have had a more loving mother. Your grandchildren and great-grandchildren adore you."

Sniffing again, he removed his own hearing aids, and read and prayed until the early morning hours. Exhausted, he fell asleep in the chair. The next thing he knew, the sun had entered their room and Jerilyn was standing over him calling his name.

"Christopher, did you sleep in the chair all night?" She asked in a soft voice.

He looked into her faded blue eyes. *She said my name. She's back ... for now.* Setting his Bible on the table, he pulled her onto his lap and held her. "I love you, Jerilyn," he said in a gravelly voice, doing his best to hold back the tears.

"I love you, too Christopher." She smiled at him. His heart overflowed with the emotion. *She's mine again, Lord, but for how long?*

Debarkation went well due to the upgrade to VIP status. They were on dry land within a few hours and getting ready for the flight back to Vancouver Hotel and Spa for the night. The next morning Marcus drove them all to Bellingham. Christopher and Jerilyn spent one night in Bellingham, and Carrie Emeline and Marcus drove them to the airport in Seattle the next morning. There were no more incidents.

Chapter Seven

Reunion Announcement

"Commit thy works unto the LORD, and thy thoughts shall be established."
Proverb 16:3

October 1998

Chris and Lori Anna called the family meeting. Included were Christopher, Lily, and her husband John, Lydia Grace, and her husband Jacob. The seven of them spread about on the sofa, two recliner chairs, and a love seat in the living room of the family home. Bobby, the family dog curled up in his over-sized doggy bed. Lori Anna had prepared two pots of Chamomile tea along with cheesecake left from dinner.

Chris nodded to his family members and set down his tea cup. "Thank you for coming to this impromptu meeting." He drew in his breath and exhaled. "Lori Anna and I are planning a ten-night reunion at Christmas Hotel this December. We plan to send invitations to guests who have stayed at the hotel two or more times over the past six decades."

Chris fingered his short brown hair and scrutinized the faces regarding the next statement. He stood to his full height of six feet two inches for added emphasis. "This reunion should be a spectacular event, and sparing no expense on our end. The reunion will be free of charge to our guests." Some eyebrows shot upward or eyes rounded. He smiled. "As the hotel's owner and manager, and my wife as marketing director, we have come up with this plan."

He reached down and patted Lori Anna's shoulder. "Each invited couple will stay at no charge, but if they bring other family, we will only charge half of the normal rate for the extra guests. Children sixteen and under will stay free. Many of the guests have been here numerous times, and Lori Anna and I thought giving something back would be a blessing for them, and for future generations of the guests' families."

He scrutinized the faces of his family. "Okay, I'm ready for thoughts."

Christopher spoke first without hesitation. "Son, I think it's a splendid idea." He rubbed his chin in thought. "However, are you prepared to take the revenue loss in December? I realize Christmas Hotel is booked to at least seventy-five percent capacity year round, but from Thanksgiving to New Years' Eve it's always booked one hundred percent."

"I get your concern, Dad, but Lori Anna and I believe the future revenue will make up for the current losses. Also, won't it be fun to relive the memories of these guests all in one week or so? Many of these people haven't met each other. I also thought it might be therapeutic for Mom."

His oldest sister Lily beamed her approval with a broad smile. "I like it, Chris. You're correct that Mom may remember many of the guests. Her long-term memory will kick in."

Lydia Grace jumped up, walked to her brother, kissed him on the cheek, and hugged him. "You're very thoughtful, Chris. I think it *will* be good for Mom, and I agree it's a great plan for future marketing. I say let's go for it! How can Jacob and I help?" She tossed her brown hair, and her blue eyes sparkled.

Chris smiled. *So like my dramatic sister.* He returned the hug and kiss. "Thanks, Lydia Grace, and all of you. I hoped you'd ask to help. We have a list for everyone, with the service you can provide. We need assistance with the guest list first. I'll let Lori Anna begin."

Lori Anna held up a legal pad and pen. "Chris and I don't want to leave out any guest who has been a regular. We've only been keeping computer files for the past decade. We have been through old check-in logs, but many of those were stored in the basement prior to 1988."

Chris smiled and gazed at his beautiful supportive wife. She had not changed much from the day they married back in '87, and she still had beautiful waist length coal black straight hair, enchanting dimples, and dark brown eyes. At barely five feet tall, she could walk under his arm. In the beginning, he felt it was wrong to date her, since she was thirteen years his junior, but the pull of love prevailed. Lori Anna was his soul-mate. Thank God, she survived the leukemia back in '88. She had now been in remission for almost a decade.

Chris picked up where Lori Anna left off. "As you know, the basement flooded in 1975, and most of the records were ruined. So, Dad, we need you to brainstorm back to 1941, when you and Mom first met. If there are any guests still living and able to travel, we want to send them an invitation. Let's fill the hotel for ten nights, beginning Friday, December eighteenth through Sunday evening, December twenty-seventh with the reunion guests, but any guests who have already booked those days will be included in the reunion. We envision this as a Christmas reunion celebration. One more thing, Dad, on the last day, Sunday, I'd like you to preach in the chapel in my place. It'll be memorable for those who recall when you did *all* the preaching."

Christopher nodded and smiled. "I'd be happy to preach on the last day, Chris."

John, Lily's distinguished former professor husband, and Jacob, Lydia Grace's artistic husband asked what they could do to help. John spoke for both men. "After all, we don't know the guests at Christmas Hotel like everyone else does."

Chris turned to him. "Lori Anna considered you two. You each have a special talent. John, you're a retired teacher, so I know you can handle public speaking, along with your wife of course." Lily smiled and placed her hand on her husband's arm. "You can give tours here in Franklin, at places of interest for the guests."

Chris then addressed Jacob. "Jacob, you and Lydia Grace are world renowned concert pianists. It would be an enormous treat for the guests to hear you and my sister play three or four nights in the chapel, and during the Sunday and Christmas morning services."

They both nodded their agreement.

"What's my assignment?" asked Lily.

"I thought you'd like to hold a three-day book reading session for the guests' children either at the hotel or at the Goodnight Memorial Library. We can also open this event to anyone in town."

"I like the idea, Chris. I'll look into my old library of books my second, third, and fourth graders enjoyed."

"Thanks, sis."

"Lori Anna plans to interview some of the guests for the *Franklin Favorite*. They can tell their story or share an experience at Christmas Hotel for the human interest section of the paper." Chris looked around at the group. "Well, if everyone is ready, let's get this list of names ready for invitations. We have the last decade on the computer. Let's begin with prior to 1988 and work our way back per decade. Are you prepared to record, Lori Anna?"

"I'm all set. Just start calling names – and if you know the city in which they reside, it would be helpful."

Chapter Eight

And Here Come the Happy People

"Blessed is the people that know the joyful sound: they shall walk, O LORD, in the light of thy countenance."
Psalm 89:15

Friday
December 18, 1998
Chris opened the double brass doors in the Christmas Hotel lobby. A light snow fell on top of the two inches already on the ground. Couples and families of all ages walked through the decorated square or on the sidewalks toward the hotel. Some pushed baby carriages or strollers, some used canes or walkers, and some were in wheelchairs.

Chris turned to his family at the front desk and announced, "They're coming. Everyone ready?"

Mr. Hanover and Mr. Adams, two of Chris's long-time assistants, walked in from the hotel's office. His parents, along with Lily, John, and Lori Anna, perched on stools behind the check-in desk.

Carrie Emeline and Marcus entered the lobby from the chapel where they had been praying for the reunion. Carrie Emeline, Marcus, and their twin daughters planned to stay on the farm with Lydia Grace and Jacob for the ten days, since all the rooms were booked.

"We're all ready," Christopher said. "We'll help you get these first guests checked in and up to their rooms."

Chris and Mr. Adams stood in the open massive double glass doors. "Welcome to Christmas Hotel," Chris announced as each family or couple stepped over the threshold. Many he knew by name from the decades he'd spent at Christmas Hotel.

"Frank and Marlene McCoy, welcome back to Christmas Hotel!"

Marlene answered with a smile, "It's good to be back, Chris."

"Pastor Chuck and Linda! It's wonderful to see you again. Did your children come?"

The pastor nodded and chuckled. "Yes, but they're no longer children. Chuck Jr., Kim, and Carrie are all grown and married with children. They'll join us shortly, along with their spouses and children."

"Mike and Virginia Dailey! How are you and your children?"

Mike shook Chris's hand and smiled. "We're all

fine, but we didn't bring the children this trip. It's a vacation alone with my wife." He hugged her to his side.

"Chevez and Cathy, you brought the baby! Lori Anna will want to hold him. Welcome back!"

Chevez shook Chris's hand, and Cathy said, "I knew she would. I can't wait to see her and your parents. We missed you, and we thank you for the invitation!"

Both Mr. Hanover and Mr. Adams carried luggage to the front desk. When the check-in line got too long, Chris sent some of the guests to the lobby to wait. Within an hour, the lobby and front desk were full of laughing, happy people, meeting other guests for the first time or just getting reacquainted.

Dona and Bob Young walked up to Chris when he was available. "Chris, the lobby is just as I remembered, if not lovelier, back when your father married Bob and me. I thought the floors so elegant with the checkered squares of black and white marble ... and the two-story lobby still takes my breath away. When the wedding march played, I descended the curved horseshoe shaped staircase from the second floor on my father's arm and into the chapel."

Dona pointed to the rounded door of the chapel. "The cherry banister is still wrapped in holly and cranberries." She turned back to face Chris. "It's all the same."

"Yes, it is, Dona. We've done our best to maintain and keep Christmas Hotel true to when it was built."

Bob pointed to the manger scene in the middle of the lobby. "The manger scene has always fascinated me. I've never seen another to compare. The life-size figures of Mary, Joseph, the shepherd men, all watching the small babe in the manger, and in the background, the barn animals ... the scene is so compelling. I feel transported back two thousand years to the birth of the baby Jesus."

Becky Ray joined the conversation. "Hello, Chris."

"Welcome to the reunion, Becky. Is your husband Randy here?"

"Yes, he'll be in shortly. He ran into Thomas Woodson outside, and they're still talking. I overheard you discussing the lobby." She pointed to the twenty foot Christmas tree in the lobby. "I've always been intrigued by the goose-feather tree. I remember your dad saying it had stood there long before he was born. I love all the handmade ornaments from different decades, but it's the angel atop the tree that amazes me. No matter where one stands, she always appears to be smiling ... and directly at the person. Years ago, when I first saw her, she was a bit unnerving, but once I got used to her, I wanted to take her home with me. I've searched, but I've never been able to find another like her. She must be one of a kind."

Chris chuckled. "You're not the first person to have the same thoughts about our angel, Becky."

Earl and Essie Carson approached. Mrs. Carson cleared her throat. "I hope we're not intruding, Chris."

"Not at all. Welcome back to Christmas Hotel, Mr. and Mrs. Carson."

"Oh, don't be so formal, Chris." She waved her hand at him. "Please call me Essie, and my husband, Earl. It makes us feel young."

Chris nodded and smiled.

Essie cleared her throat once more and pushed on the thin graying bun knotted at the back of her head. "I suppose the winter chill might be getting to me. Since we've moved to Sarasota, Florida ... it's nice spending the winter there. I do like to be home in Franklin, Kentucky in December though, and I do like a little snow, but just a little." She drew her forefinger and thumb about an inch apart.

Chris just smiled and nodded. Essie Hendricks Carson was born and raised in Franklin, and the townspeople loved her. However, everyone knew how Essie could "run on," as they'd say. Back when they lived in Franklin, the two of them would spend every anniversary at Christmas Hotel.

"Now *personally, I* like the lobby furniture," she continued without taking a breath. "It's comfortable and always looks like I should have a seat and sit a spell. You know what I mean, Chris?"

"Yes, Mrs. ... I mean, Essie. I do know what you mean."

"I like the groupings of the leather sofas, high back chairs with the oriental rugs in each grouping." She stopped a moment to catch her breath and once again cleared her throat. "However, it's the stone fireplace that sets off the room." She paused a few seconds. *She must be gathering her next set of thoughts.* "I see you keep a roaring fire in the fireplace just like your dad did and the Bazells, too. Yes, I remember the Bazells, but they were *many* years before your time, Chris."

"Yes, ma'am, they were."

"Essie. Call me Essie." She narrowed her eyes in a stern look and adjusted her glasses. "How long is the fireplace again and how tall is the mantel? I can't seem to recall." With her cane, she pointed in the direction. Earl placed his arm around Essie, smiled at Chris, and waggled his bushy, white eyebrows.

Chris placed his hand briefly over his mouth to hide his grin. "Well, Essie, the hearth is roughly seven feet wide, and the mantel stands about six feet above the fireplace opening."

Essie studied the fireplace another minute. "I see you've added more stockings since we were here last. I suppose some more babies have been born. When God said to go forth, be fruitful, and multiply, you Wrights paid attention." She laughed at her own joke.

Chris had to chuckle along with the group of about twenty more people who had been listening in on Essie's chatter. "Yes, Essie, quite a few more babies have been born. You and Earl have been gone from Franklin about ten years ... right?"

"Ten years last October. Are the names of the new young 'uns on the stockings?"

"Yes, ma'am ... I mean, Essie."

She narrowed her eyes in another stern look when he said ma'am.

"You'll find all the stockings in birth order going back to 1936."

She grabbed her husband's hand. "Come on, Earl. We've got to go see the new stockings. I want to sit a spell on the furniture, too."

Chris shook his head and grinned. *Essie and Earl. I certainly have missed them in Franklin.* "Welcome to Christmas Hotel!" Chris said with enthusiasm to the next group of guests.

Chris, Lily, Christopher, and Jerilyn stood together,

while Lily gave the speech her mom used to give after check-in. "Breakfast is at six o'clock in the morning. We serve a noon meal and dinner is at six. At each meal, two families will be invited to sit at our family table during the ten days. We want to become reacquainted with all of you, and we thank you for attending this reunion. Please feel free to enjoy the lobby and the chapel during your stay."

Jerilyn smiled at each guest, but she remained silent.

Chris interjected. "There will be extra festivities here at the hotel, and many of the businesses around the square will provide celebrations and shopping discounts during your stay. The daily flyer information will be slipped under your door by five o'clock each morning. Above all, have a wonderful time!"

More guests continued to arrive throughout the day. Mr. Thompson and Mr. Clark, two more of Chris's assistants, arrived at five o'clock to relieve Mr. Hanover and Mr. Adams. Christopher hoped he and Jerilyn would be able to have all the noon meals with two families, and Chris and Lori Anna planned to have dinner with two different families at each evening meal throughout the reunion. The other four siblings and their spouses planned to rotate breakfast or fill in for noon or dinner if needed.

Chris stood when one of the families arrived for their first evening meal. Chris smiled and shook Mr. Woodson's hand. "Thomas and Alice Woodson. Thank you for joining us at tonight's dinner." Lori Anna hugged Mrs. Woodson.

Mr. Woodson gripped Chris's hand. "Thank you for having us." Mr. Woodson turned to more of his family who approached. "I'd like you to meet our son David, his wife Rebecca, and their oldest son Noah and his fiancée Melanie. Noah and Melanie are on your schedule to marry them at Christmas Hotel during their stay. We brought three generations from Houston for this reunion." He swept his hand towards his family. "Alice and I were married here at Christmas Hotel by your father back in '47. When we told Noah and Melanie about it, they also wanted to be married here." He laughed. "Maybe this will continue through the generations."

Chris shook Noah's hand. "I am honored to marry you two."

"Thank you, Mr. Wright."

"Please call me Chris, and my wife Lori Anna."

Eugene and Cecilia Scott approached them. Cecilia hugged Mr. and Mrs. Woodson. "I'm so happy we could have dinner with you tonight." She turned to Chris and Lori Anna. "Thank you so much for inviting us."

Chris smiled at her. "Cecilia, you and Eugene could never have been left off the reunion list." Chris knew Cecilia stayed with the Woodsons' back in 1967 in Houston, following a very troubling time in her life. She had met Mr. Woodson when he drove her in his taxi cab to a seedy section of Houston. Cecilia and the Woodson family became friends during this disturbing time in Cecilia's life. The Woodsons' church sponsored Cecilia's stay at Christmas Hotel. Eugene shook Chris's hand. "That was very considerate of you, Chris. Cecilia and I appreciate your kindness."

Lori Anna hugged Cecilia. "It's nice to meet you, Cecilia. Let's all have a seat."

Cecilia congratulated Chris and Lori Anna. "When Eugene and I moved away from Franklin, Chris, you didn't own Christmas Hotel nor were you married." She smiled and winked at Lori Anna. "I was beginning to wonder if someone was ever going to capture Chris's heart. So much has changed in eleven years. You have done some very special things with the hotel, adding the basement darkroom and gym. However, I'm pleased the hotel itself hasn't changed."

"I agree," added Mrs. Woodson. "The lobby and chapel look just as they did when Thomas and I honeymooned here in 1947. Christmas Hotel will always hold a special place in our hearts."

Cecilia smiled. "In my heart and Eugene's, too. We met and married here, and your father married us too, Chris." She turned to the Woodsons. "I see the marriage traditions will continue with your grandson, Noah, and Melanie."

Melanie took a sip of her sweet iced tea. "Chris is marrying us in the chapel tomorrow at two. I hope all of you will come to our wedding."

Cecilia looked over at Eugene and he nodded. "We'll be there. Thank you for inviting us, Melanie. Chris, I haven't seen two of my best friends I met here at Christmas Hotel back in 1967: Loretta and Gloria. Of course, we correspond and call each other. Do you know if they're coming to the reunion?"

Chris laughed. "Well, since Loretta is married to my brother Ken, their attendance is required. They'll be here late tonight and staying in Loretta's room from 1967: room ten. Gloria and Matthew are also checking in tonight and will be in room nine, and you and Eugene will have your original room number eight."

Lori Anna jumped in. "Oh, by the way, Loretta and Ken *and* Lydia Grace and Jacob are hosting the breakfast here at the family table in the morning. Per their request, Gloria and Matthew *and* Cecilia and Eugene are to join them at this family table.

They wanted to kick off their reunion with the four of you."

"Wow, this is definitely going to be a splendid reunion," said Cecilia. "I can't wait to see Loretta, Gloria, and Lydia Grace again, and their husbands. It'll be 1967 all over again." She laughed and added, "Just an older version of us, with children and grandchildren."

Conversation halted when their waiter brought the plates of roast beef, mashed potatoes, carrots, onions, turnips, green beans, and cornbread.

Eugene sniffed the aroma and rubbed his belly. "I can already see I'll be gaining at least ten pounds while I'm here."

The others laughed and dove in heartily.

Chapter Nine

Happy Occasions

"But as it is written, Eye hath not seen, nor ear heard, neither have entered into the heart of man, the things which God hath prepared for them that love him."
1 Corinthians 2:9

Saturday
December 19, 1998
By five o'clock the next morning, Chris and Lori Anna delivered the announcement flyer under the doors of each room with the daily events. Their three children were at home in bed and Jerilyn, too. Only Christopher was awake when they left the house at 4:30 for the walk to Christmas Hotel.

* Every Saturday and Sunday is "Omelet Day" at Christmas Hotel, prepared by our amazing chefs. Please join us in the dining room for your omelet any way you want it at six o'clock this morning.

* *Bridgette's Books on the square at 114 West Kentucky Street is having a 25% discount on books today, and only for the Christmas Hotel reunion guests. Just bring this flyer to use for a coupon.*

* *The Flower Patch at 128 North Main Street will have a 15% discount on all arrangements for the duration of the stay of the Christmas Hotel reunion guests.*

* *Jan's Bridal Boutique at 116 W. Kentucky Street will have a 15% discount on all items for the duration of the stay of the Christmas Hotel reunion guests.*

* *At 2:00 in the chapel, Noah Woodson and Melanie Carrigan would like to invite reunion guests to witness their wedding vows. World renowned concert pianists Jacob Carlisle and Lydia Grace Wright Carlisle will provide the music. Pastor Chris Wright will officiate. Seating will be available in the chapel, and overflow seating available in the lobby.*

* *Tonight at 8:00 in the square, the Leroy and Bobbi Ann Band will play Christmas Hymns and some of their favorite country songs. Park benches and fold-up chairs will be provided for your use.*

Dress warm and bring a blanket from your room! Come and enjoy the music, the beautifully decorated square, and the courthouse all dressed up for Christmas along with the decorated businesses around the square. The retail businesses will stay open until 9:30 every night until Christmas Eve, when they'll close at 5:00. They will also be closed on Sundays and Christmas Day.

Sincerely,
Chris and Lori Anna Wright

At 6:00, most of the guests gathered for breakfast. When Cecilia and Eugene and Gloria and Matthew arrived in the dining room, Ken and Loretta, and Lydia Grace and Jacob, rose and hugged them. Cecilia glanced around the dining room. "At dinner last night, I realized nothing has changed. I always loved this dining room. The white table cloths are so crisp and the red runners draped across each table ... and the poinsettia centerpieces." She looked up. "Yes, the chandeliers are still sparking clean. Christmas Hotel is the best place in the world to stay. If my parents had not entered the nursing home in Houston, Eugene and I would not have left Franklin and moved back to Texas. We really loved are home and our friends in Franklin. We've missed you all."

Gloria nodded. "Sometimes it's hard to believe it's only been eleven years since we've all been together, but other times it seems longer.

Cecilia looked across the room and pointed. "Our son Brandon and his wife Brooke, along with their three children: six-year-old Lucas, four-year-old Emily, and ten-month-old Aiden are over at the table across the room. They wanted us to have our smaller reunion with just the eight of us. I'm sure we'll all get together with our children and grandchildren in the next ten days."

"We've missed all of you," Loretta agreed. Phone calls and letters just aren't the same." "This reunion was such a good idea and so capably planned by Chris and Lori Anna. They make a great team as owners and managers of Christmas Hotel." She pointed at another table. "Our three daughters and their husbands are several tables over. They said the same thing about some privacy for us four couples. Our two older daughters are pregnant with our first grandchildren and both are having baby girls".

Gloria opened her purse and pulled out a packet of pictures. The women laughed when she dropped one end and about five feet of attached pictures encased in plastic fell. "You've got to see the latest pictures of our children and grandchildren."

Matthew, Ken, Eugene, and Jacob groaned and rolled their eyes at one another. "You can't get women together without showing pictures," said Ken, but he smiled and shook his head. The other men nodded in agreement. The other three women now had their pictures out and passed around.

"Okay, guys. The women will be preoccupied through breakfast," said Ken.

"How about my Duke Basketball team?" Matthew wiggled his eyebrows. "They're killing your University of Kentucky team, Ken."

"All right." Ken frowned. "I'll *maybe* give you the win *this* season but wait until next year. Kentucky will clobber Duke."

Eugene shook his head. "I've got to side with Ken. Besides, Matthew, I realize you've lived in Durham, North Carolina for thirty years, but you were born and raised in Indiana; aren't you loyal to your home state of Indiana anymore?"

Matthew grinned. "Only when they're winning – and it certainly isn't this year."

Jacob looked from one man to the others. "Growing up in New York City, I didn't have a great college basketball team to follow, but I certainly had some major league baseball teams. So, I'll say, how about those New York Yankees? They swept the World Series in four games this year. It was also their second world series in three years. There's my bragging rights, boys."

Ken and the others laughed. "Okay, Jacob, you win the sports conversation banter."

The waiters brought the omelets, and the women and men quieted, along with the guests around the dining room, as they savored their breakfast.

*****

By 11:00 the Christmas Hotel staff and Wright family members finished decorating the chapel for the wedding. Chris and Lori Anna opened the arched door and entered the chapel to view the bedecked room. With Chris's arm around Lori Anna's shoulder, together they gazed around the beautiful chapel. "Let's sit on the last row of pews." Taking her hand, he led her to a seat. "*The Flower Patch* did a beautiful job with the pots of red and white poinsettias."

"Yes, they did, Chris. I also like the white bows the hotel staff tied to the six pews on each side of the main aisle." Lori Anna sighed and laid her head on her husband's shoulder. "It takes me back to our wedding, Chris."

He laughed. "Minus our dogs Fritz and Bella for the ring bearers?"

Lori Anna laughed, too. "Yes. We've probably had the most unique wedding *ever* in this chapel in the hundred and forty-eight years of its existence."

Chris looked straight ahead on the wall behind the pulpit where the large wooden cross hung. "Ever since I was a little boy, this chapel has provided peace for me, my family, and the townspeople. Numerous people have come here to pray and over the years many have found answers to their prayers; so many found their miracles here and realized all along their miracle was in Jesus and not a place. I found the answer to my most important prayer in this chapel." He turned to face her. "Lori Anna, I was here on the front pew with our baby daughter ten years ago when I asked God to spare your life from the leukemia, but it's also when I said, Thy will be done, Lord. I knew I needed to place my trust in Him, no matter what His decision would be; whether He took you home to him or gave you back to me. So many miracles have occurred here at Christmas Hotel. People have prayed for the guests and our family throughout the years." He cupped her cheeks in the palms of his hands. "I thank God every day for your remission. I love you so much, Lori Anna." He kissed her lips.

"I love you too, Chris. You are my life."

"You are my life, too. Let's pray for Noah and Melanie's wedding and their future." They bowed their heads. "Dear Heavenly Father ..."

*****

The reunion guests gathered for the wedding, and

Thomas and Alice Woodson approached Christopher and Jerilyn. "We just want to thank you for holding this reunion." Thomas placed his arm around his wife. "I can't tell you how much this means to us. We have never forgotten our wedding and honeymoon here. We brought the pictures to show Noah and Melanie ... and you two."

Alice continued her reminiscing. "You two set a wonderful example for our marriage. We saw how in love and devoted you two were to each other and to your children."

Christopher nodded. "Thank you, Alice."

"You're welcome. Thomas and I committed to the same promise in our marriage. I remember the year prior, your newborn baby had been kidnapped, and our heart broke for you both. However, your faith in God kept a peace in your heart. We were so happy to find out she was returned to you eight years later, *and* your little girl Lydia Grace grew up to become an accomplished pianist. We've attended two of her concerts. God is so good."

Christopher hugged Jerilyn to his side. She closed her eyes and buried her face into his shoulder as she often did to tune out chatter. She entered the world only she visited. Sometimes he wished he could join her. *Where does she go, Lord?*

However, he was in the here and now. He

needed to comfort Jerilyn and politely respond to the guests. "Yes, He is good. I'd say we both were blessed with wonderful marriages, children, grandchildren, and great-grandchildren. I'm happy my son Chris and his wife Lori Anna thought of holding this reunion." Christopher chuckled. "At our ages, it will probably be our final earthly reunion with all these friends together in one place."

Thomas nodded in agreement. "You're probably right, Christopher. I'm so glad Alice and I have lived long enough to see our grandson Noah married, and he chose such a lovely young lady for his wife. It was special for us when you married us fifty-one years ago, and now your son, the preacher, is marrying our grandson. What a day this will be."

"Indeed, Thomas, indeed it will be. By the way, you'll have two photographers on hand to commemorate this day. Lori Anna, who happens to be a professional photographer, and I will take plenty of photographs for their album, *and* my grandson Brian is making a video."

"Oh, how wonderful." Alice clapped her hands to her chest. "We thank you again for this unforgettable time at Christmas Hotel." She smiled at Jerilyn. Jerilyn returned the smile but said nothing.

Christopher knew the Woodsons must be

wondering about Jerilyn. In the past, she was always so outgoing and a terrific hostess. Thankfully, he had Lily, Lori Anna, and Lydia Grace to fill in for her, but it was Jerilyn who always made the guests feel extra special. He just hugged his wife closer to his side.

The wedding went off without a hitch. The bride had brought nothing blue, but as usual, Lily took care of it and provided the blue garter she purchased from *Jan's Bridal Boutique* earlier in the morning. "Lily, thank you so much, and you must let me pay you for it," said Melanie.

Lily flashed her winning smile. "Oh, no you won't." With a gleam in her eye and a wink she added, "I've provided the blue garter for many brides at Christmas Hotel, my family included. After all, Noah would be the one disappointed at not being able to remove your garter later."

Melanie blushed but returned the smile.

Chapter Ten

Offering Assurance

*"And the work of righteousness shall be peace;
and the effect of righteousness quietness and
assurance forever."*
Isaiah 32:17

Sunday
December 20, 1998
At 5:00 a.m. Chris and Lori Anna again placed the
flyers under the door for the day's events.

** Remember, reunion guests, every Saturday and
Sunday is "Omelet Day" at Christmas Hotel,
prepared by our amazing chefs. Please join us in
the dining room at six o'clock this morning for
your omelet any way you want it.*

** Sunday school is held in the chapel at nine
o'clock, and the worship service is at ten o'clock.
World renowned concert pianists Jacob Carlisle
and Lydia Grace Wright Carlisle will provide the
music.*

* Captain and Mrs. Rawlings are scheduled as Christopher and Jerilyn's guests for the noon meal, along with Jerilyn's best friends from her youth in Dayton, Ohio – Emma and Jack Showalter. Christopher and Jerilyn Wright look forward to welcoming both couples at their dining room table.

* Since it's Sunday, and the retail businesses are closed, please join the walking tour beginning at 2:00 this afternoon with my sister Lily Wright Demeter and her husband John as your tour guides. They will provide you with historical information of businesses around the square and our old courthouse. You will also visit the beautiful Greenlawn Cemetery.

* Tonight at 8:00 in the square, entertainment will be provided by Jonathan and Marianne. This will be another special treat with Christmas and Southern Gospel Hymns. Remember, the benches and fold-up chairs are available for your use. Don't forget to dress warm and bring a blanket from your room!

Have a blessed day!
Sincerely,
Chris and Lori Anna Wright

Marcus and Ken taught Sunday school, and Chris preached for the morning worship service. At the end of Chris's sermon, he announced he would preach again at the traditional Christmas Eve and Christmas morning worship service, and his dad, Christopher Wright, would preach the Sunday morning worship service on December, twenty-seventh. His three sisters and brother-in-law Jacob Carlisle would sing songs of farewell Monday morning, December, twenty-eighth, while the reunion check-out took place.

In the dining room, Christopher and Jerilyn greeted Jackson and Carolyn Rawlings with hugs, and Jerilyn kissed her life-long friends, Emma and Jack.

After the formal introductions were conducted, Christopher asked Captain Rawlings, "How are you and your lovely wife enjoying the reunion so far?"

"Oh, we are having an amazing time. It's the perfect wintertime respite at your lovely hotel. Carolyn and I could not be happier we were invited to the reunion."

"We were happy you could come," added Jerilyn. "And what about my two best friends from Dayton, Ohio?"

Emma grabbed Jack's hand. "We are grateful to have received the invitation, too. Now, since Jack and I have been retired for nearly ten years, we should get together more than every five years. Why don't you two come and visit us in Dayton in the spring? Jerilyn, you and I can visit our favorite old haunts – at least the ones still standing. The so-called modern buildings and parking lots have replaced many of our landmarks. They're now talking about tearing down the *Rike's Department Store* building *and* Memorial Hall. At least the Victory Theatre was saved. I hear they'll be remodeling the Victory Theatre next year and changing its name back to Victoria when it reopens."

She paused just a moment to catch her breath, and Christopher and Jack smiled at each other. Emma was known to talk ... a lot.

"Do you remember when we'd go downtown at Christmastime with our moms and view the Santa and reindeer flying up the side of *Rike's*? How about the amazing *Rike's* display windows with the mechanical figures, each depicting a family Christmas setting? The windows reminded me of Norman Rockwell paintings. Well, I hear the mechanical figures are out for repair. I wonder if we'll ever see them again. I certainly hope so." Emma stuck her lower lip out to display her sadness.

Christopher watched Jerilyn as she tried to absorb everything while Emma rattled on, but it was too much for her. Jerilyn took his hand, smiled at Emma with a nod, and turned to Christopher without a word. He recognized the pleading look in her eyes and answered for his wife.

"Emma, Jerilyn and I would like to visit with you and Jack in the spring. We should discuss this further before you leave." He saw the puzzled expression on Emma's face and changed the topic. "Did all of you attend the Sunday school and hear Chris's sermon this morning?"

"We were there." Carolyn swallowed a bite of her omelet and dabbed at her mouth. "I especially liked Chris's sermon. He's become quite the fiery preacher. Not a boring moment. We both enjoyed the Lord's message."

Christopher smiled. "I suppose he's become a 'chip off the old block.' I'll tell him what you said. He'll be pleased."

Jack jumped into the conversation. "I liked the Sunday school lesson your son-in-law Marcus and your older son Ken taught. They asked their audience for interaction, unlike our Sunday school teachers at home. I appreciated the class participation."

"I'll pass on your positive critique to Marcus and Ken. I know the two men prepared several hours for the lesson." Christopher stopped to take a bite of his meal, swallowed, and wiped his mouth.

"Will all of you go on this afternoon's tour and the evening singing in the square?"

"Wouldn't miss either," both couples replied.

"Lovely reunion activities," commented Carolyn.

"Totally agree," added Emma.

Jerilyn said nothing, so Christopher squeezed her hand for assurance and smiled at her. He said a silent prayer for Jerilyn, and he made a mental note to let the Rawlings, the Showalters, and some of the other reunion guests know about Jerilyn's condition ... especially the close friends.

Chapter Eleven

Story Time and a Christmas Hotel Tour

"This is the day which the Lord hath made;
we will rejoice and be glad in it."
Psalm 118:24

Monday
December 21, 1998
Chris and Lori Anna placed the flyers under the guests' doors by 5:00 in the morning.

* This morning at 10:00, Lily Wright Demeter will hold a reading in the Christmas Hotel conference room for the little ones. Moms and dads, please stay for the reading. Franklin townspeople are welcome to bring little ones.

* At 3:00 all guests are invited for a guided tour of Christmas Hotel – all five floors and the basement. Chris and Lori Anna Wright will be your tour guides.

* World renowned concert pianists Jacob Carlisle and Lydia Grace Wright Carlisle will hold a one-hour recital Monday through Wednesday at 8:00 p.m. this week in the chapel, playing selections of Southern Gospel and Christmas Hymns. Extra fold-up chairs will be provided for overflow in the lobby. Feel free to sing along!

* Lily and John will host two families at breakfast: Ralph and Irene Reynolds and Pastor Warren and Bertha Johnson.

* Christopher and Jerilyn will host Bob and Dona Young and Michael and Anise Rouse for the noon meal.

* Chris and Lori Anna Wright will host Mr. and Mrs. Paul Cooper and their children along with Emmet and Martha Randolph at 6:00 p.m.

Sincerely,
Chris and Lori Anna Wright

Lily didn't have to go far for the book she decided to read in the three sessions. Her parents still had her original copy of *The Lion, the Witch, and the Wardrobe* from 1950 in their family home library on South College Street. Lily was fourteen years old when she entered the enchanted world of Narnia, and she read all seven novels in the series from 1950 through 1956. The books were still in mint condition, and they all remained in her parents' library.

The weekend would be busy with the check-in on December eighteen, nineteen, and twenty, so Lily decided the readings should take place on Monday, December twenty-one and end on Wednesday, December twenty-three. She scheduled Monday in the conference room at Christmas Hotel, and Tuesday and Wednesday at the Goodnight Memorial Library, with up to an hour and a half for each reading.

At ten a.m. the parents brought their little ones to the hotel's conference room. Lily had pushed the chairs and sofas back against the wall, so the children could sit in a semi-circle on pillows on the floor in front of her. The parents sat in the chairs and sofas against the wall.

Each day, following a reading, Lily asked the children about their thoughts or questions. After the first day, a little boy named Paul cocked his head and frowned. Finally, he raised his hand. Lily called on him, and he stood. "Mrs. Demeter, my name is Paul. I don't have a question about Narnia. My question is why the children were sent to the professor's country home? You read in the story how in 1940 children were evacuated from London during World War Two to escape the Blitz. What was the Blitz?"

Lily studied the serious-minded little boy who was among the oldest of the children in the room. His parents who sat on one of the sofas looked at each other. Silence filled the room for several long seconds. "Paul, it's interesting you picked up on that part of the story. You are very astute, and I commend you for your thoughtful question. I taught school for nearly forty years, and I've read this story more than a hundred times myself and later to my students. You're the first to ask this question.

"There's a great many stories about the Blitz, so I'll give you a shortened version. The Blitz, from the German word 'Blitzkrieg' meaning 'lightning war', was the name borrowed by the British press and applied to the heavy and frequent bombing raids carried out over England in 1940 and 1941, during the Second World War. The heaviest air raids were often targeted especially on London. Have you studied Great Britain and the Second World War in school?"

"Not the war, but I know where London, England is from geography class. I'm in the sixth grade. I'm told both of my grandfathers fought in the Second World War."

"Well, Paul, you have some basic knowledge. I will just suffice it to say, during the war, many towns and cities were heavily bombed. Parents who had relatives or friends who lived out in the countryside, sent their children there to protect them. Many children were sent to stay with people they didn't know, but some had to remain in the cities with their parents."

Paul shuffled his feet, looked down, and then looked directly back at Lily. "What did those parents do with their children when there were air raids, Mrs. Demeter?"

Lily sighed. "Those parents had to keep their children with them and use underground shelters when the air raid warnings sounded. Paul, tomorrow morning we will be having our reading at the Goodnight Memorial Library. There are some excellent books for your age group about the children of World War Two. Your parents and I can help you choose a book to read during your stay at Christmas Hotel. Would you like me to help you?"

His face brightened. "Yes, Mrs. Demeter, I would."

Lily checked her watch. "In the meantime, it's lunchtime. Let's all head to the hotel dining room."

"Yay," or "yippee," shouted the excited children as they scrambled to their feet. Paul's parents stopped Lily. "Thank you so much, Mrs. Demeter. You handled Paul's question perfectly."

"Yes, you did," added Paul's father. "Actually, my father is English, and he, Air Commodore Jonathan Cooper, was in the Royal Air Force. My wife's father, Lieutenant Colonel David Timmons, was in the American Air Force, but they met and became friends during the war. My family left England and moved to New York where my dad's job took him after the war. My wife's family hails from Tampa. Both men and our families are friends to this day, and because of our father's continued friendship, I met my wonderful wife. It was during a reunion of the two men here at Christmas Hotel back in 1976 when her parents and my parents vacationed here. We were both college students and on Christmas break, so we joined them. We fell in love, corresponded for a year, and returned to Christmas Hotel. Your father married us in the Christmas Hotel chapel two years later in 1978."

Lily removed her handkerchief from her purse and dabbed at her eyes. "It's a lovely story. My sister-in-law Lori Anna is featuring stories this week in our local paper from our reunion guests. May I submit your story to be featured?"

"We'd be honored." Mrs. Cooper looked up lovingly at her husband.

Another little girl, five-year-old Jenny, who

overheard added, "You can share my parents' story, too. My mommy says every time she and Daddy visit Christmas Hotel in December, they have a baby the next September. My mommy says it's something in the water at Christmas Hotel. All four of us kids are born in September."

Lily's left eyebrow shot up, her chin quivered, her eyes blinked, and she did her best to avoid a chuckle. Lily and Mr. and Mrs. Cooper looked over at Jenny's mom and smiled. Jenny's mom's face turned bright red, and she stared wide-eyed and open-mouthed at her daughter.

Finally, Jenny's mom was able to speak. "Come along, Jenny, it's time for lunch." The little girl skipped gaily beside her mommy and out the door.

At 3:00 Chris and Lori Anna met the tour guests in the lobby. "Welcome to the Christmas Hotel tour, reunion guests! I know many of you have been on this tour in years past, and many of you with my father Christopher. He so very much enjoyed conducting the tour, but he passed it this year to my lovely wife Lori Anna and me.

"You're going to hear some canned speeches by me which you've probably heard at prior visits, but I know many of you brought guests who haven't been to Christmas Hotel. We thank you, because Christmas Hotel has been a generational place to visit from the day it was built. Follow Lori Anna and me, and we'll begin on the fifth floor and make our way down to the basement. If you're not up for all the steps, we have two elevators."

Chris pointed in the direction of the elevators. "When you exit the elevator, please just wait for us, and we'll meet you shortly."

Those who were able followed Chris and Lori Anna up the steps to the fifth floor, and the older guests and those with small children headed to the elevators.

When they reached the fifth floor, Chris pulled the brass handle on one oak door engraved with the letter C and one brass handle to the second door engraved with the letter H. He and Lori Anna used the wall hooks to hold each door open revealing a ballroom with a wide plank southern pine floor and six elegant crystal chandeliers. Plush green velvet high back chairs lined the walls.

Chris pointed to the portraits and the landscapes around the walls. "The portraits you see here are of the previous owners here at Christmas Hotel: Thomas and Lucy Goodnight Hoy, Captain Jacob Barnabas Bazell and his wife Mary Eve Winters Bazell, and of course my parents Christopher Joseph and Jerilyn Marlene Wright."

He looked over at Lori Anna. "I suppose we need to add our portraits eventually, honey." Lori

Anna nodded. "The landscapes are of different scenes around Simpson County throughout the one hundred forty-eight years of the existence of Christmas Hotel. There are two pictures of our courthouse: the original one that burned over a century ago, and the current building. The fourteen columns in this room are braces for the structure. I'm told, the architects of Christmas Hotel didn't want them to look like support beams in an elegant ballroom. Therefore, all the beams were encased in the columns."

The guests uttered their oohs and aahs, before discussing the beauty and elegance of the room among themselves.

Chris began the speech he'd heard his dad give from the time he was a toddler as he followed his dad around the hotel in the late fifties. "This antebellum hotel was built in 1850 prior to the Civil War, thus the word antebellum. It was built by a prominent Christian family in the community, the Thomas Hoy family. Mr. Hoy's wife, Lucy, was born into the Goodnight family, and to this day you'll see the Goodnight name around Franklin. Those of you who walked the Greenlawn Cemetery tour yesterday with my sister and her husband probably saw the Hoy and Goodnight graves, and family and friends' graves."

Many in the group nodded.

"The Hoy family's intentions were for all who stayed at Christmas Hotel, no matter what season of the year, to find their Christmas miracle. They prayed for each guest to experience the love of our Lord Jesus. They hoped all who visited would appreciate the daily miracle of Christmas, not just on the celebrated birth of Jesus. This is exactly why the Thomas Hoy family named their hotel Christmas Hotel.

"By the way, we're planning a ballroom night for our guests, so get your dancing shoes ready. On Saturday night, an orchestra from Nashville will be here to play the big band music of the thirties and forties, along with some professional ballroom dancers to teach us some dance steps."

Smiles and excitement reverberated through the crowd. Thomas Woodson even twirled his wife Alice and dipped her over his arm. He smiled at his surprised wife. "We'll be ready, won't we dear?" The other guests grinned and clapped.

Chris led the guests out and closed the ballroom doors. The guests followed Chris and Lori Anna down to the fourth floor. Chris continued his narrative. "Notice the artwork as you walk through the halls of each floor. Each picture is labeled for the year, who or what the picture is regarding, along with the photographer or artist. You'll find more portraits of the previous owners and their children throughout these floors. You'll also find paintings of our town square in each decade since the hotel's inception. All the business spaces have changed ownership throughout the years except the corner where Christmas Hotel stands."

He unlocked the door to one of the guest rooms. "Fifty-nine of the rooms on the second, third and fourth floors are identical, and are decorated in a twentieth century up-to-date fashion. Each of the rooms is redecorated approximately every ten to fifteen years. However, each room still has the small, original water closet, along with the antique tub with attached shower and sink. Guest rooms are larger than a room in an average sized hotel. In addition, long before the Gideons began placing Bibles in hotel rooms over eighty years ago, this hotel had a King James Bible placed in all sixty rooms, in the chapel, and in the lobby, from its inception. Now let's head down to the second floor. You'll see a far different room."

They descended the steps or rode the elevator, then walked along the hallway and stopped at room number seven. Chris reached in his pocket and extracted an antique oversized key engraved with the number seven and held it up to show the guests.

"As I previously stated, fifty-nine rooms at Christmas Hotel are periodically updated. However, room number seven is still bedecked in the nineteenth century and always will be. Lori Anna and I are the fourth owners of Christmas Hotel, and like the previous three owners we have no intention of changing this one room. It's never rented, and only used by the Wright family."

Chris opened the door, struck a match, and lit the kerosene lamp on the table by the door before asking his guests to enter the darkened room in groups of twenty. When each group stepped over the threshold, Chris and Lori Anna watched their facial expressions.

"Wow, have we entered another time era?" asked one guest. All eyes were drawn to the high four-poster oak bed with a sheer curtain around it and a marble top oak dresser which held an attached matching oak framed mirror. A lady's vanity sat next to the dresser, and it held a silver tray which contained a mother of pearl hairbrush, comb, and hand mirror. Two brocade chairs with a table between them and with a very old kerosene lamp atop the table sat in front of the window. Chris also lit the second lamp. Heavy deep green velvet drapes pooled on the floor from four floor-to-ceiling windows. In the middle of the four windows, french doors led to a small balcony.

Chris saw one lady viewing the drapes, and he strode over to open them. The woman walked up beside him, and she gasped. He smiled at her amazed expression, and others walked to the window to look over their shoulders. "You're in one of the two special rooms overlooking the square on North Main Street. From this vantage point you can look down on the square, see all the Christmas decorations, the townspeople milling around the square, and the numerous decorated businesses."

He showed the guests how the windows and french doors opened and locked. Four guests at a time stepped onto the balcony and glanced at the people strolling around below. When all had viewed the sights from the balcony, Chris locked the doors and closed the drapes.

Lori Anna pointed out another wall where a writing desk with very small drawers and pigeon holes stood. "My mother-in-law, Jerilyn, Chris's mom, arrived at Christmas Hotel back in December of 1941. She was only twenty years old, recently widowed, depressed, and pregnant. In this desk, she discovered a secret compartment. Let me show you."

Lori Anna showed them the spring which activated the secret cubicle, and continued with the story.

"Jerilyn found the diary of Carrie Emeline Bazell, the daughter of Captain and Mrs. Jacob Bazell, the second owners of Christmas Hotel. This diary had been hidden away for fifty-eight years until Jerilyn discovered it. It was through this diary Jerilyn found her miracle at Christmas Hotel. It was as if the diary had waited for her all those years. If you walked the Greenlawn Cemetery tour, you saw the graves of Carrie Emeline Bazell and her parents."

One of the guests asked, "Isn't one of your sisters named Carrie Emeline, Chris?"

"Yes, you're correct. As Lori Anna pointed out, my mother arrived at Christmas Hotel widowed and pregnant. When she married my widower father, Dad already had a daughter: five-year-old Lily. Mom birthed twins nearly five months after their marriage and she named one Kenneth Elliot for her deceased husband and my dad's first wife Ellie, and she named the other Carrie Emeline whose diary she found. My mom always considered Carrie Emeline a sister from another century."

"Wow," said another guest, "what a marvelous story."

"Yes, it is," agreed Chris.

Beside a large armoire, Chris opened a closed door. "This room also has the original water closet, or lavatory as it was also called, just like the other fifty-nine rooms," he explained.

There were three pre-teen children in the group and several teenagers. Chris addressed them. "I'm sure all of you children grew up with indoor plumbing, but indoor plumbing was almost unheard of in the nineteenth century and prior. You've probably heard of an outhouse or privy, but nowadays you'll only find them sometimes out in the country.

"Back in 1850, when Christmas Hotel was built, I'd guess only five percent of the population in the United States had indoor plumbing, and in cities only. What you see here at Christmas Hotel is the nineteenth century architect's answer to this novelty, and he used the latest technology of the time. You'll see the pull chain over the bowl used to flush the toilet. We also have the original tubs with a shower head that creates what was a called a rain shower in those days. In 1850, the water was stored in a huge cistern. You can learn a great deal about water closets or indoor lavatories at the library if you have further questions. I'm not an expert, and this is the best explanation I can provide.

"The three previous owners, and Lori Anna and I, kept the water closets for each of the sixty rooms, which helps generate the character of Christmas Hotel. People come from many states around the United States and the world to experience the ambiance of this unique hotel. Weddings have been performed here in our chapel from the hotel's inception, especially at Christmas. Many of you had the pleasure of attending the Woodson wedding this past Saturday."

Heads nodded in agreement.

Chris showed the final group out of room seven, snuffed out the lamps with a quick puff, locked the door and met all the people in the hallway. "Please follow Lori Anna and me downstairs, or take the elevators, and we'll continue the tour in the dining room."

When the group reached the main floor, they walked through the lobby and into the hotel's dining room. "I know you have dined in here, but I wanted you to see the room from the staff's perspective. Look up at the ceiling and observe this room. Like the ballroom, it contains six crystal chandeliers. These chandeliers are cleaned weekly by the hotel's excellent staff." Chris smiled at one of his employees on a ladder who was cleaning a chandelier. "Meet Ralph Emerson up there on the ladder. He's been with Christmas Hotel for thirty-eight years. Am I correct, Ralph?"

"Yes, sir, you are. Christmas Hotel is a great place to work."

"Thank you, Ralph. We appreciate you, too."

Ralph's face radiated.

Chris turned back to the guests. "Tables for two or four persons fill the room, all draped with crisp white linen tablecloths and matching white napkins." He held up a napkin. "You can see the monogram CH embroidered in the corner of each napkin and each tablecloth while a red runner extends across the middle of the tables with a holly and cranberry or poinsettia centerpiece. The ornate silverware is also engraved with CH. This room has been decorated similarly since Christmas Hotel opened in 1850. We know this because the Hoys and the Bazells kept meticulous records. This silverware is the original pieces from 1850."

Three men stood at the waiters' station polishing the silverware. Chris waved his hand toward the men. "I'd like you to meet Dave Bledsoe, Peter Scranton, and Sam Pinson. They've all three been a major part of Christmas Hotel for many years. They polish this silverware each day and make certain everything in the dining room is in order before every meal. Thank you, Dave, Peter, and Sam."

The three men smiled. "You're welcome, Chris." Two other men set crystal glasses on the tables.

"Reunion guests, I'd like you to meet Steven Henson and Michael Frawley." The men nodded toward the guests. "Steven and Michael work in the kitchen making certain the china, crystal, dishes, pots and pans are clean."

Chris pointed out the glasses. "Note each glass is embossed with a replica of the hotel and the letters CH."

Lori Anna waved her hand toward the windows. "Do you see the floor-to-ceiling windows overlooking the hotel's courtyard? Observe the two french doors leading to the courtyard and the red velvet drapes pooling on the floor. In the nineteenth century, extra-long drapes were a sign of wealth. In the summer, out in the courtyard, tables are set up around the decorated pine tree for those wishing to dine outside."

She noticed the surprised look on some of the faces. "I realize many of our Christmas guests have not visited in the summer, but the courtyard contains manicured flowerbeds and hanging potted plants with roses trailing from the pergola and trellises. Maybe some of you would like to visit in the summer. It's quite beautiful." She pointed in the opposite direction. "The corner fireplace is used in the winter, and as you see, our detailed staff has a roaring fire set." She chuckled. "They also clean the ashes each morning."

Chris and Lori Anna led the group through the third exit from the dining room and into the modern kitchen. Chris pointed out the copper pots and pans hanging on ceiling hooks and the oversized refrigerators, range top, and the six ovens. Ten men were busy preparing the evening meal for the guests: some whistling and others humming songs. The chef and his nine assistants paused while Chris introduced them to the guests. "These ten efficient men are the best cooks in Simpson County. They are the ones who ensure your meals are top-notch."

The men smiled, nodded to the guests, and thanked Chris for his compliments. Chris thanked each of them for their service at the hotel.

"Including the dining room door, six doors lead from the kitchen," continued Chris. He proceeded to show where the other five doors led. He opened the first door, and the group noted the large well-stocked walk-in pantry.

"Most of the items in this pantry were grown in the garden behind the hotel and out at my farm. The preserves and vegetables were canned at harvest time by these well-organized men, their wives, and my family members. We also have a cold meat locker on the other side of the pantry where the meat is hung until ready for meals. Most of the beef, chicken, pork, and even the freshwater fish come from local farms. We try to keep the Simpson County farmers busy. The second door is the supply room for the housekeeping staff. The third door opens to a staff break room, and the fourth door leads to the courtyard, so meals can be served straight from the kitchen to the guests seated in the courtyard on warm days. The fifth door leads to the basement steps." Chris turned on the light, and Lori

Anna and the group followed him down.

Lori Anna explained more about this area. "The housekeepers wash, dry, and fold the hotel linens over there." She pointed in the direction of the washers, dryers, and folding tables. Several of the men stooped. "I'm sorry, but the low ceilings can't be helped. It was built this way, and I apologize to you men over six feet eight inches."

"Not a problem, and that would be my brother and me," one of the two very tall men commented. "We'll just duck."

The crowd chuckled.

"The large enclosed area is a storage area for the hotel. You'll see the locked, fenced-in area containing several crates marked CEB. Those crates still contain the items which belonged to Carrie Emeline Bazell. They've been stored here since her death in 1884. There's an old safe there, too. We can only assume it contains items which belonged to the Bazell family, but no one in the Wright family has been able to open it. The combination is unknown."

Chris pointed to a room with a closed door. "Twelve years ago, I installed a darkroom. My dad, Lori Anna, and I are photographers, and it saved time not having to develop our pictures at the *Franklin Favorite*. At the same time, we installed the ten treadmills and the mirrors along the final wall. Please feel free to use the treadmills while you're here."

He pointed in another direction. "Behind those two doors are men's and lady's dressing rooms, each with showers. There's also another entrance to this basement off from the lobby. Those steps are over there." He pointed in the direction. "If you use the treadmills, you'll probably want to use the lobby entrance."

They headed back up the steps and passed through the kitchen into the lobby.

"I have only one other room to show you," Chris said. "Many of you have spent time here over the years."

They walked across the lobby. Chris opened the arched door of the chapel, and the group stepped in. Straight ahead on the wall behind the pulpit hung a large wooden cross, the focal point of the chapel. One main aisle split the room, with six pews on each side.

"This is where the small weddings are held, and my father has preached many sermons here," Chris said reverently. "Numerous guests and the townspeople come here to pray, and over the years many have found the answer to their prayers." He looked to Lori Anna, remembering their earlier talk. She smiled and nodded.

Chris glanced at his watch. "Well, it appears our

time is up. Lori Anna and I hope to see all of you for dinner at six and the concert at eight. Please enjoy the rest of your day."

Chapter Twelve

God at Work: The Years the Locusts Ate

*"And I will restore to you the years that the
locust hath eaten, the cankerworm, and the
caterpillar, and the palmerworm, my great
army which I sent among you."*
Joel 2:25

Tuesday
December 22, 1998
Chris and Lori Anna placed the flyers under the
doors by 5:00 in the morning.

** This morning at 10:00, Lily Wright Demeter will
hold her second reading at the Goodnight
Memorial Library for the children. Moms and
Dads, please stay for the reading.*

** World renowned concert pianists Jacob Carlisle
and Lydia Grace Wright Carlisle will return for
another one-hour recital tonight at 8:00 in the
chapel, playing Southern Gospel and Christmas*

Hymns. Extra fold-up chairs will be provided for overflow in the lobby. Feel free to sing along!

* Lydia Grace and Jacob will host two families at breakfast: Robert and Joan Cunningham and their six children, and Lyle and Priscilla Adamy and their two children.

* Christopher and Jerilyn will host Bob and Dona Young, and Randy and Becky Ray for the noon meal.

* Chris and Lori Anna Wright will host John and Tammy Damron, and Scott and Debbie Klepinger for the 6:00 meal.

* Private interview with Bruce and Ginny Sutton who arrived at Christmas Hotel the first time in 1979 will be conducted by Lori Anna Wright and held in the conference room. The conference room will be closed this afternoon during the interview.

Sincerely,
Chris and Lori Anna Wright

Lori Anna's first reunion guest interview for the *Franklin Favorite* was scheduled at 3:00 with Bruce and Ginny in the stylish conference room at

Christmas Hotel. On one side of the room, the conference table extended for the use of up to forty guests. On the other end four brown leather sofas and six matching swivel rockers surround a stone fireplace creating a cozy gathering area.

A log popped and crackled, and soft Southern gospel hymns played through the six overhead speakers. Lori Anna chose a seat in one of the swivel rockers near a sofa where Bruce and Ginny the forty-something couple sat close together holding hands.

Lori Anna opened the conversation. "I'd like to thank both of you for this interview. There are many people returning to Christmas Hotel for this spectacular reunion. The editor of the *Franklin Favorite*, our local paper, thought it would be a nice touch to interview some of the guests about their life before or during their first stay at Christmas Hotel. My father-in-law Christopher Wright informed me you two wanted to share your story with our newspaper readers. Do you mind if I record this interview?"

"Not at all," said Ginny, and Bruce offered the same response.

"My first question: how did you two meet?"

Bruce spoke first. "Ginny and I met twenty-three years ago back in 1975. Neither one of us were Christians at the time. We're from Lancaster,

Kentucky, and both of us went to a nightclub in Lexington for an evening of drinking, dancing, and meeting someone."

Ginny picked up from there. "I was with three of my girlfriends, and we were dressed in our favorite cowgirl outfits, having a good time laughing and talking. Bruce sat at the bar with a friend of his. I heard this roar of laughter, looked to my left, and that's when I first laid eyes on Bruce. He stood to get some money from his pocket and saw me looking at him.

"When our eyes met, I turned back to my friends. I wasn't flirtatious, but I definitely saw what I liked. He wore a checked cowboy shirt, jeans, cowboy boots, and a cowboy hat. The next thing I knew, he was standing beside me at the table. 'Hi,' he said, 'would you like to dance?'

"'Sure,' I said. When I got up, he took my hand and moved me to the dance floor where a line dance was in progress. When it ended, a Texas two-step began."

Bruce grinned and for a moment Lori Anna thought the years had fallen away for Bruce. He looked almost boyish with his dark but gray-streaked, neck-length hair and just a bit of protruding belly. "Ginny was gorgeous. I remember exactly what she wore: a cowgirl hat and boots, a short blue denim skirt, and a ruffled red plaid top just short enough to expose her belly when she raised her arms. Her hair was long, blonde, and straight."

Lori Anna thought Ginny was still a beautiful, but mature woman. She wore her blonde hair shoulder-length with subtle curls, and her figure was still slender.

Ginny blushed and touched his cheek. "Bruce and I spent the remainder of the evening together. We moved to a private table, talked and drank way too much. I went to his Lancaster apartment with him which was only ten miles from my parents' home where I still lived." She stopped and smiled at Bruce.

Lori Anna interjected during the pause in the conversation. "Evidently, the relationship grew or you two wouldn't be sitting here now. So what happened after the first night?"

Bruce smiled and brushed an unruly lock of hair from Ginny's cheek. "We were together for the next two weekends at my apartment. Within a week, I knew I was in love with Ginny, and I asked her to move in with me. I was a driver for an over-the-road nationwide trucking company, so I was only home on weekends. On the fourth weekend, we married at a justice of the peace in Lancaster."

Ginny chuckled and flipped the ends of her hair. "I was pregnant within a month. My parents, devout Christians, were not happy with our relationship, but were pleased knowing their first grandchild was on the way ... and I was married *before* I was pregnant." She looked down and then back up and met Lori Anna's gaze; her expression now sober. She sighed and continued. "However, I spent most of my time alone. After a couple of months, when Bruce came home on the weekends, he wasn't really home. He spent time with his friends at the bars, and getting high on drugs. He blew money we couldn't afford. We had three eviction notices during the first year and a half of our marriage, and the electric and gas were shut off several times."

Bruce hung his head. "I'm certainly not proud of how I treated Ginny. She tried so hard to be a good wife, but I suppose I wanted freedom again, and we fought. The worst night happened when she was eight months pregnant with our first child. I came home drunk on a Saturday night. I said to her, 'I bring home a paycheck ... what more do you want?'"

"He slapped me, and I fell into the wall. I went into labor, and Bruce passed out on the kitchen floor. My parents drove me to the hospital, and our son Matthew arrived one month early."

Bruce kissed Ginny's hand. "I met my son six hours after he was born. I apologized to Ginny, and as usual, she forgave me."

"Bruce was much better after the incident – at least for a few months. Bruce started running with a different crowd and listening to dark music. I was pregnant again, and our daughter Gabrielle was born thirteen months after Matthew. Bruce rarely saw us when he was supposed to be home. I suspected other women, but I wasn't certain until my brother Peter saw him out with a woman. I cried, not knowing what to do. Peter said to leave him, and my mom and dad would take in the children and me.

"On a Monday, when Bruce left for the week, I packed up everything the children and I needed, and moved back home. Bruce was furious when he returned Friday evening. Knowing he might show up at my parents' home, Peter and two of his closest friends stayed the weekend."

During a lull in the story, Lori Anna softly asked the next question. "What happened next, Bruce?"

He looked at Lori Anna and then back to his wife. With her other hand, Ginny squeezed his. "Tell her, honey. It's okay."

"Ginny's right. I was furious. I drove to her parents' home, and her brother Peter met me at the door. 'What do you want, Bruce?' he asked. He wasn't mean, but he was firm. However, I was belligerent. 'I'm here to get my wife and kids.' As I said it, I tried to step past him, but his friends stood behind him. I said to them, 'I'll be back.' I drove off, squealing my tires.

"I was angry. I met up with some friends, drank and smoked some weed. At midnight, I was banging on her parents' door. This time, Ginny opened the door with Peter, his friends, and her parents behind her. I grabbed her arm roughly and said, 'Get the kids. We're going home.'"

"I wasn't having any part of his bad behavior. I was done with Bruce. We'd had a family meeting when Bruce left earlier. I knew he'd be back, but my family and Peter's friends told me not to worry. They would not let him harm me or the children. When Bruce pounded on the door, Peter and his friends were there and had been watching for him. They saw Bruce was alone. I told them I'd go to the door. I'd hoped to calm Bruce. When he grabbed my arm and gave me the ultimatum to come with him, he slurred his words. I knew there would be no reasoning with Bruce. Peter stepped forward, and Bruce took a swing at him, but he was so drunk he missed Peter and hit me. My parents called the police, but Bruce left before they arrived."

Bruce shook his head. "I started drinking and carousing at night during the week. I was spiraling down into a deep hole, and I didn't care anymore. I'd lost my family. Life no longer had meaning. I could barely get up in the morning to report to the trucking company. After a couple of months of going into work hung-over or drunk, I lost my job."

Lori Anna quit asking questions and let the story unfold at Bruce and Ginny's own pace.

Ginny held up her hand. "In the meantime, the children and I were going to church with my parents and Peter. I had attended church as a child but strayed in my latter teen years. One Sunday, Christ saved my soul, and I dedicated my children to the Lord for His help in raising them. I knew with the Lord at the helm, I could do this. I joined a mothers' prayer group who met every Thursday evening at different houses. I prayed for Bruce constantly. I didn't want a divorce. I wanted my family, but I wanted a family like the family in which I was raised."

Bruce nodded. "While Ginny prayed for me, I'd become homeless. I panhandled for alcohol and drug money during the day and drank and slept in an alley at night, rolled in a threadbare blanket in a cardboard box. I had hit rock bottom. One morning I awakened, my head aching and I retched near where I had slept. I knew then I couldn't get much lower. My body and clothes were filthy. My beard and hair had grown long and tangled. I missed Ginny, Matthew, and Gabrielle something fierce. I prayed. 'Lord if you're really up there, please help me. I can't do this alone. I want my family.' And then I broke down and cried."

Bruce paused as his eyes teared. "When I looked up, two clean-cut older men were walking toward me. I stared at them, and they smiled. I said to them, 'If you're thinking about robbing me, I have nothing.' One of the men answered and said, 'No, son, we're here to help you. We heard your prayer. We're on our way to *House of Bread Mission* about two blocks from here. If you want the Lord's help, He's ready to help you. Will you come with us?'

"Wow, I thought. Did this prayer thing really work? I stayed with them at the house for two months. I was detoxed, fed, clothed, cleaned up, but most importantly, I accepted Jesus Christ as my Lord and Savior. I was given a job at a small factory in town, and I saved just about every penny. There were no longer drugs or alcohol on which to waste my money."

Ginny nodded. "One Sunday, about eight months after I left Bruce, I was at church with my parents and Peter. We were in line to say goodbye to our pastor and thank him for the service. I spotted Bruce about five people ahead of us. When I walked out, he was waiting. He politely addressed my parents, and Matthew ran to him. 'Daddy, Daddy,' he yelled as he hugged his father around the knees. Bruce knelt and picked up his son. I saw the tears on Bruce's cheeks. I stared at the well-groomed and sober man before me. I turned to my parents hoping they'd suggest what to do. They did not disappoint.

"'Why don't you two walk over to the park across the street,' said my dad. 'Your mother, Peter, and I will be nearby with the children.'"

Ginny laughed and turned back to Lori Anna. "To make this rather long story shorter, Bruce, the children, and I spent nearly every evening together at the mission, and later at my parents' home. We worshiped at church together. This pattern went on for about three months. We still hadn't spent a whole night alone. We were all so happy.

"In December, our fourth anniversary was approaching. My parents surprised Bruce and me with a five-day second honeymoon here at Christmas Hotel. They took care of Matthew and Gabrielle while we spent time at this amazing hotel getting reacquainted. We were in room number forty-four where we're again staying this week. Your father-in-law, Christopher Wright, preached on Sunday in the chapel. I remember the sermon so well. It was titled—"

Bruce finished her sentence. "'... I Will Give You Back the Years the Locusts Ate.' Yes, the Lord indeed gave Ginny and me back those wasted years."

Lori Anna wiped tears, sniffed, and Bruce continued. "Lori Anna, your father-in-law Mr. Wright preached about how sin could destroy a marriage, but God could restore the marriage and then some. Mr. Wright said, 'God must deal with sin, but when His people repent, they find abundant blessings which more than compensates for what was lost in the sinful years. His grace abounds.' God gave us back our lives, and we were blessed with three more children: Jonathan, Samuel, and Rebecca. Matthew is here this week with his wife and their three-month-old daughter Mary Elisabeth. All five of our children are Christians. We *have* been blessed."

Ginny gazed upon her husband, and Bruce wrapped his arm around her. "We were also blessed with the best marriage a couple could have. When the Lord is put first in life, nothing can break the binding ties. Christopher also remarried us in the chapel at Christmas Hotel on our fourth anniversary."

Lori Anna grabbed the tissue box on the coffee table, dabbed her eyes, and cleared her throat. "Your story has really touched me. I thank you for sharing it with me and our paper's readers. God bless you and your family, and enjoy the reunion."

Chapter Thirteen

The Lord's Timing

*"But they that wait upon the Lord shall renew
their strength; they shall mount up with wings as
eagles; they shall run, and not be weary; and they
shall walk, and not faint."*
Isaiah 40:31

Wednesday
December 23, 1998
Chris and Lori Anna placed the flyers under the
doors by 5:00 in the morning.

** This morning at 10:00, Lily Wright Demeter will
hold her third and final reading at the Goodnight
Memorial Library for the children. Moms and
Dads, please stay for the reading.*

** World renowned concert pianists Jacob Carlisle
and Lydia Grace Wright Carlisle will return for
their final one-hour recital tonight at 8:00 in the
chapel, playing Southern Gospel and Christmas*

Hymns. Extra fold-up chairs are provided for overflow in the lobby. Feel free to sing along!

* *Ken and Loretta Wright will host two families at breakfast: Kelley and Beverly Moore, and Ruthanne Etter and her daughter Betsy Etter.*

* *Christopher and Jerilyn will host Bill and Ginger Chandler, and Win and Shelly Kovar for the noon meal.*

* *Chris and Lori Anna Wright will host Vickie Hensley and her daughter Sarah Hensley, and Ron and Joy Lightcap for the 6:00 meal.*

* *At 1:30: photograph of reunion guests in front of Christmas Hotel. Meet out front of the hotel, and Megan, Franklin Favorite's photographer will take the commemorative photograph.*

* *Private interview with Beverly Brewster will be conducted by Lori Anna Wright and held in the conference room. The conference room will be closed this afternoon during the interview.*

Sincerely,
Chris and Lori Anna Wright

Lori Anna readied the conference room for her next interview, and checked her prepared introduction for the next interview. *Our Christmas Hotel reunion has turned out well. The hotel is full, and the reunion guests are having a great time. Several guests have shared a period in their lives and memories of their special time at Christmas Hotel for the Franklin, Kentucky paper – people like Mrs. Brewster. She asked to meet me alone without her husband.*

Lori Anna welcomed Mrs. Brewster with a smile and a handshake. Mrs. Brewster, a beautifully coiffed woman, wore a fashionable and sophisticated suit, and she returned the smile. "Mrs. Brewster, it's so nice of you to meet with me and share your memories of your mother. Please have a seat." Lori Anna set the recorder, with Mrs. Brewster's permission.

The sixty-something, well-spoken woman began in a soft voice. "One year ago, my mother died. She was ninety-five, and I was sixty-four at the time. I wish I could tell you we were close, but unfortunately it was not the case. Ours was a strained relationship and rarely affectionate. In fact, as a child, I can't ever remember running into my mother's arms for a hug and a kiss. She was distant toward me. As a child, I remember many nights crying myself to sleep. In my young mind, I thought Mom considered me a nuisance.

"When she was ninety, she entered the nursing home. I'd visit once a week, try to talk to her, and usually leave depressed, carrying her dirty laundry to wash over the next week. Sometimes, I think she tuned me out during our visits by turning up the television volume. She had great pride and would never admit she enjoyed my company. I had my own pride, and I would not admit how much I longed for her love.

"As she grew older, her health rapidly deteriorated. I thought about our intertwined lives. You see, my parents divorced when I was ten. Divorce was unheard of in the forties. My brother and I were the only children in our school having only one parent at home. When I was fourteen the school held a father-daughter dance, and the mothers helped by serving refreshments. I didn't even tell my mother about the event. My dad lived nearby in the same county in Kentucky, worked the second shift at the factory, and would never have taken off work for something he'd call frivolous. I didn't ask him.

"Following the divorce, my mother worked two jobs. I only saw her first thing in the morning and at bedtime. She wasn't the type to tuck me in and kiss me goodnight. She only asked if I'd finished my homework and what I'd prepared for dinner for my brother and me."

Mrs. Brewster shifted in her seat, crossed her legs, and folded her hands. She licked her lips, closed her eyes for a second, and sighed.

Lori Anna stood. "I'll pour us a glass of water."

"Thank you, Lori Anna." She took a sip and continued.

"By the time I was eighteen, I was ready to leave home. I refused to go to college, as my mother hoped, but I worked and lived on my own. However, something was missing. I owned a dog, but I wanted a real human relationship. When I met Mark, I thought I was in love. When I discovered I was pregnant, I told him, hoping he'd be pleased. He fled. I never saw him again.

"Mother had a traditional upbringing, so you'd think she'd have disowned me. However, when folks looked down their noses at me *and* my young daughter, she'd grab my arm and say, 'It's time to go, Beverly.'

"After she'd been in hospice care about six months, my mother's health quickly declined. She had some dementia, but she always knew me. I realized she wouldn't be alive much longer, so I needed to find some personal closure with her, or our abnormal relationship would haunt me forever. We began to talk more. One day I kissed her on the cheek before I left and told her I loved her. She smiled, her eyes teared, and she told me she loved me, too. In the last couple of months, it became our ritual of saying goodbye." Mrs. Brewster stopped, pulled a monogrammed, starched handkerchief from her purse, and patted around her eyes.

"The day before she died, hospice called me. They assessed the end of her life was a matter of hours. I entered her room, Bible in hand. I remembered the day I got saved, forty years earlier. She was the person I told first. I actually didn't know she was a Christian until I asked her. Mother was such a private person. She took me to church occasionally, but I'd never heard her testimony. She said her salvation was between her and God.

"When I arrived on her final day, she was asleep. I read my favorite Bible passages to her, hoping she'd somehow hear and know I was there. When she awakened, she merely said in a disgusted voice, 'They think I'm dying.' Mother always needed to be the one in control. However, I risked her insolence by brushing her hair, adjusting her pillows, and gently rubbing lotion on her swollen ankles, legs, and hands. I noticed her legs and hands were unusually cold. Not a good sign." Mrs. Brewster paused again and sipped some water.

"I stayed with her until one o'clock in the morning. She hadn't been conscious for at least eight hours. A couple hours earlier, the hospice nurse suggested to me, 'Go home. I'll call you when her time is over.' Shaking my head, I said, 'Not yet.' I pulled my chair closer to her bed. The nurse discreetly left the room. With tears running down my face, I talked to her. 'It's okay, Mom. I want you to know I'll be okay. It's time for you to relax. It's your time.' I didn't want my final words to her to be accusatory about her poor mothering. I just wanted her to know I was there for her, and if she was holding on for me, it wasn't necessary.

"I thought about her lack of hugging and kissing me when I was a little girl. Was it possible she learned the emotionless behavior from her own mother? I thought about her working two jobs after the divorce. She had to have been extremely tired, and I was too young to realize the effects the divorce had on her. I thought about the times she protected me from the judgmental people when my daughter was born. In her own way, she was protecting me like the mother bear with her cub. I look back now and I realize she was always there for me. Why did it take me all these years to figure her out?" Mrs. Brewster's eyes glistened, but she blinked twice, sniffed, and continued.

"At three o'clock in the morning, two hours after I'd left, the hospice nurse called. 'Your mother has passed. I'm sorry.'

My only response was, 'Is she still warm?'

"'Yes, but you need to hurry.' I awakened my husband, and we drove the twelve country miles in about nine minutes. The Hospice nurse met me at the door, and I walked straight to Mom's room and held her hand. It was still warm. The tears rolled down my cheeks. "'I love you, Mom. I'll see you on the other side. I wish we could have had a better mother/daughter relationship, but it was not for us. I'm just glad we completed our journey well.'

"Following the funeral, my husband asked me what I'd like to do. 'I want to visit Christmas Hotel in Franklin, Kentucky, where people find peace – where we honeymooned. Will you go with me?'" I asked.

"He hugged and kissed me. No words were necessary. I waited on the Lord, and I realized He had blessed me with a husband who healed my need for love." Beverly wiped the tears now trailing down her cheeks, and Lori Anna did the same.

"Your story was beautiful," whispered Lori Anna. "I thank you for sharing this difficult but poignant memory during the Christmas Hotel reunion. I'm certain your story will touch the hearts of many mothers and daughters. I appreciate your candor."

She nodded. "You're welcome, Lori Anna."

*****

The day's events went well, and at 7:30 folks

gathered for the final night concert featuring Lydia Grace and Jacob. Just like the previous two evenings, guests squeezed into the chapel, and the overflow spilled into the lobby. Years ago, Chris had placed monitors and speakers around the lobby, so when there was overflow, the guests could watch and hear chapel events from the lobby.

Monday and Tuesday night, Chris and Lori Anna attended the concert and Christopher stayed home with Jerilyn. The reunion was wearing her out, and she only stayed a couple hours each day for the noon meal. She spoke very little today and was not even receptive to her own children and grandchildren.

Back at home, Lori Anna hugged her father-in-law. "We want you to attend tonight, Dad. Chris and I will stay home with Mom. In fact, please take the children. School's out for Christmas break, so they can stay up late. I know they'll love watching their aunt and uncle. Also, for this final night, I hear Lily and Carrie Emeline are going to sing."

Christopher arrived with his three grandchildren, and they were early enough to get seats in the chapel three pews behind the piano. John, Marcus, and Ken lit the candles in the lobby and chapel, turned off the electric lights, and squeezed in behind Christopher and the children.

The three sisters and Jacob took the stage.

Jacob wore his black concert tuxedo with a white carnation, and the three ladies wore strapless, floor-length silk evening gowns: Lily in ruby red, Carrie Emeline in forest green, and Lydia Grace in midnight blue, and all with a white carnation pinned to the bosom of their dresses.

Lydia Grace spoke the greeting. "Thank you all for coming to our final concert this week. My husband Jacob will again sit at the piano."

The audience applauded, Jacob stood, took a bow, and sat back down, flipping his coattails over the piano bench. "Tonight we have an added treat for our reunion guests. My sisters Lily and Carrie Emeline will sing the hymns, and I will play the violin."

The audience clapped again, and the girls smiled and curtsied. "The first half of the evening we'll play and sing Christmas hymns, and the second half some of our favorite Southern Gospel and traditional hymns. Please feel free to sing along.

"Okay, up first is our oldest sibling Lily's favorite Christmas hymn, 'O Little Town of Bethlehem.' In fact, growing up, the Christmas season began in our family, the day after Thanksgiving with Mom, Dad, and my siblings singing Christmas hymns, cutting down a tree at the McLemore farm, trimming the tree, and singing more Christmas hymns. As the oldest, all hymns began with Lily's favorite. After, 'O Little Town of Bethlehem' was sung, the other Christmas hymns could be sung, and the Christmas season officially began."

Lily smiled. "Did my younger sister stress enough I was the *oldest* child in the family?" The audience chuckled.

While they sang the hymn, Christopher smiled, remembering a long-ago conversation with Lily. At the age of two, Lily sat on a bed pillow on the piano bench so she could reach the keys, and he sat beside her. She then spent a year practicing her notes and scales. By age three she had practiced enough. It was time to play a hymn. "What would you like to play first, Lily?"

"I want to play 'O Little Town of Bethlehem,' Daddy. It's my favorite. We can't have Christmas, Daddy, until we play, 'O Little Town of Bethlehem.'" She said it so matter-of-fact, he smiled then, as he did now.

Lydia Grace's voice interrupted the pleasant memory. "Now we're going to play *my* personal favorite: Franz Schubert's 'Ave Maria.' My sisters will sing the vocals while my husband and I play the music."

Christopher closed his eyes. Lydia Grace eight when she asked him about Jesus and salvation. She had recently found out Rose Clark, the woman who raised her and loved her, was not her real mama. They agreed that for future conversations they would address Rose Clark as Mama Rose.

"He really does hear us, doesn't He, Daddy?" she'd asked.

"Yes, honey, He does. Jesus came to earth as a baby to save us from our sins. He's our protector, like your dog Bullet was your protector. But unlike Bullet, He will never die. He'll always be here for you. Jesus is eternal. Do you want Jesus to save you, honey, so you can be with Jesus forever?"

"Yes, Daddy, but how?"

I know Mama Rose took you to church, but I don't know how much you've learned and what you believe. Do you believe in your heart Jesus can forgive your sins and allow you to live with Him forever?"

"Yes, Daddy, I believe it."

"Do you believe Jesus died on the cross for your sins and rose to Heaven three days later?"

"Yes, Mrs. Scott told us so in Sunday school. She said He could forgive all our past sins and our future sins." She hung her head. "Sometimes I didn't always tell Mama Rose the truth. Sometimes I was late coming home from school because I was watching the television at Lerman's Department

Store. On Saturday, I'd sneak out to watch the Roy Rogers show. I didn't always tell my mama the truth about where I was. I just loved to watch *his* Bullet. He looked just like *my* Bullet. Did you know that's why I named him Bullet?"

Christopher laughed. "We suspected such, honey." He smiled from the lovely memory, and his focus returned to the beautiful, adult Lydia Grace on stage.

Lydia Grace transitioned into more family favorites. "Next, my two brothers, Ken and Chris, have their favorite hymns, too: 'O Holy Night' and 'O Come all Ye Faithful.'"

As they sang, Christopher reminisced again. Over thirty years ago, his son Ken was trying to win the affections of the petite and raven-haired beauty, Loretta, whom he eventually married. Chris was twelve, and he worked the front desk at Christmas Hotel. The two brothers conspired to entice Loretta on a date with Ken, and Christopher overheard part of the conversation.

"You have to have lunch, so you may as well have it with me," Ken reasoned with Loretta, and he winked at his little brother.

"My brother's right," said Chris, taking the hint. "We don't want any of our *special* guests passing out from hunger."

Loretta had to laugh despite herself. "Okay, you

both win. Are we eating here at Christmas Hotel?"

"Actually, I thought I'd take you somewhere different. There's a little place over on Kentucky Street I like, and it's called ... drums please ..." Chris tapped his hands rhythmically on the desk. "Kentucky Grill!"

Loretta laughed and shook her head. "You're both nuts. Okay, I'll give it a try."

He took her arm. "Goodbye, little brother."

Chris winked at him, and Loretta laughed again. "You two are in cahoots," she said.

Ken guided her to the front door. "Well, we *are* brothers."

Christopher's memories ended abruptly when those on stage finished the hymns and the applause died down.

Lydia Grace turned to her husband. "We can't end the Christmas hymns without Jacob's favorite, although it seems to change from year to year." The audience chuckled. "Okay, love of my life, what's your favorite hymn this year?"

"This year I choose 'Hark the Herald Angels Sing,' and I'll require enthusiastic participation from everyone here."

Christopher's thoughts drifted to December, 1941. He'd recently met the young widow Jerilyn Marlene Seifert. His own daughter Lily was just five years old, and she'd invited Miss Jerilyn to dinner.

After the three of them cleaned the kitchen, they made hot chocolate, let Daisy, Lily's dog out of the basement, and retired to the living room. When they finished their hot chocolate, Christopher sat down at the baby grand piano, and Lily sat beside him. He motioned for Jerilyn to join them. She stood beside the piano, and he opened his hymn book and played, "O Come, All Ye Faithful," encouraging Jerilyn and Lily to sing with him.

Jerilyn chose next with "It Came upon the Midnight Clear." Lily naturally chose "O Little Town of Bethlehem." Christopher ended with "Silent Night."

Christopher checked his watch. "Lily honey, it's time for bed."

Lily's face scrunched, her eyes drooped, and her chin quivered.

"Maybe we can get Miss Jerilyn to help you into your gown tonight and watch you brush your teeth. I'll join you two soon."

Lily's face brightened, and she jumped up from the piano bench, grabbed Jerilyn's hand, and pulled her to the stairway.

Ten minutes later, Jerilyn and Lily sat on the edge of the bed. Jerilyn brushed Lily's hair, and Lily turned and hugged her. "I'm glad you're here, Miss Jerilyn. My daddy is tired so much, but he wasn't tonight. He was happy. I think he likes you. I like you, too."

Jerilyn smiled and returned the hug. "I like you too, sweetheart," she answered softly. "What's next in your bedtime ritual?"

"I need to say my prayers, and Daddy always listens. Then he tucks me in and reads to me until I fall asleep."

Christopher entered the room after waiting for the right moment. He didn't want to embarrass Jerilyn and have her think he was hovering.

He walked to the bed and hugged Lily. "Well, Lily, are you ready to say your prayers?"

"Yes, Daddy. Will you listen to my prayers, too, Miss Jerilyn?"

Jerilyn nodded, and all three knelt on the floor beside the bed with Lily in the middle.

"Dear Heavenly Father, thank You for bringing Miss Jerilyn to Franklin. Daddy and I like her, and I think she likes us. I really liked Christmas shopping with her today. She's fun ... just like Ruth's mommy. I like it when she hugs me, and she smells really nice. God, please bless Miss Jerilyn, my daddy, and Mrs. Evans, and my dog Daisy. Oh, and Miss Jerilyn said the sewing machine was expensive, but Daddy says all things are possible with You. Please give her the sewing machine for Christmas; and God ... if it's not too much trouble, please give me a mommy for Christmas. In the

name of Your Son Jesus I pray ... Amen."

Christopher hugged Lily when she finished, and saw Jerilyn sniff, wipe a tear, and look away. Children's prayers could be so open and honest, with no pretense. Christopher picked up Lily and laid her in the bed, placing her head on the propped pillows. He walked around on the other side, and Jerilyn helped tuck her in.

Christopher pulled up the chair, and Jerilyn sat on the bed beside Lily. "All right, Lily," he said. "What story do you want to hear tonight?"

"Would you read me *Curious George*, please?"

"My dear Lily, I think I have read you that story twenty times since we bought it at the bookstore this year. I'd think you would have it memorized."

"All right, Daddy. Maybe Miss Jerilyn could read the story tonight. Then it will sound different!"

Returning to the present, Christopher used his handkerchief and wiped a tear after this particular memory. Jerilyn was so fragile that Christmas. Many times he wanted to hold her and let her grieve. Lily was the one who helped Jerilyn more than anyone. *Thank Thee, Lord, for my precious little Lily.*

Christopher composed himself just as Lydia Grace turned to Carrie Emeline. "Carrie Emeline, which of the Christmas hymns should we end this half of the evening?"

"Well, in my opinion all Christmas concerts must include 'Silent Night.'" It was so beautifully harmonized by all three sisters it silenced the audience.

As Christopher watched his daughter on stage, the poised Carrie Emeline, he remembered a time when she was not so poised. It was thirty years ago when she met her first husband, Staff Sergeant Andrew McConnaughey.

They all turned as a blast of cold air hit them when the front door opened. In walked an army soldier with a large pack thrown over one shoulder. As soon as he stepped over the threshold, his cap was immediately in his hand. Carrie Emeline checked out the tall figure with the muscular build and the military-short blond hair. He stomped the snow from his boots and brushed the snow off his shoulders onto the large mat. When he looked up, his blue eyes landed on Carrie Emeline. He smiled with a slow crooked grin, and she blushed.

He addressed her father. "I'm Staff Sergeant Andrew McConnaughey," he announced in a commanding voice while shaking Christopher's hand. "A buddy of mine stayed here with his family several years ago. He told me about Christmas Hotel and how special it is. I'm on leave, and I thought this is where I'd like to spend my leave. Would you have a room available for the next twenty days?"

"Yes, we have a room for you, and we'd all like to welcome you to Christmas Hotel. My name is Christopher Wright, and this lovely lady is my wife Jerilyn." He hugged Jerilyn to his side.

"Welcome to Christmas Hotel." Jerilyn shook the sergeant's hand.

Twelve-year-old Chris stepped forward. "I'm one of their two sons, and you can call me Chris."

Sergeant McConnaughey shook Chris's hand. "It's nice to meet you, Chris."

"This young lady is one of our three daughters: Miss Carrie Emeline Wright," said Christopher.

Sergeant McConnaughey took Carrie Emeline's hand, but instead of shaking it, he drew her hand to his lips, and tenderly kissed it. "It's a pleasure to meet you, *Miss* Carrie Emeline."

The sergeant's blue eyes twinkled, and his lips curled into a crooked grin when he accented Miss.

She laughed and blushed again. "It's my pleasure to meet you, also, Sergeant McConnaughey."

Christopher cleared his throat, interrupting the meeting between the sergeant and his daughter. "If you'll step over to the front desk, we'll get you checked in."

Back in the present, the audience's applause echoed throughout the chapel and the lobby, interrupting Christopher's trip down memory lane. Lydia Grace continued, "This concludes the Christmas hymns, so now we'd like to sing some family favorite traditional Southern Gospel hymns. Our Mom and Dad's favorite hymn is 'Farther Along,' which we'll begin with, and then you, our audience for this final evening may choose. After each hymn, just yell out the next one you'd like to hear."

Shouts for "He Touched Me", "How Great Thou Art", "Count Your Blessings", and "Amazing Grace" ended the evening.

A rousing applause along with a standing ovation commenced from those in the chapel and in the lobby. Jacob stood beside his wife and her sisters. He took a bow, the three women curtsied, and Lydia Grace addressed the audience.

"I thank all of you for attending our three concerts. We have been honored to provide these concerts during the Christmas Hotel reunion. Thank you so much for joining us at this special reunion. Look for your flyer tomorrow morning for the Christmas Eve events. Have a blessed evening."

Chapter Fourteen

A Time of Tribulation and Comfort

*"Who comforteth us in all our tribulation, that we
may be able to comfort them which are in any
trouble, by the comfort wherewith we ourselves
are comforted of God."*
2 Corinthians 1:4

Thursday
December 24, 1998
Christopher rose before Chris and Lori Anna had
printed the flyers. He met them down in Jerilyn's
former office, now the family home office. Chris
and Lori Anna were the main ones to use the room
since Jerilyn no longer wrote novels. Jerilyn still
entered the room, but she'd sit and stare at her
Brother Word Processor.

Much of her last story had been completed
before Jerilyn became ill, and Lori Anna, the other
writer in the family, planned to finish the
manuscript for her mother-in-law when the
reunion was over.

When Christopher walked into the office at 4:00
a.m. he was just in time before they hit print. "I'm

149

sorry, but I think you need to take my name and your mother's off the flyer as host and hostess for the remainder of the noon meals. I think it's become too much for Jerilyn. She's getting quieter and quieter."

"We've noticed too, Dad. Do you still want to do the woodworking project today from 2:00 - 5:00 this afternoon?"

"I do, as long as someone will be here in the house with Jerilyn."

Chris nodded and pursed his lips. "Lily and John are hosting breakfast. I know Lily, Carrie Emeline, and Lydia Grace will be in Bowling Green this afternoon serving at the soup kitchen, so I'll see if John can stay with Mom. Olivia will help him, and Abigail and Michael will be with you in the woodworking class. Lily and John are normally awake by now, so I'll give John a call. I'm sure Ken and Loretta will host the noon meal. I'll call them, too." Chris placed his hand on his dad's arm. "We'll get through this, Dad."

Christopher nodded. "I know, son, and thanks."

Chris and Lori Anna placed the flyers under the doors by 5:00 a.m. as usual.

* Lily Wright Demeter and her husband John Demeter will host two families at breakfast: Jim*

and Kim Sexton, and Chuck Jr. and Denise Zimmerman.

* Ken and Loretta Wright will host Pastor Jack and Josephine Little, and Pastor Dave and Tera Heltsley for the noon meal.

* Chris and Lori Anna Wright will host Gilbert and Ruby Dailey, and Samuel and Anna Parks for the 6:00 meal.

* From 2:00-5:00 Christopher Wright will hold a woodworking class at the Wright family home at 210 South College Street. All participants should meet at the back of the residence in the backyard workshop. Today's project: Cutting out and painting replicas of the Christmas Hotel facade as a commemorative Christmas ornament.

* This evening, at 7:30 in the Christmas Hotel chapel, Chris Wright will read Matthew Chapter 1 Verses 18 to 25, and Matthew Chapter 2 Verses 1-11, at our traditional Christmas Eve service. Please join us.

Sincerely,
Chris and Lori Anna Wright

At 9:30 a.m., Lily, Carrie Emeline, and Lydia Grace met at Christmas Hotel to drive to Bowling Green. Lily waited in the hotel's lobby for Lydia Grace and Carrie Emeline to arrive, with a package on the floor beside her wrapped in bright pink and blue birthday wrap. The two sisters were laughing when they joined their older sister. Lily grinned at them.

"Okay, little sisters, what's so funny this morning?"

Carrie Emeline answered, still laughing, "Staying with Lydia Grace on the farm is a hoot. Growing up in a seacoast town, Elise and Erica are certainly not used to farm life. I must say though, my sixteen-year-old twins are adventuresome. This morning they followed Jacob, Anthony, Lydia Grace, and me to the barn to watch while the cows were milked. After watching a few minutes, they asked to help.

"Once they got the rhythm down, they performed the task quite well. However, after about fifteen minutes, when some milk sprayed Elise, she shrieked, jumped up, spilled her bucket of milk, fell over her sister, and both wound up in a heap on the barn floor. While they were on the floor laughing from their mishap, two barn cats licked the milk off Elise's face."

Lydia Grace laughed. "The girls did better than Jacob, Anthony, and me when we first moved to the farm. Chris was patient teaching us about barnyard animals. Poor Chris, he had to come every morning for a month. We knew nothing about cows, pigs, horses, and chickens – and especially Jacob and Anthony, both having been born and raised in New York City. At least growing up, the Wright family visited farms in the country, so we were around the barn animals and were aware of the chores."

Lily listened to her two younger sisters. Although, she was not blood related to Carrie Emeline they were as close as two full-siblings could be. She and Lydia Grace were half-siblings both having Christopher for a father, and she felt very close to Lydia Grace, too. There was no denying it; God blended this amazing family together.

Carrie Emeline turned to Lydia Grace and hugged her. "Thank you so much for letting Marcus, the girls, and me stay with you this trip. With our family home *and* Christmas Hotel full, I'm just glad you had the room for us. What a jam-packed house, but what fun. There's never a dull moment on the farm."

"It's been great for me, too, sis. Maybe after Christmas, and when the reunion is over, we can have Lily over and kick everyone else out. It would be fun for just the three of us to spend a night together again. Or we can all three stay in our family room number seven here at Christmas Hotel."

Lily smiled and nodded. "Sounds like fun. By the way, Lydia Grace, here's your birthday gift from John and me. I've taken up painting in my old age. I hope you like it."

The three sisters sat together in the lobby while Lydia Grace tore into the wrapping. "Sometimes it's hard to believe I'm now fifty-two."

"What a child," scoffed Carrie Emeline. "I'm fifty-six!"

Lily shook her head. "You're both such children. At sixty-two, I feel every year. My bones even creak. Where did the time go? It just doesn't seem so long ago when we all lived in the family home on South College Street. I miss those days."

Lydia Grace and Carrie Emeline concurred, while Lydia Grace finished tearing off the wrap of the birthday package. "Wow, Lily, this is incredible. You have real talent."

All three sisters studied the collage painting of the family home on College Street, the square with the courthouse, and the façade of Christmas Hotel. In the square, Lily even included the special park bench where their parents became engaged, as did John and Lily, Carrie Emeline and her first husband Andrew, Lydia Grace and Jacob, and also Chris and Lori Anna – along with a holly wrapped light pole with a big red bow near the top.

"You know the city can never remove *our* bench or the light pole," continued Lydia Grace. "The Wright family would have to buy it. There are so many wonderful memories in your painting: our family home, the bench, the old courthouse on the square, the decorated light post, and Christmas Hotel. This will go in a special spot just like the painting I received on my birthday many years ago of the fountain in Bowling Green and of my first dog Bullet."

She paused and cleared her throat. "Excuse me. All at once, I feel very sentimental." A tear slid down her cheek, and her two sisters hugged her.

Pragmatic Lily jumped up first. "We'd better get to the soup kitchen in Bowling Green. It's time to feed our homeless friends."

As they walked to the front door, Lily added, "I'm glad we made this day with the homeless a Christmas Eve tradition all those years ago. It's nice to have something consistent to do each year with my sisters and such a special tradition. I hope my three girls do something like this in the years to come."

While the three sisters were serving the homeless at the special Christmas Eve Soup Kitchen lunch in Bowling Green, John arrived for the afternoon to relieve Christopher and help his young niece Olivia as Jerilyn's caregivers.

"Are you certain you're okay with this, John?" Christopher ran his fingers through his hair. "Jerilyn can be challenging. One never knows how she'll react when she awakens. I can always cancel the woodworking today."

John wrapped his arm around the shoulder of ten-year-old Olivia. "We will be fine, Dad." He smiled at Abigail and Michael who fidgeted beside Christopher. "I know Abigail and Michael have been looking forward to this woodworking class. It's not every day a commemorative ornament of Christmas Hotel can be cut out and painted."

While he spoke, men and children gathered out back. "It looks like about twenty so far, Dad. I hope you have room in the workshop for all of them."

"Yes, I see. I didn't expect so many, but this is wonderful. We'll fit them in. Thanks again, John."

"Don't mention it, Dad."

Christopher turned to Abigail and Michael, who skipped off ahead of him toward the back door. John overheard his father-in-law. "Welcome, and let's head into the workshop. I have everything ready."

Jerilyn still had not awakened from her nap, so John and Olivia made hot chocolate, added marshmallows, and carried their mugs into the living room to wait. Bobby, raised his head and resettled on the hearth in front of the fireplace with a heavy moan.

Olivia frowned, her chin quivered, and she stared at her uncle. "Is something wrong, Olivia?"

A tear slid down her cheek, and she wiped it away. "Sometimes I don't think Grandma loves me anymore." She set her mug down and shifted in her seat. "She used to hug me and kiss me and tell me she loved me, and Abigail and Michael, too. She doesn't do it anymore. Sometimes she doesn't know I'm here. She mostly just sits and stares. Every now and then I hear her in her bedroom crying." Olivia paused and then looked at her uncle. In a shaky voice she asked, "Did I do something wrong, Uncle John?"

John set his cup down and moved to the sofa to hold his niece. Olivia cried and shook in his arms. "Olivia, you did nothing wrong. A disease has attacked your grandma and unfortunately there is no cure. Have your parents explained any of this to you?"

"I've been afraid to ask. I ... I thought it was me."

"Oh, honey, it's not you. Your grandma will probably never again be as you remember, and it's not her fault. She can't help the way she acts. Just know if she could be like the grandma you knew and loved, she would."

"So Grandma may never hug and kiss us again?"

"I'm not saying *never*, Olivia, but this disease is harder on the family than the victim. Always remember how much she's loved you, and she'd tell you if it was possible for her."

Olivia sniffed, wiped her eyes, and sat straighter when she heard the bed squeak upstairs. "Thank you, Uncle John. Listen, I hear Grandma getting up. We should go help her. She'll need us."

He rose. "I'm right beside you, Olivia," and he took her hand. "Don't worry, because we'll take care of her. No matter what happens, we love her, whether she knows us or not. Someday we'll look back and say we loved her when she could not know or love us."

Together, and hand-in-hand, they climbed the steps.

At 7:00, folks gathered in the Christmas Hotel chapel for the Christmas Eve service. Jacob sat at the piano, Lydia Grace played her violin, and her two sisters, Lily and Carrie Emeline, sang Christmas hymns.

Chris walked to the podium promptly at 7:30. He looked around at his family, friends, townspeople, and the reunion guests; most dressed in reds and greens for Christmas. The Blakely boys, both under age ten, even sported matching bow ties. *How I love them all, Lord.* He bowed his head for a silent prayer. *Lord, let me get out of the way, so You can deliver Your message through me to these wonderful people.*

He looked out to the congregation. "Good evening, reunion guests, family, and friends. As you know, it's been a tradition at Christmas Hotel to read part of the Christmas story on Christmas Eve, and the remainder on Christmas morning. Please stand for the reading of God's Word in Matthew chapter one, verses eighteen to twenty-five, and Matthew chapter two, verses one to eleven."

Chris closed his Bible after he completed the reading, asked the congregation to be seated, and a flash of memory crossed his thoughts. Ten years earlier, when Lori Anna was enduring leukemia treatments, and Olivia was just a couple months old, he was tired and losing faith in God. His wise father spoke to him about adversity.

Chris took a seat on the sofa in the family home. "How was Olivia while I was gone, Dad?"

Setting his Bible on the end table and removing his reading glasses, Dad said, "She was wonderful, Chris. She drank all her formula at her evening meal. How's Lori Anna?"

"If I could use one phrase, I'd say content with

her situation."

Dad sat up straighter in his chair and rubbed his chin in thought. "I see Lori Anna's disease as adversity, but adversity is what defines us, son. I sometimes think about all the adversity your mother and I went through over the years, especially when Lydia Grace was kidnapped and the two miscarriages your mother suffered. It's hard to think in the present how much stronger adversity makes one but, when looking back, it made your mother and me stronger.

"When adversity strikes, we sometimes forget to rely on God. It's important to recall past answers to prayers, guidance provided by the Holy Spirit, and what we learned in prior crises. Don't let your distressed emotions impede clear thinking, son. Whatever happens, you and Lori Anna will be fine. Know God is *always* with you. Have faith in Him."

"Thanks, Dad. It's hard. I watch Lori Anna feeling and looking better one day, and the next day she's back at the starting point." He sighed and rubbed his temples. "I wish I knew how and when this will all end." He told his dad about Lori Anna's ominous letter to him.

"It sounds to me as though Lori Anna is ready to accept whatever fate the Lord hands her. You must be strong, son. You must let her know you'll be okay. I think that's what she needs to hear from you. It's not giving up, Chris – it's letting go and letting God do what's needed for Lori Anna ... and you."

Chris hung his head. "I don't know if I'm ready, Dad." He stood. "Tell Mom I love her, and I'll call tomorrow." He picked up his sleeping daughter and left for home.

Chris shook off the past memories from a decade ago, and he looked out on his congregation. "It's been a custom of ours to speak about this precious Baby Jesus and what He means to all of us. First and foremost, He was God's gift to us. Since I was a small boy, I observed my parents walk with God and their unwavering faith. When I was a teenager, I asked my dad how he and Mom never appeared to argue, fuss, and fight. His answer was immediate: 'We pray together daily. We went into the marriage knowing we'd never give up on each other. My parents and grandparents felt the same, and so were your mother's parents and grandparents. Never give up, son, always pray. Make certain God is in the marriage triangle with you.' Recently Dad said to me, 'A song was written titled "A Long Line of Love". When I hear the song, I think of your mom and me. We come from a long line of love." Chris paused and took a sip of the water at his pulpit.

He smiled and looked out upon his attentive

congregation. "I know God brought my parents together, who had been mentally crippled by the deaths of their first loves. So, what do I know about this Baby Jesus? He grew up to change lives, as He did for my parents. His most precious gift for us is the gift of eternal life with Him. When He knocks on our hearts, we can choose Him – or not. Many have chosen the riches of this life and walked away from Him. Believe me, when we *do* walk away, He is saddened. He does not want any of us to perish but to have eternal life with Him. Do you prefer riches and this world, over eternal life with Him? I know it must break His heart, but He gave you the freewill to choose your destiny.

"Your walk begins when you admit you are a sinner, when you ask forgiveness, repent, and ask for salvation. Then get close to Christ, pray, and build a relationship. Don't stay a baby Christian. One can't live on milk forever – we need solid food. Many people have given testimonies during this reunion. My sister Lydia Grace asked to share her testimony tonight, which happens to be her birthday. Lydia Grace, please come forward."

Lydia Grace walked up the few steps, hugged her brother, and he took a seat behind her. She inhaled a deep breath and slowly exhaled. "I could have been bitter. Yes, I was born on Christmas Eve in 1946. However, for the first eight years of my life,

I thought my birthday was December first. You see, I was kidnapped from the hospital in Nashville where I was born, and taken to an apartment in Bowling Green."

She stopped a moment as gasps sounded throughout the room from those who were unaware of her story.

"I was so close in miles to my real parents, yet so terribly far. For eight years, I was raised by Rose Clark, a troubled woman whose baby and husband died shortly before I was born. In her disturbed mind, she desired to use me to replace her own baby, so she snatched me from the hospital nursery where she was a resident nurse.

"She got away with her crime for eight years, but thankfully she had a change of heart after she was saved at a church near our Bowling Green apartment. When she was dying, she wrote a letter to my real parents and admitted what she had done."

Ladies pulled out handkerchiefs and dabbed at their eyes.

"Following her death, I was returned to my true parents, Christopher and Jerilyn Wright. However, I then hated Rose Clark for what she'd done. Jesus came into my heart and changed my eight-year-old hardened heart. I was able to forgive her.

"I could have remained bitter, but I chose Jesus,

forgiveness, and His gift of eternal life. In return, He has given me an incredible life. I have the most wonderful parents, siblings, husband, and son. God is good. If you have bitterness in your heart or need to forgive someone, I implore you to call upon Jesus tonight to change your heart. He will comfort you in your suffering. If you have not received His gift of salvation, He has His hand out to you. All you must do is say yes to Him. I did, and I've never looked back. Thank you for allowing me to share on my birthday."

Lydia Grace stepped down to the front pew and sat between her husband and son, who each hugged her, and the applause subsided.

Chris stood at the pulpit and smiled at his sister. "Thank you, Lydia Grace for sharing. It's unwise and unhealthy to hold onto bitterness. It only cripples one's spirit." Chris looked upon the congregation. "If any of you are holding onto bitterness or unforgiveness, ask God to help you let it go today. I promise you, your Christmas will be much more peaceful. If you have not yet asked for His gift of salvation, there's no time like the present. Like Lydia Grace said, 'You'll never look back.'

"Let's pray. Dear Heavenly Father...."

Chapter Fifteen

God's Amazing Gift to Us

"I have shewed you all things, how that so labouring ye ought to support the weak, and to remember the words of the Lord Jesus, how he said, It is more blessed to give than to receive."
Acts 20:35

Friday
December 25, 1998
By 5:00 a.m., the flyers were placed under the doors.

* Today, the only activities asked of the reunion guests is for all to have breakfast with their own families and to come to the Christmas service in the chapel at 8:00 a.m., following breakfast.

Sincerely,
Chris and Lori Anna Wright

Jacob played Christmas hymns at the piano, and the three Wright sisters sang while worshippers entered the chapel. Chris stood behind his pulpit as "Joy to the World" ended.

"Merry Christmas to all of you, and I hope you savored some wonderful omelets this morning prepared by Christmas Hotel's chefs, *and* opened a few presents."

The congregation murmured, smiled, and nodded their heads.

"Last night we read Matthew's account of the birth of Jesus, so it's our tradition at Christmas Hotel to read the continuation of the story on Christmas morning: Luke's account. Please stand in reverence of the Word of God and open your Bibles to chapter two of Luke, verses one through fourteen."

Chris read the fourteen verses and asked everyone to be seated. "My sermon this morning is simply titled 'Gifts'." Chris gazed around the little chapel. "Let's pray. Dear Heavenly Father, help me to get out of the way, so this will be Your message. You know what words are needed to be spoken. I am only the messenger. It's been an astounding week at Christmas Hotel, leading up to the day belonging only to You each year. However, we at Christmas Hotel celebrate Your birth each day. We appreciate the sacrifice Your Son Jesus Christ made for His children. Thank You, Jesus, for Your blessings on the people who enter Christmas Hotel every day of the year. In Your name, we pray, Jesus, Amen."

The crowd echoed Chris's Amen.

"Last night in reading Matthew's account of Jesus' birth, we learned about wise men bringing gifts. No doubt, many gifts have been unwrapped all over the world today. We all know Jesus' words, 'It is more blessed to give than to receive.' Do you believe it? Do each of you prefer to give a gift, rather than receive a gift? I had an elderly and lonely widow once say to me, 'I like to give gifts, but when I receive a gift, I know someone thought of me.' I do appreciate what she said, and I understand. In this particular circumstance, the giving can work both ways, if one is thoughtful of others. You heard my sister Lydia Grace's testimony about bitterness, forgiveness, and salvation last night. Keep her testimony in mind when I tell you this story."

Chris paused for a moment as he looked at the rows of eager faces. "This story is about my three sisters, and I'll try not to embarrass them. When Lydia Grace was ten, Carrie Emeline was fourteen, and Lily was twenty, they were out shopping on Christmas Eve – Lydia Grace's birthday. My three sisters came upon the soup kitchen just up 31-W in

Bowling Green. The situation was more pitiful for Carrie Emeline and Lily than it was for Lydia Grace. The two older sisters had not been around the homeless, poor, and outcasts of society, but it was familiar to Lydia Grace. When she was kidnapped by the widowed, former nurse, she was raised her first eight years in poverty. Lydia Grace was drawn to the destitute people."

Chris picked up his microphone and walked down the few steps to the front row.

"As the people filed into the soup kitchen for their warm Christmas meal, she begged her sisters to go in, too; not to eat, but to help serve. The two workers were frazzled, as some helpers had not shown up. At eleven o'clock the food was not nearly ready. The bread had been baked earlier but vegetables were still being added to the soup. The sisters tied on aprons and went to work. Carrie Emeline and Lily finished peeling carrots and potatoes, while Lydia Grace added tablecloths, dinnerware, napkins, and centerpieces to the four large rectangular tables. By noon, everything was ready on time.

"It became a Christmas Eve tradition for my sisters. Each year they serve in the soup kitchen. It's their gift to these people. Over the years, they have collected little presents from these good people. Lydia Grace has said many times her favorite gift was from a six-year-old girl. The child had cut a star from cardboard and colored it with her one crayon: white. The star still hangs on the Christmas Hotel tree in the lobby."

Chris climbed the few steps and returned to his pulpit.

"What I'm trying to say is, find a tradition for your family. Christmas was never meant for families to go into debt. Sacrifice some of your time for others. It'll be a rewarding gift for them and you. Sacrifice is what Jesus did for us. It's not hard to sacrifice for others. Give generously. Remember, generosity does not need to be in an overabundance of money. Give from your heart. How often do we look at giving as a privilege? When the offering plate is passed in church, give a little extra. You'll be surprised at how the Lord will reward you.

"However, I urge you to give from your heart, not in anticipation of a reward. Little acts of kindness matter. Have you ever seen someone struggle to pay their water or heat bill? Maybe a single mother has to decide whether to pay one of these bills or give her children food or a Christmas gift. If you are able, pay the bill for her. If someone is a shut-in, shovel the snow from the sidewalk for them. Take a lonely person a cake, a pie, or decorated cookies you've made with your children or grandchildren. Visit someone in a nursing home, especially someone with no family or someone who has been forgotten by family. Remember, Christmas can be a sad day to someone who's lonely. Maybe even someone who is here now … in this service."

He stopped a moment to look around his congregation. He smiled when a mother stood to quiet her crying baby.

"Generosity comes in many forms, but it's always a reflection of our Lord in us. Let people see Jesus in you. It could be a chance to give your testimony and present the plan of salvation. Don't forget your greatest gift. 'For unto you is born this day in the city of David a Saviour, Who is Christ the Lord,' from Luke chapter two verse eleven. Remember, He took your sins upon Himself. *He* didn't deserve this, but *you* did. That's our Savior and your gift from Him. Remember, 'Every good gift and every perfect gift is from above, and cometh down from the Father of lights, with whom is no variableness, neither shadow of turning.' That's from the book of James, chapter one and verse seventeen. Remember, the greatest gift we receive is God's love. The greatest gift we give is our love for one another. May the Lord shine His grace upon you this Christmas. God bless all of you."

Chapter Sixteen

A Day of Mixed Events

*"Hear my prayer, O LORD, give ear to my
supplications: in thy faithfulness answer
me, and in thy righteousness."*
Psalm 143:1

Saturday
December 26, 1998
At 4:00 in the morning there was a knock on the door of the Wright family home. Only Chris and Lori Anna were awake, getting dressed to head to Christmas Hotel and deliver flyers to the reunion guests.

"Chris, who could possibly be at our door at this hour?"

"I don't know, but you check on the children, while I answer—"

His parents' bedroom door swung open. "Chris, your mom is not in bed."

The two men rushed down the steps. Chris flipped on the outside light, and there stood Sheriff Joe Palma. "Good morning, Christopher – Chris," he nodded at each man.

Within seconds, Lori Anna was down the steps. "The children are in their beds."

The sheriff tipped his hat. "Ma'am." He then turned to Christopher. "I found your wife about forty-five minutes ago. She was sitting on the bench inside the square facing Christmas Hotel, wearing nothing but her nightgown, robe, and house slippers. No coat. When I approached her, she was shivering, crying, and terrified. I called her by name, but she stared at me blankly, just blinking her eyes. It was obvious Jerilyn didn't know me, but she allowed me to throw my coat around her shoulders and walk her to my cruiser. I seated her in the back and turned up the heat. I called the information to my dispatcher, and Jerilyn began crying uncontrollably. I was afraid she was in shock and hypothermic, so I thought it best to drive her straight to the Franklin Medical Center. She's in the ER, Christopher."

"Thank you, Sheriff Palma. I'll head on over there."

The sheriff left, and Christopher turned to Chris and Lori Anna. "I know you both want to come with me, but one of you will need to stay with the children, and the other deliver the flyers. The ballroom still needs the final prep for tonight. I'll call here and at the hotel as soon as I know something about your mother. Please don't change the day's events."

Chris nodded, and Christopher rushed up the stairs to dress.

*****

By 5:00, the flyers were placed under the doors

Ken and Loretta Wright will host two families at breakfast: Pat and Eveanna Barry, and Jerry and Ann Bradley.

Lily and John will host Frank and Marlene McCoy, and Todd and Carla Ann Anderson for the noon meal.

Chris and Lori Anna Wright will host Thomas and Vivian Dailey, and Jerry and Linda Mintz for the 6:00 meal.

Please join us in the ballroom after dinner tonight from 7:30-11:00 p.m. for a 1930s/1940s night of music and dancing. If you don't know ballroom dances, two professional dance couples from Nashville will be here to teach you the steps. Ladies, Jan's Bridal Boutique at 116 W. Kentucky Ave carries suitable dresses for this special occasion. Jan is offering a 25% discount today for reunion guests. For the children, the shop next door: Pistols 'n' Petticoats, will fix you right up and with a 25% discount today. Hayes Shoes at 122 N. Main Street can help the family with shoes at a 15% discount today for reunion guests. They also sell ice skates.

* Join Lydia Grace and Jacob, Carrie Emeline and Marcus, Chris, Lori Anna and their three children, and Ken and Loretta from 2:00-4:00 this afternoon at the Wright family farm on 31-W for ice skating on the pond. Maps to the farm are available at the front desk.

Sincerely,
Chris and Lori Anna Wright
*****

Christopher knew he appeared frazzled when he entered the ER at Franklin Medical Center and walked to the information desk. He provided his name and Jerilyn's name to the receptionist, and she ushered him to a curtained-off room. His mind flashed back two years earlier when he had his heart attack at home. He had been taken by ambulance to this ER. Then and now, four nurses' stations took care of approximately 60 curtained-off cubicles.

Huddled under blankets, Jerilyn peered wide-eyed around the cubicle, her eyes darting back and forth throughout the enclosure. She focused on the IV line and its bag of nutrients. Christopher's heart went out to this woman he loved. He closed his eyes. *Dear Heavenly Father, please help me to help my wife. I love her more than life itself. I vowed on our wedding day to protect her from all harm and* ... he stopped to wipe his eyes and sniff back tears ... *Lord, I can't protect her from this harm. Only Thou, Lord, can fix this situation, and I plead for Thee to give Jerilyn Thy blessed peace.*

He opened his eyes, and Jerilyn's beautiful blue eyes stared back. *Oh, how I have loved this woman. Please, Lord, don't let her see me cry. Help me to be strong for her.*

"Daddy, is it you?" Jerilyn asked in a little girl voice, cocking her head and raising her eyebrows in question.

Christopher released a big sigh. Jerilyn's dad had been dead almost twenty years. He pulled up the chair beside her bed. "It's me, Christopher."

Her eyes focused on him, and a frown lined her forehead. "Christopher? I don't know a Christopher."

His heart broke. *I won't cry. I'll just give her comfort.* He took her hand. It was so cold. He wrapped her hand with his other hand to add warmth. "I'm here to help you."

A nurse walked in. "Mr. Wright?"

"Yes. How is she?"

"Can we speak privately?"

The nurse and Christopher stepped out of the cubicle, left the curtain open, and stood by her station. "Mrs. Wright was very cold when she arrived. We've been wrapping her in heated blankets every fifteen minutes, and she's wearing foot warmers. Her vitals are stabilized, and we're rehydrating her. She didn't know her name when she arrived. How long has she had dementia?"

Christopher sighed again. "Several years now. This is the first time she's left home in the night."

The sympathetic nurse rubbed his shoulder. "I know it's difficult. My grandfather has dementia – probably Alzheimer's. It appears Mrs. Wright has entered a new stage. I have a pamphlet to give you."

She handed Christopher the brochure. Christopher read the title. *Stages of Alzheimer's and Coping with a Loved One.*

He looked back at the young nurse and read her name tag. Elizabeth Jennings, Registered Nurse. "I believe I know your grandfather. Is his name Martin Jennings?"

Nurse Jennings smiled. "Yes, he's such a dear, but now he's in the nursing home over at Woodburn. We could no longer properly care for him."

Christopher winced. "I'm trying not to send my

wife away."

"I understand, but sometimes it's best." She paused and asked, "How do you know my grandfather?"

She's good at her job. She's distracting me. "We graduated high school together here in Franklin. Class of 1931."

She smiled again. "The doctor will be in shortly. As long as Mrs. Wright is warm, her vitals remain stabilized, and she's rehydrated, you'll probably be able to take your wife home. Did you bring her coat, warm clothes, and shoes and socks?"

"Yes." Christopher nodded and pointed over on the chair where he set Jerilyn's things.

"God bless you, Mr. Wright."

"God bless you, too, Nurse Jennings."

On the short drive home, Jerilyn didn't look at him. She stared out the window and was quiet. He didn't try to engage her in conversation, but he wished he knew her thoughts. For the umpteenth time he asked, *Where does she go, Lord?* In their bedroom, he helped Jerilyn into a clean nightgown and tucked her into bed. She still said nothing but stared into his eyes, and soon fell asleep. *Does she know me? Does she realize I care and want to help her?*

He sat in the chair across the room and took the opportunity to gaze at his sleeping wife. He couldn't pray. He was too choked up and couldn't think. So he softly sang the hymn, which described how he felt at the moment.

Precious Lord, take my hand
Lead me on, let me stand
I'm tired, I'm weak, I'm lone
Through the storm, through the night
Lead me on to the light
Take my hand, precious Lord, lead me home.

When my way grows drear precious Lord
linger near
When my light is almost gone
Hear my cry, hear my call
Hold my hand lest I fall
Take my hand precious Lord, lead me home

When the darkness appears and the night
draws near
And the day is past and gone
At the river I stand
Guide my feet, hold my hand
Take my hand precious Lord, lead me home

Aloud, he began to talk to the Lord. "It's my prayer, Lord. I need Thee, Lord." He stopped a moment to catch his breath and wipe the tear trailing down his cheek. "Take my hand, and help me do right by Jerilyn. Please give me an answer regarding the nursing home. Take my hand, and let me lean on You. Hear my cry to You."

The doorbell rang. Christopher took the handkerchief from his pocket, wiped his tears and blew his nose. He hurried down the steps. His good friend, Dr. Beasley, stood on the front porch. "Dr. Beasley, welcome. Come on in."

Dr. Beasley stamped the snow from his feet and entered the Wright home. "I heard about Jerilyn. I came to help."

Christopher shook his head and smiled. "Sometimes I forget how fast good or bad news travels in our small town. Please come in and have a seat. I was just considering a cup of coffee. Would you like a cup?"

"I'd love a cup."

Christopher returned with a tray holding two mugs of coffee and the cream and sugar. They settled back in the two lounge chairs. Christopher sighed and gazed into Dr. Beasley's concerned eyes. "It's hard watching Jerilyn go downhill. Sometimes I think this reunion at the hotel was too much for her. Maybe I shouldn't have involved her. She's gotten quieter over the past week." Christopher ran his fingers through his hair. "I should have realized the change in her sooner."

"Christopher, don't berate yourself. You can't control the progression of Jerilyn's dementia." Dr. Beasley's voice softened. "She very likely has Alzheimer's. There's no test to make a determination, but I feel there will be in the next ten years. Although I'm retired, I still receive reports of new medical breakthroughs." He took a sip of his coffee. "Have you considered a nursing home?"

Christopher sighed and set his mug down. "Until today, it had not crossed my mind. However, after what happened, and speaking with Nurse Jennings...." Christopher picked up his mug, took a sip, and wrapped both hands around it to warm a sudden chill.

He set the mug back on the coffee table, stood, walked to the fireplace, opened the screen, and lit the preset paper and twigs. He waited for it to flame, threw on a small log, and closed the screen. His faithful old dog Bobby raised his head. Christopher patted Bobby's head, and he settled back down on his doggy bed.

Christopher paced a couple of times and looked back to Dr. Beasley. "Nurse Jennings, over at the Franklin Medical Center told me her grandfather has Alzheimer's. He's now in the nursing home at Woodburn."

Christopher sighed, raked his fingers through

his hair again, and sat back down. "I was in high school with Martin Jennings, and he was a long ago friend. I knew he and his wife Mazie left Franklin about the time I entered the Army Air Corps after high school. Martin and Mazie moved to Chattanooga. They only had the one son ... George. I know that the rest of the family, brothers, uncles, aunts, and cousins remained in Simpson County."

Dr. Beasley smiled. "I doctored the Jennings family and delivered most of their babies, including Martin's granddaughter Nurse Elizabeth Jennings. George moved to Franklin after he graduated from high school in Chattanooga. He took a job at the Kendall Company."

"Dr. Beasley, I regret I didn't visit Martin while he was still lucid."

"Christopher, when Mazie died, George moved Martin back to Franklin. Mazie had been Martin's caregiver until she died. Martin was already in the middle stages of the disease. George confided with me and said he should have moved them here several years before Mazie died. The caregiving wore Mazie's health down. Martin wouldn't have known you when he arrived back in Franklin. George and his wife Pam tried caring for him in their home for a year, but it was too much for them. Martin nearly burned the house down when he left some vegetable soup on the stove. George and Pam realized his caregiving had become too much for them. They moved him to Woodburn."

Christopher mulled over this information. He thought back to when Jerilyn had left beans on the stove – and not so long ago. Also the incident this morning. "I've got some thinking to do, Dr. Beasley."

Dr. Beasley nodded. "In the meantime, I brought you some hook and eye locks." Dr. Beasley reached in his pocket and pulled out a small sack. "Alzheimer patients tend not to look up. I want you to fasten them at the top of your doors every night before bedtime. At least Jerilyn won't be able to get out again until you make your decision, Christopher. I'll help you attach them if you like."

"Thanks, Dr. Beasley. Let's get to work."

*****

Following breakfast, the reunion guests hit the stores around the square. All the stores were open the day after Christmas, still decorated, and with wonderful discounts promoted in the morning flyer. The guests discovered first hand why Franklin was voted "The Friendly City" for many consecutive years. The women took advantage of the discounts and purchased ballroom gowns and accessories for later in the evening, and ice skates for the children going to the Wright family farm in the afternoon.

Three inches of snow caked the ground, while

more fell. Chris, Lori Anna, and their three children finished decorating the ballroom by 11:00. Christopher had already informed them Jerilyn was home and sleeping.

Most of the family headed to the farm at 1:00 after the noon meal. They wanted to be ready to greet the reunion children and their parents when they arrived. It was a perfect afternoon for skating. The light snow continued to fall, but the sun peeked through the clouds intermittently. With a steady temperature around twenty-five degrees over the past four weeks, it had been cold enough to keep the pond frozen.

The family arrived in plenty of time ahead of the guests to set a fire in the trash barrel and surround it with lawn chairs. Stationary benches were scattered around the pond, along with several boulders. Chris had used the farm's tractor and placed the boulders there over twenty years ago. Christmas music blared from the backyard speakers, and Lydia Grace, Jacob, and Anthony had decorated pine trees several weeks earlier.

"The fire in the barrel should keep those guests warm who need a break from the skating and the cold." Chris turned around when he heard car doors open and shut. "Okay, they're coming."

He waited until all had arrived before giving his speech he'd given many times over the years for guests. Chris asked the children, "Have you ever skated on a pond versus an ice rink?"

All the children looked at each other and shook their heads.

"Well, the main thing to remember is the ice will have some bumps. It won't be smooth like in a rink. However, on the plus side, you get to skate in the wonderful outdoors."

"It's lovely on your farm," said one of the parents.

"Actually, this past year the farm was passed to my sister Lydia Grace and her husband Jacob." He placed an arm around each of them. "They're the two who all of you have enjoyed in concert in the chapel this week. I lived here for twenty years before them."

"Do you have horses?" asked one of the children.

Chris turned to Jacob and Lydia Grace. "I'll let them answer your questions, since it's their farm, now." Chris winked at his sister and her husband.

"Yes, we have three horses," said Jacob.

Olivia jumped in, "There are three ponies for my sister, brother and me, too. We don't live here now, but we get to visit a lot, and feed, ride, and brush our ponies."

"Wow," said one of the little girls. "Can I have a pony, Mommy?" She looked up at her mom.

Her mom smiled down at her daughter. "We live in an apartment in Chicago, honey. We don't have room for a pony."

The little girl thought about it. With a huge smile she said very matter-of-fact, "We can move to a farm, Mommy."

Her mother hugged her and smiled. "I'll discuss it with your dad."

"We also have cows, pigs, and chickens," added Michael. "Wanna see?"

"*Yay*," several children yelled.

Chris put his hand up like a stop sign. "Let's wait and see if we have time after ice skating. It's best that we all stay together. By the way, there's a fire in the barrel over there if anyone gets cold out here or needs a break. Also, there are plenty of chairs set up around the barrel, and lots of boulders and benches around the pond for a quick break. So you can put your skates on without sitting on the ground. Let's head to the benches and boulders and get our skates on!"

"Yippee," the children chorused, and ran to the benches and boulders.

Little six-year old Betsy Robbins was the first to fall on the ice, but her eight-year old brother Johnny picked her up. Chris called out to the children. "I realize some of you are not expert skaters, but I know how to help. I want the expert skaters to skate toward me."

Over half of the group skated up to him.

"Now turn around and look at the ones left, and two of you experts can buddy up with one of them. I want to see a beginner holding the waist of an expert and an expert behind the beginner holding his or her waist. You beginners will soon pick-up the rhythm, and before you know it you'll be an expert, too."

After the children had finished skating *and* visited the barn animals, all the parents thanked the family for a lovely afternoon.

Olivia acted as the spokesperson for her siblings and parents. "You should come back to Christmas Hotel this summer, and we can go fishing in the pond and ride the ponies."

Several of the children asked in excitement, "Yes, can we?" as they looked up to their parents.

Lori Anna turned to Chris and rolled her eyes. "Sorry," she said to the guests. "I think our daughter is drumming up summer business for us."

The parents laughed. "A return visit in the summer just might happen," some of the moms and dads said to their sons and daughters.

The parents shook all the family's hands and thanked them again for the enjoyable afternoon.

"Don't forget to come to the ballroom tonight,"

added Chris.

"Wouldn't miss it," answered several of the parents.

Promptly at 7:30, the guests began arriving in the ballroom. Chris and Lori Anna were proud of the decorations they had created with their staff and children. Four ornamented Christmas trees stood in each corner of the huge room. Wreaths adorned the walls and the two entrance doors.

Lori Anna found a box of old ornaments in the attic of Christmas Hotel years ago, so whenever they held these balls, a variety of colored ornaments embellished the trees and the wreaths, many handmade. Red and green ribbons hung from the chandeliers along with mistletoe hanging in several strategic places from the ceiling.

Chris took the microphone. "I'd like to welcome all of you to the Christmas Hotel ballroom. Tonight, we have for your entertainment, and a tribute to the thirties and forties era, one of the best big band groups from Nashville. Please give a round of applause to the Pete Wilson Orchestra."

The fifteen band members stood, bowed, and nodded to the applauding audience.

"Next, I'd like to introduce two couples who are professional ballroom dancers, and also from Nashville. Please welcome these incredible dancers from the Kendall Ballroom Dance Studio in Nashville."

The two couples bowed to the applauding audience.

"Throughout the evening they will dance waltzes, jitterbugs, the foxtrot, and maybe some other ballroom dances. Don't be intimidated if you don't know how to do any of them, because the professionals will teach the steps on the left side of the ballroom, while you who know the steps can dance on the right side of the room."

He looked down at Lori Anna smiling up at him. "Also, this is the eleventh wedding anniversary with my beloved Lori Anna. We decided we didn't want to spend our anniversary anywhere but with all of you at Christmas hotel. If you need anything tonight, you'll find my three sisters: Lily, Carrie Emeline, and Lydia Grace, and my brother Ken, along with their spouses here to help – and of course Lori Anna and me."

He turned to the orchestra. "Let the music begin!"

Chris stepped down from the platform as the band began with "Chattanooga Choo Choo." The ballroom professionals taught the steps of the Foxtrot. He took Lori Anna's hand and raked his eyes over her. "You look spectacular in your strapless red gown, Lori Anna."

She dropped his hand, stood on tiptoes, and adjusted his red bow tie. "You look quite dapper yourself, Chris, in your white tuxedo with the red carnation."

They turned when they heard a throat clearing. "Are we interrupting?" Dr. Beasley stood in front of them, along with his six adult children: Betty, Barbara, Susan, Beth Ann, Bonnie, and John.

"Not at all, Dr. Beasley." Chris again held Lori Anna's hand and smiled. "Thank you for coming."

"Chris, I'm sorry your mom and dad couldn't be here. I know they would have loved this evening. I remember those two used to slip off to Nashville back in the forties whenever possible to enjoy an evening of big band music and spend a night alone. They had a special song ... but I can't recall the title."

Chris smiled. "'I Know Why (and So Do You)' is the title. Lily said she can remember them dancing to the record back in the forties and fifties after she, Ken, and Carrie Emeline were supposed to be in bed." Chris stopped to chuckle. "When my three oldest siblings heard the record begin playing, they'd go to the top of the steps and watch our parents dance in the living room."

Dr. Beasley joined in the laughter.

"I have some good news to add, Dr. Beasley. Megan and Amy from the *Franklin Favorite* are photographing tonight's event, and my nephew Brian is recording the sound. *All* of our guests will be able to take home pictures and a copy of the music. I'll get a copy of the music for Dad to play for Mom tomorrow." Chris's eyes glistened just a tad. "Such good memories."

"I know, Chris. I have those good memories about Mrs. Beasley. Your mother and dad raised five wonderful children, and Mrs. Beasley gave me six. Those are the best memories," he said, as he patted Chris's arm.

Chris turned to Bonnie. "You'll have to save me a dance. We're probably the only graduates here of the class of '73 at Franklin Simpson High School."

Bonnie smiled. "I'd love to dance with you, Chris."

Chris looked out again, and County Attorney for Simpson County, Sid Broderson and his lovely wife Jill walked toward their little group. Jill hugged Betty and Barbara. "Chris, I heard what you said about the class of '73 at FSHS. I suppose the three of us will represent the classes of '67, '68, and '69. We can't leave out the sixties generation."

Chris laughed. "I suppose with all the Beasley children here and the Wright children, we can represent graduation classes in three decades."

Barbara turned to her dad. "Daddy, I hear a jitterbug. Maybe I can entice my brother to dance with me and learn the steps from the professionals."

"You children go on ahead." Dr. Beasley waved them on with a flip of his hand. "I'll wait for something slow, like 'Dancing Cheek to Cheek,' or 'Sentimental Journey,' or Chris's parents' special song. The band will probably get around to those, and each of you girls can save a dance with dear old Dad."

The Beasley and the Broderson families stepped away to dance or visit with other townspeople while Chris and Lori Anna greeted more of the reunion guests.

"Chris and Liz Wright from England," Chris acknowledged, as the couple walked toward him. Chris pulled Lori Anna closer to him. "Lori Anna, you didn't get a chance to meet them when they checked in last week, so I'd like to introduce this wonderful couple. As you heard, Chris from England, Dad, and I share the same name." Chris offered his hand to Chris from England.

"Thanks, Chris," said the English visitor, as he shook Chris's hand. "It's wonderful being back at Christmas Hotel. It never disappoints."

"It's my pleasure to welcome you both to Christmas Hotel," Lori Anna shook their hands, too.

"It's our pleasure to meet you, too, Lori Anna,"

and Liz echoed her husband's greeting.

"I'm so sorry my father will not be here tonight," continued Chris. "He always enjoyed your company and the discussions you shared about England. However, my mother is not well."

"I heard about her illness. You and your family have our deep regrets. We enjoyed your mother immensely the times we visited Christmas Hotel. Your parents are a lovely couple.

"Regarding conversations with your father, I, too, have enjoyed those discussions. I always said we should both research our roots. We may find out we're sixth or seventh cousins."

"The plaque of the Wright family crest you gifted my dad on your second visit back in '85 is still proudly displayed behind the Christmas Hotel desk."

"We saw it when we first checked in. Liz and I want you to know we haven't been ignoring all the reunion festivities. We did come to the Christmas Eve service and your Christmas morning service, and we plan to attend the worship service in the morning. I understand Christopher will preach."

"Yes, I asked him to preach Sunday morning. He said the Lord has already given him a special message."

"Liz and I will look forward to it. We rented a car this week, and we plan to visit Mount Vernon

Missionary Baptist Church out in the countryside tomorrow morning. Christopher told me about the little church the first time Liz and I visited Christmas Hotel back in '74. He explained close friends of his have ancestors who are founding members at the old church. The service at Mount Vernon doesn't begin until eleven tomorrow, so we'll have plenty of time for both services." He chuckled. "I just have to keep remembering to drive on the right side of the road. Liz is a great navigator. Every time I turn a corner, she yells, 'Go right!'"

"Well, enjoy the evening, both of you. I think the band is beginning 'In the Mood,' which sounds like a waltz. I need to grab my wife for a dance."

"Thank you again, Chris, for inviting Liz and me. We have enjoyed our stay."

"Thank you for coming. We may have another reunion after the millennium. I hope you'll come for your fourth visit to Christmas Hotel."

Chris hugged Liz close. "If the Lord is willing, Liz and I would love another visit. We'll see what the new millennium brings. Enjoy the waltz with Lori Anna."

Chris smiled and twirled Lori Anna out to the dance floor. He stopped under one of the spots where the mistletoe hung. "Look up, Lori Anna."

She smiled at him displaying the amazing

dimples and twinkling dark brown eyes he adored. "What would Christmas Hotel be like without your mistletoe, my wonderful husband?"

He kissed her, and they danced to the waltz.

Chapter Seventeen

Heaven

"After this I looked, and, behold, a door was opened in heaven: and the first voice which I heard was as it were of a trumpet talking with me; which said, Come up hither, and I will shew thee things which must be hereafter."
Revelation 4: 1

Sunday
December 27, 1998
Christopher awakened before Jerilyn on the morning he would preach at the nine o'clock Sunday worship service. "I guess I'll start a pot of coffee." He chuckled. "They say when you talk to yourself you're getting old ... just don't answer. Oh well, I may be getting old."

When the coffee was ready, he poured a cup and sat at the kitchen table. He sipped his coffee, read a passage in his Bible, his devotional, and then bowed his head. *Dear Heavenly Father, I thank Thee for the long and wonderful life Thou hast given me. Words can't express the love I have for Thee, for Jerilyn, my children, their spouses, my grandchildren, and great-grandchildren. I know this old heart of mine will give out someday. The heart attack weakened it. I'm asking for a special blessing on Jerilyn, a blessing of which she'll be okay if I'm gone before her.*

He stopped a moment and wiped the tear trailing down his cheek. *I suppose okay isn't the word for someone with Alzheimer's, so how about content and well-cared for? I know our children will love her and provide for her needs, but it won't be the same as me being there for her. I love her, Lord, and our fifty-seventh wedding anniversary is coming up on New Year's Eve. Dost Thou think we could have a few more days or even hours together in which Jerilyn knows me? I've watched her deteriorate rapidly this month. I'd love to spend a few hours with my lovely wife. It's my prayer, Lord.*

Footsteps sounded on the stairs, he turned, and looked at the kitchen clock. Six o'clock. Chris and Lori Anna had left for Christmas Hotel, and the grandchildren didn't get up this early during Christmas break. So, it must be Jerilyn. The kitchen door opened.

"Where am I?"

He sighed when he heard the question.

Jerilyn looked around the room. Even in her nightgown with uncombed hair, she was still the most beautiful woman he knew. His heart swelled with love.

She stared at Christopher and asked, "Who are *you*?"

The heart-breaking question. There was no improvement with this disease. She had progressively gotten worse. *Lord, help me. I don't want to put Jerilyn in the nursing home, but I fear for her safety. Help me decide what's right for her.*

Several hours later, Christopher was seated beside Jerilyn in the chapel, watching as Jacob took his place at the piano. His three daughters sang, and Lydia Grace strummed the hymns on her harp as the folks gathered in the Christmas Hotel chapel and spilled over into the lobby. She had brought the harp from home for the special Sunday morning service her dad would preach. They were singing "Joy to the World" when Christopher left Jerilyn's side.

He walked up the few steps to the pulpit and shook Chris's hand who had just introduced him. He took a few seconds to clear his throat while his daughters, Chris, and Jacob headed for a seat in the pews. He smiled as he looked upon the congregation in the chapel. He had stood in this spot many times over the past fifty plus years. Jerilyn was now sitting with their three daughters and their husbands. He'd already explained to them what happened earlier with their mother. Lily had arrived at the house to help get Jerilyn ready for church.

Their son Ken sat with his wife Loretta, Lori Anna beside them, and Chris sat down to join his wife. Behind all of them sat their grandchildren and great-grandchildren. *Family*, thought Christopher. *There's nothing better besides my relationship with Thee, Lord. I'm a rich man. Thou has blessed me greatly.* Christopher looked up at the ceiling. *Lord, help me through Thy message.*

He cleared his throat again and addressed the congregation. "I don't preach too often anymore. When Chris asked me to preach at this Sunday morning worship service, the Lord laid the message on my heart. Today I will preach about Heaven. Please turn to Revelation chapter twenty-one verse four. When you have found the verse, please stand in honor of the Word of the Lord God."

Christopher again cleared his throat. "'He will wipe every tear from their eyes. There will be no more death or mourning or crying or pain, for the old order of things has passed away.' Heaven," Christopher repeated and he paused. "Please be seated."

He waited until the chapel became quiet. "Do you ever think about Heaven? I suspect if you've been alive fewer years than fifty, you probably do not. However, I'm now eighty-five, and *I* think about Heaven. I think about going home. When I see Jesus, I pray He'll say, 'Well done, thou good and faithful servant.' I have loved Him since I was saved at age twelve. Am I perfect? No. Did He expect me to be perfect? No. Did He expect me to trust Him? Yes – and I *do* trust Him.

"Life isn't always easy. Sometimes children die young and we wonder why. There are terrible diseases in this world," – he paused and looked at Jerilyn – "and we ask why. My daughter Carrie Emeline's first husband died young and we asked why. We all know someone battling cancer and we ask why. What we do know is sometimes bad things happen to good people. We, as Christians, are not immune to these bad things, but we know we are saved. No matter what happens, we will someday be with Him. If your Christian loved one is in the throes of a terrible affliction, we know that whether your loved one is healed and continues life on earth or the Lord takes the loved one to the Heavenly home, either way, he or she is a winner. Someday He will wipe away *all* our tears."

Christopher paused a moment while a young mother rose to take her crying baby out of the chapel.

"That was appropriate timing." Chuckles were heard in the congregation. "We have His assurance. I trust Him knowing He will wipe away my tears when I reach Heaven. I am a rich man. He has blessed me in many ways, and I have no regrets about my life. Proverbs chapter ten and verse twenty-two: 'The blessing of the LORD, it maketh rich, and he addeth no sorrow with it.'

"I had a beloved friend, Brother Willard Thomas from Georgia, who wrote beautiful poetry. He has now gone home to be with the Lord. I'd like to share with you a poem he penned." Christopher lifted a notebook and adjusted his glasses. "It's titled 'My Emotions.' Please let the words gel.

"'It puts the water in my eye,
When we sing about our Home in the sky,
Where I know I'm going by and by.
When my time shall come, to walk the vale,
I will follow the Saviour's blood-stained trail,
Holding His nail-scarred hand – all is well.
When my heart is touched, and the tears
start to flow,
Sometimes to reap, sometimes to sow.
Please, Lord, let my devotion – be touched by
emotion.'

Christopher gazed around the congregation. "Someday, when I hold His hand, I know I will be in awe as I walk beside Him. I look forward to meeting His mother, Mary. She was the only member of His family who stood at the foot of His cross. I can't help wonder ... where were His brothers and sisters? Why didn't they stand with their mother? All I can say is she was a tremendously strong woman. I want to meet Mary.

"Why am I excited about Heaven? For many reasons, but I'm especially excited because I was washed in the blood of the Savior. Someday, I'm headed for a reunion with Christ and those who have gone before me. We've enjoyed a reunion with our many guests this week – those people who have previously visited Christmas Hotel. As wonderful as this has been, can you imagine what it will be like when we *see* Jesus? What it will be like when we have supper with Him *and* the loved ones who went before us?

"I realize some of you may be thinking, 'Christopher is eighty-five, and that's why he's thinking this way.'" A few chuckled at his comment and nodded their heads at one another. "You may be correct. Remember, I opened this sermon by saying, 'I suspect if you're fewer years than fifty, you probably do not think about Heaven.' However, we don't know when our time is up. I look at the obits in the paper, and some who have died are a few days old, a few years, in their twenties and in their seventies or eighties. We do not know when the end of our time on earth will come – only God knows. What's important is to know where you're heading: Heaven or Hell. If you don't know, I implore you to come forward, and I or one of the members of my family will take a Bible and show you how to receive His gift of salvation. Please stand while we sing 'At the Cross,' or come forward to this old-fashioned altar if you're under conviction. Seize the moment. Don't delay."

While the congregation sang, and Jacob played the organ, twelve people: nine adults and three of them around age twelve came forward. Christopher, Chris, and Ken prayed with the four men and two boys and Lily, Carrie Emeline, and Lydia Grace prayed with the five women and one girl.

While they continued to pray, Jacob played Fannie Crosby's "Near the Cross," and the congregation sang.

"Jesus, keep me near the cross,
There a precious fountain –
Free to all, a healing stream –
Flows from Calv'ry's mountain.

Near the cross, a trembling soul,
Love and Mercy found me;
There the bright and morning star
Sheds its beams around me.

Near the cross I'll watch and wait
Hoping, trusting ever,
Till I reach the golden strand,
Just beyond the river."

Christopher and his children finished praying with the twelve. To the congregation, Christopher announced, "I give you twelve new souls for whom the Heavens are rejoicing."

The congregation broke out in applause.

While his children and the twelve took their seats, Christopher continued. "Today, I've asked my daughters to sing acapella another one of my many favorite hymns ... 'What a Day that Will Be.' I think of it when I think about Heaven. Enjoy."

When their dad was seated, Lily, Carrie Emeline, and Lydia Grace stepped behind the podium and sang.

"There is coming a day,
When no heart aches shall come,
No more clouds in the sky,
No more tears to dim the eye,

All is peace forever more,
On that happy golden shore,
What a day, glorious day that will be.

There'll be no sorrow there,
No more burdens to bear,
No more sickness, no pain,
No more parting over there;
And forever I will be,
With the One who died for me,
What a day, glorious day that will be.

What a day that will be,
When my Jesus I shall see,
And I look upon His face,
The One who saved me by His grace;
When He takes me by the hand,
And leads me through the Promised Land,
What a day, glorious day that will be."

Christopher looked at Jerilyn beside him. Her eyes were closed. *Is she hearing the words, Lord? I hope so. Jerilyn loved this hymn, too.*

The Wright family had no guests at their supper table at Christmas Hotel for the final evening of the reunion, so tables were pulled together to accommodate only the family. With grand and great-grandchildren, they comprised of forty-nine in all. Jerilyn had heard the words in the hymn earlier. She'd actually been coherent since the morning service, able to have a conversational noon meal, and now dinner with all her family.

"Mom, wasn't the service lovely with Dad preaching today?" asked Lily.

Jerilyn smiled at Lily, and placed her hand over Christopher's. "Yes, it was, dear. I also enjoyed the singing my three daughters provided. I'm so proud of my family. I love you all."

"We love you, too, Mom."

One by one the family said, "We love you very much."

Jerilyn's sons and Christopher's eyes glistened with tears and tears spilled down their daughters' cheeks.

Jerilyn turned to Christopher, and frowned. "Where have you been lately?"

Christopher smiled and patted her hand. "Darling, I've been by your side all along. You just didn't realize my presence."

Is this my answer to my earlier prayer, Lord? I don't know how much time Thou has given me with Jerilyn today, Lord, but I'm grateful for these past few hours.

The chefs prepared an elaborate dinner on the final

night of the reunion. Lydia Grace set her fork down. "Hmm ... it's been a long time since the chefs fixed roast duck with orange and ginger. So festive, so good." She closed her eyes and licked her lips.

Chris laughed. "Would you like to write a culinary article for the *Franklin Favorite*? Christmas Hotel is slow in January, so maybe it'll help reservations."

Lydia Grace paused. "Oh Chris, you're teasing me. You must admit this is amazing. Look around the dining room. Conversation has come to a halt. The guests are chowing down."

Chris shook his head. "You have always had a way with words, Lydia Grace."

Carrie Emeline took up for her sister. "I'm with her." She looked to Marcus. "We need to get the recipe and take it back to our restaurant in Bellingham. I don't ever remember serving duck."

Marcus smiled at his wife. "We *are* a seafood restaurant, dear."

"Well, we have turf, so let's add some fowl."

Christopher smiled as he gazed upon his family. The banter was picked up by all his children and their spouses, and some of the grandchildren joined in. *Thank Thee Lord for this special day and the time I've had with Jerilyn. Thou provided me with a family of which to be envied. As I said earlier, I'm a rich man.*

The family members headed to their homes. Jerilyn asked Christopher to walk her into the square and sit on their bench facing Christmas Hotel. They put on overcoats, hats, gloves, and scarves. Once they were seated, she shivered, and he wrapped his arm around her. "Are you too cold, dear, to sit outside?"

"No, I'm fine. I'm just happy to be here with you. God is good, Christopher."

Hot tears filled his eyes, but he couldn't help himself. He'd prayed in earnest for this special time with his beloved Jerilyn. With his other hand, he took hers. "Yes, He is, my love."

They stopped speaking for a few minutes, cuddled together, and reveled in the moment.

Christopher took a deep breath. "The air is so clean and crisp. I do love the Christmas season."

Townspeople walked by and smiled. Some greeted with "Merry Christmas!"

"You know, Jerilyn, sitting here brings back memories of fifty-seven years ago. You were only twenty, but I knew without a doubt we were meant to marry and raise a family. I was nervous the night I proposed to you on this very bench." He chuckled. "We should call this the Wright family bench, since it was used by three of our children for proposals, too."

Jerilyn turned to him. "You were nervous that

night?" Her soft voice warmed his heart. "I thought I was the nervous one. You've never told me this."

I can't believe I'm sitting here and carrying on a normal conversation with Jerilyn.

"I was twenty-eight-years-old. I suppose I wanted you to have confidence in my decisions. You were so mentally wounded when you arrived at Christmas Hotel. I wanted to be your knight in shining armor."

She took her free hand and placed it on his cheek. "You *have* been my knight in shining armor. I'm so happy the Lord sent me here all those years ago. I never thought being penniless would be a good thing, but it brought us together. Our Lord brought us together. I'm so thankful, Christopher."

"So am I, my darling, so am I."

She placed her head on Christopher's shoulder, and they took a moment to gaze up at the sky. "It's so clear tonight, Christopher. The stars are putting on a light show for us."

Christopher pointed up. "I know that one's the North Star, but tonight, for us, it's the star of hope. Hope for us and the future of our family."

"I love you, Christopher."

"I love you, too, Jerilyn. I want you to remember our love, at least for tonight. I've never in all our years together tired of telling you I love you." He kissed her.

"I want to pray together in the Christmas Hotel chapel, Christopher. Let's go in. Maybe we'll be alone."

Jerilyn was granted her wish. The chapel, filled earlier to capacity was now silent. They each lit a candle and a third candle for the Lord, their special triangle. Seated on the front pew, they stared at the cross, holding hands.

"In this season of giving, I think of His amazing gift." Christopher took Jerilyn's hand. "How blessed we and our family are because of knowing Jesus Christ. The perfect gift: forgiveness of sins, salvation, peace of God, and joy in the Lord. All our children were saved at a young age, they are married to Christians, the grandchildren are all saved, *and* even the great-grandchildren who are at the age of accountability."

"Yes, Christopher, we've truly been blessed. No matter what happens after tonight, I'm thankful for this precious gift of being with you tonight."

"I'm thankful for being with you tonight, too, my darling Jerilyn."

"Christopher, can we spend the night here at Christmas Hotel in room number seven? I want to sleep here tonight where we met."

He cupped her cheeks in his palms and kissed her. "Yes, dear, nothing would make me happier." Looking up at the empty cross, he said, "Thank

Thee, Lord." He turned back to Jerilyn. "However, there is something we have to do first." They snuffed out the candles and headed to the lobby.

Christopher looked both ways to make sure no one saw them. He grabbed Jerilyn's hand and they headed to the elevator. "Where are we going, Christopher?"

"I have a surprise for you in the ballroom."

She giggled like a teenager. "I feel mischievous, Christopher."

On the fifth floor, he opened the "C" door and let it close behind them. He flipped the switch for the chandelier lights and he and Jerilyn stepped over the threshold.

"Oh, Christopher, the ballroom decorations are so beautiful."

"I asked Chris and Lori Anna to leave it decorated, just in case I was able to bring you here." He walked to the CD player. "Chris also left a recording of the music the orchestra played, and it's set for a particular song."

He cued the music and Jerilyn smiled when she heard the first few notes to their song. "I Know Why (and So Do You)." Christopher took her hand. "May I have this dance?"

She curtsied. "Yes, you may."

Christopher twirled her to the middle of the floor, and he held her close. She rested her head on his shoulder.

"Christopher, I know my ... condition ... has been hard on you."

He tightened his hold on her and looked her in the eyes. "I love you, Jerilyn. I would not change a moment of our time together. Yes, at times it's difficult, but I trust in Him. He's always here whenever I need him. The Lord will see us through this."

"Christopher, He's my rock, but I have to say I've been scared of someday outliving you. I know it's selfish of me, but I don't want to outlive you." She bowed her head, and then looked back up at him. "I've also feared you'd quit loving me." Her lip quivered and she blinked back tears.

He said nothing but pulled her closer to him and kissed her lips.

A few minutes later he turned off the music and the lights, and they were now standing in the lobby. Mr. Hanover was the manager on duty this evening, but he was nowhere in sight when Christopher stepped behind the front desk and snatched the antique key to room number seven off the wall.

Christopher grabbed Jerilyn's hand and led her back to the elevator. He opened the door with the old key, and reached into the bedside table drawer for the matches and lit both kerosene lamps. The yellow glow filled the room. Jerilyn tittered.

"Christopher, I feel naughty. Nobody knows where we are, especially our children. It's like a second honeymoon."

"They'll probably scold us in the morning when they find out." He pulled her close to him. "I don't care. Right now, I just want to spend this lovely gift I've been given for tonight, holding you in my arms, my darling." He kissed her with all the passion he possessed. "I'm still in awe you're really here with me. If this is a dream, I never want to awaken."

"I completely understand, Christopher."

He opened the dresser and handed Jerilyn a Christmas Hotel nightgown. In the bathroom hung the "his" and "her" Christmas Hotel robes. He handed Jerilyn the "her" robe.

"We have everything we need, Christopher."

He took her in his arms. "Yes, I do, my darling. You're all I need."

They spent the next hour sitting in the two brocade chairs by the window, talking, holding hands, and reminiscing by the light of the kerosene lanterns.

"I remember those first few nights I spent in this room fifty-seven years ago," Jerilyn said at last. "I was still struggling to function. What kept me going was my pregnancy, *and* when I found the diary in that desk in the secret drawer Carrie Emeline Bazell had written years earlier. God certainly lit my path straight to you, Christopher. I may awaken tomorrow and remember nothing about this special night. I realize your heart breaks when my memory leaves me. Please know how much I love you. I could not have had a better husband, lover, and friend. Thank you for loving me."

"Thank you for being the perfect wife, Jerilyn. You complete me in every way. We have raised a great family, and just look at all of us at supper tonight – forty-nine of us. What a legacy. When we are gone, the Wright family legacy will continue. Chris and Lori Anna will continue with the mission of Christmas Hotel: Where Jesus's birth is a daily celebration."

He reached in his pocket. "My friend Willard Thomas in Georgia wrote another poem. I saved it to read to you at the right moment." He cleared his throat and began.

"'Two Lives Together'

"'The years have passed but not in fear,
As they look around, at all they hold dear.
The treasure chest of life in final measure,
Goes to the one each love and treasure.
Many years, side by side, they walked on,
Sometimes there's heartache; sometimes a song.'"

He stopped a moment, looked at Jerilyn, and smiled. Her faded blue eyes were focused on him.

"'She's been right there, a faithful best friend,
As steady as a river, to reach its last bend.
Then there's the children, we can never repay,
For the sons and the daughters, that come this
way.
Then the fine grandchildren, blessings indeed,
As they are trained in the family creed.
But it all comes back to her and me,
'What did we want? What do we see?'
Two old saints, struggling along,
'Hey, look up, Honey, it won't be long.'"

"Oh, Christopher, the poem is so beautiful." She wiped a tear. "Willard wrote such lovely poetry. I know he penned the poem for his wife, but it fits us, too. Thank you for sharing it with me."

He took her hand and led her to the bed. "I'll leave the one lantern by the window burning, and extinguish the one by the bed. If you awaken in the night, you'll have light."

"Thank you, Christopher. You're always protecting me. I have been blessed with a considerate, old-fashioned husband. Old-fashioned is good."

He kissed her and whispered, "Goodnight, my

lover and best friend, until we meet again in the morning."

He removed their hearing aids, placed them on the nightstand, and by 8:30 they drifted off to sleep wrapped in each other's arms.

Chapter Eighteen

Alarm!

"Let us therefore come boldly unto the throne of grace, that we may obtain mercy, and find grace to help in time of need."
Hebrews 4:16

Sunday evening
December 27,
and the wee hours of Monday
December 28, 1998

Chris hurried to Christmas Hotel at nine o'clock in the evening as soon as he received the emergency call from his assistant manager. He greeted Mr. Hanover at the front desk. "Is the water shut off to the hotel?"

"Yes, Chris. Due to the extended freezing weather conditions, the two mains water pipes have burst where they enter through the basement. They're old and rusty, and can't be repaired. The basement flooded and we immediately lost the supply to the whole building. Our maintenance men couldn't stop the leaks, but it's turned off in the street."

"Okay, it's a disaster, but let's not panic. We have to cope somehow. Type a notice to all the guests so they're aware of the situation, and place it under each door. In the meantime, I'll call several close-by businesses and ask them to open up and provide us with buckets of water. We can set a bucket of water outside each room to use if necessary to flush a toilet tonight. I'll also offer the four bathrooms at my house for shower use in the morning. We can also add the three bathrooms at the farm. Fortunately, tomorrow morning is check-out. These pipes will take a while to replace. I hope we can get the plumbers in here tomorrow morning."

Mr. Hanover nodded grimly. "That's what they've promised. I'll add the two bathrooms at my house, and I'll call the other assistants to see if we can add their bathrooms. I'll prepare an announcement immediately, Chris."

"I'll watch the front desk and call Mr. Thompson in early to help distribute the notices. I'd have Lori Anna come in but then my dad would have to watch the children. I think my parents must have gone to bed early tonight. I didn't hear a peep out of them when Lori Anna, the children, and I arrived back home after our big family dinner here at the hotel. The light was already out in their room, except Mom's night light."

"Chris, speaking of your parents, your mom seemed to be her old self today. What a wonderful gift for your father ... and all you children, too."

"Thank you, Mr. Hanover. It *was* a special day ... another miracle at Christmas Hotel."

By 10:00 the printed announcements appeared under the guestroom doors with instructions for toilet use and morning showers at all the assistant managers' homes, the farm, and the Wright family home. Four local businesses opened to provide buckets of water.

While Chris took care of the Christmas Hotel emergency, Lori Anna prepared their children for bed. By 9:00 they were bathed, teeth brushed, and the four of them settled in Olivia's room for story time. Lori Anna always read the stories in Olivia's room, and Abigail and Michael often fell asleep. They were easier to carry off to their rooms than Olivia.

Lori Anna gathered all three of her children on Olivia's bed. "You kids are getting spoiled, getting to sleep at 9:30 instead of 8:30. What will you do when school begins again in January?"

The very mature ten-year-old Olivia answered for her brother and sister. "We'll be fine, Mom. It will just take a little adjusting."

Lori Anna smiled at her precocious daughter and wiped the hair away from her daughter's face. She was such a good big sister to Abigail and Michael. Olivia was just five when she and Chris adopted the two siblings. Their mom died from a drug overdose, and their father was serving life in prison. Abigail was two and Michael was four months old when Lori Anna met the children while photographing patients at Vanderbilt Hospital. Michael was born drug addicted, but the doctors at Vanderbilt Hospital in Nashville were able to detox and heal his body. Abigail was malnourished.

Guests seeing them today would never know they had ever been afflicted with health issues. Adopting the children was not a difficult decision. Chris and Lori Anna wanted more children, but she had been unable to conceive following her leukemia attack. Both children had dark hair like Lori Anna and Olivia, and actually looked like they could have been Chris and Lori Anna's biological children.

"What story did you pick out for tonight?"

"I found a box of books in the basement yesterday, and I pulled out a couple." Abigail jumped off the bed and ran to the bookshelf. She returned with a well-worn copy of *Curious George*.

"It's one of your Aunt Lily's books when she was a little girl. Why, the book is well over fifty years old. Excellent choice, Abigail. *Curious George* is a classic. Let's all kneel beside the bed and pray first."

Lori Anna had not finished the story when Abigail and Michael were fast asleep. One at a time, Lori Anna carried each child into their bedrooms, tucked them in and returned to Olivia.

She tucked Olivia in, swept her bangs back, and kissed her on the forehead.

"Mom, is Grandma going to be okay now? I mean, all today she acted like our old grandma."

Lori Anna leaned back down on the bed, gathering her thoughts, took a deep breath, and slowly exhaled. "Your grandma has an ailment and there is no cure. It's called Alzheimer's, honey, and it attacks one's memory. Grandma will gradually get worse. At some point, she'll even forget how to walk, talk, and eat. She won't get better. I'm sorry, but it's time you knew."

Olivia frowned. "Yes, but ... but ... what about today?"

Lori Anna shook her head. "I don't know what happened today, honey. I think God gave us all a Christmas gift. For decades, miracles have occurred at Christmas Hotel. I think today was no exception."

"So you think she won't remember me tomorrow?"

"I'm saying ... I don't know. I don't want you to

get your hopes up, honey." She tucked a stray curl behind her daughter's ear.

Olivia looked down, wrung her hands, a tear fell, and she sniffed. Lori Anna wrapped her arms around Olivia. "I know it's hard, honey. I'm sorry you have to go through this at such a young age."

"Can we pray again, Mommy?"

"Yes, sweetheart." Olivia rarely ever called her Mommy anymore. Lori Anna knew Olivia was hurting for her grandma. "Dear Heavenly Father...."

*****

At the farm, a similar conversation was taking place between Lydia Grace, Jacob, Carrie Emeline, and Marcus. Elise and Erica had gone to bed early, and Anthony was in his room composing music on his guitar.

"Before bed, Elise and Erica asked me about their grandma," said Carrie Emeline while the foursome sipped hot Chamomile tea in the kitchen.

"Let me guess," interrupted Lydia Grace. "They wanted to know if their grandma was healed."

"Exactly. They're sixteen now. They're not little children. They need to know the whole truth about Alzheimer's disease. I explained to them what a horrible disease it is, how it robs people of their thoughts, memories, and hurts the people who love them most. I told them I didn't know what took place with their grandma today, but I could only thank God it happened – especially for their grandpa. We love Grandma but it will never compare with the love Grandpa holds for her. They've had a special love for many years. Today was an exceptional gift for Grandpa. I thank God for His gift, but I will not shake my fist at God tomorrow if Grandma slips back. I know Grandpa won't either."

Jacob rose. "Let's go into the living room. We can talk and get comfortable. I'll add another log on the fire."

Marcus scooted his chair out. "I'm right behind you, Jacob."

"I'll make hot chocolate and bring it on a tray," added Lydia Grace.

Two doors opened and closed and Elise, Erica, and Anthony rushed into the room laughing and joking. "We just came for hot chocolate," the girls said simultaneously.

"I'll get the marshmallows to roast in the fireplace," added Anthony.

Lydia Grace cocked her head. "We thought all of you were in bed for the night."

"We heard hot chocolate," said Elise.

"I heard hot chocolate and thought marshmallows and camping," said Anthony. "I'll grab the graham crackers and chocolate. We can make s'mores, too."

The parents just shook their heads and laughed. "Okay, I'll grab the roasting sticks," said Jacob. "Let's get this campfire going." He stoked the fire and added a second log.

*****

At 2:00 in the morning, Lydia Grace awakened and sat up. Jacob slept beside her. Moonlight filtered through the window blinds and she squinted. In the mirror she could see that perspiration dotted her forehead. Over in the corner chair sat a man in a plaid shirt, bib overalls, sporting a long, gray beard. He held his floppy hat in his lap. She blinked a couple times and rubbed her eyes.

When he spoke, he said softly, "It's all right, Lydia Grace. The Wright family will be okay."

He disappeared.

A minute later, Carrie Emeline couldn't sleep and looked at the clock. She had been tossing and turning, thinking about her mom and dad. *Maybe a glass of warm milk will help.* She looked over at Marcus and he was sound asleep. *Well, at least he can sleep just fine.* When she threw back the covers, she saw a bearded old man sitting in the chair wearing a plaid shirt and bib overalls. "Mr. Gabe?" she whispered.

"It's all right, Carrie Emeline. The Wright family

will be okay," then he vanished.

At 2:02, the sisters met in the living room. "I saw Mr. Gabe," murmured Lydia Grace. "I haven't seen him since I was eight, but I know it was him."

"I saw him, too, Lydia Grace."

"What did he say to you?"

"He said 'The Wright family will be okay.'"

"He said the same thing to me. What could he mean?"

Carrie Emeline shivered. "I don't know, but I suspect something dreadful has happened. Why else would he revisit both of us on the same night, and at the same time?"

"I feel it, too. What should we do?"

"Let's pray."

The phone woke Chris from a deep sleep. Still groggy, he felt for it several times through the pitch black and barely had a chance to answer when Mr. Hanover yelled, "Christmas Hotel is on fire!"

Lori Anna sat up, and Chris threw back the covers, jumped out of bed, snatched his pants and pulled them on. "Lori Anna, the hotel is on fire!" He threw on a sweater and tennis shoes. "Stay with the kids, I'll get Dad up."

He ran down the hall to his parents' bedroom and swung open their door.

Their bed was empty and still made.

He ran the three blocks to Christmas Hotel. Sirens screamed in the night air from fire trucks, ambulances, and police vehicles. Flames shot high and lit up the night sky. An ambulance pulled away from the hotel, lights and sirens blasting. The reunion guests stood outside the hotel in their night clothes, women and children cried and shrieked in terror, and husbands and fathers did their best to comfort their loved ones. Townspeople who lived nearby stood in the square and looked on in horror, many in agony and sobbing.

Chris grabbed Mr. Hanover's arm and almost fell at his assistant's feet. "Did all the guests get out?" He gulped for air.

"The guests ... yes, I think so, but ... a couple from your family ... I'm sorry, Chris. They must have been in room seven. I didn't know until I saw the missing key. When the firemen checked the rooms, they found two people in the room ... dead. I'm so sorry, Chris. They were carried away in the ambulance." He pointed in the direction of the ambulance heading to the medical center.

Chris stared at him in shock and disbelief. He ran his fingers through his hair, sucked in deep breaths, and expelled them rapidly. He bent over, with his hands on his knees trying to catch his breath. "My parents were not in bed when I checked their room at home. They wouldn't have heard the smoke alarm." He shook his head. "Dad always removed his and Mom's hearing aids at bedtime, and they're both nearly deaf without them."

He thought about the fire sprinkler system and shouted above the screaming people. "The sprinklers wouldn't have worked with the water shut off." He stood watching the burning building. Tears rolled down his face, and he gasped for breath.

Ken and Loretta yelled Chris's name as soon as they saw him. Like the other guests, they were still in their nightclothes. Chris turned as they ran toward him. "Ken, I think Mom and Dad were in room seven. They aren't at home. The bodies of two people were taken away in the ambulance just now."

Ken gaped at his brother. "Please ... tell me they were alive?"

Chris shook his head, still crying.

"Oh please, God, not Mom and Dad," cried Ken. The brothers and Loretta held each other, sobbed, and watched as the fire destroyed Christmas Hotel.

Chapter Nineteen

The Morgue

*"The LORD is good, a strong hold in the day of
trouble; and he knoweth them that trust in him."*
Nahum 1:7

Monday
December 28, 1998
By 5 o'clock in the morning, all the Wright family
members had gathered at the Wright family home
on South College Street. Chris had informed the
others in the family by phone call two hours earlier.

The siblings and their adult children gathered in
the kitchen for a family discussion while the small
children were sent upstairs.

"It had to have been Mom and Dad." Chris
sipped his coffee and drummed his fingers on the
table. "The only family who would have taken the
room key is sitting here now ... or Mom and Dad.
Nobody has seen them since last night at supper."
Chris looked around the kitchen at his family; eyes
were swollen and most still wept.

John wiped the tear that trailed down his cheek. "Lily and I drove by Christmas Hotel on the way into town. The building is still smoldering. The roof collapsed into the fifth floor, and the fifth floor into the fourth floor; maybe into the third floor, too. The firemen and the fire marshal are still sorting through the ruins, but they have the fire contained. We asked, and they still haven't found the cause. Every inch of the building is soaked from their fire hoses."

Chris sighed as he looked around the kitchen at his family. "Someone needs to go to the hospital morgue this morning." His eyes landed on his brother. "Ken, are you up to joining me?"

Ken looked as badly as Chris felt. "Yes, little bro. We'll go together."

At 6 a.m. the story was reported on the local radio station, not only for Simpson County but it was picked up by radio and television stations around the country, the world, and reported throughout the day and evening. The early morning reading for the local radio station at 6 a.m.:

"Last night our beloved Christmas Hotel at 100 N. Main Street on the square, burned beyond recognition. It's suspected, but unconfirmed, former owners Christopher and Jerilyn Wright perished. All other guests and staff survived. The

good people of Franklin have taken the Christmas Hotel guests into their homes or driven them to a Bowling Green hotel or motel and provided clothing for the day. The fire marshal still has not determined the cause of the fire. We will keep you updated."

At 6:30 a.m., Chris and Ken drove by Christmas Hotel on the way to the hospital morgue, and stopped. Some of the salvaged items were strewn along North Main and East and West Cedar Streets. Several police officers stood guard, not allowing anyone near the structure. People sat on benches in the square crying and holding each other. Christmas Hotel was a beloved landmark in Franklin, and the brothers could see how hard the townspeople were taking the demise of the hotel.

They continued on to the hospital. Staff, patients, and visitors hugged them and offered their condolences. In the basement, at the hospital morgue they spotted their old family friend Dr. Beasley.

"I wanted to be here this morning for you." The good doctor hugged them. "You know how much I loved your parents," he said through teary eyes as he sniffed. "Lily called me, told me what happened, and said you two were on your way. I'd already heard the radio report at six o'clock."

"Our parents knew you loved them, sir," responded Ken.

The morgue attendant, Lee Parsons, waited. Ken had graduated high school with him at Franklin Simpson High School back in 1960. Lee shook their hands, hugged each brother, and offered his condolences. "The bodies are unrecognizable, entwined together, but I have the wedding rings, and I cleaned them as best as possible." Lee sniffed, his chin quivered, and his eyes glistened. He reached in his smock's pocket.

Two warped gold bands and a sapphire and diamond engagement ring sat in his open palm.

The brothers turned to each other and cried.

Dr. Beasley accepted the rings and thanked Lee. "They're Christopher and Jerilyn's rings. I'd recognize Jerilyn's engagement ring anywhere. I'm sure the family will contact you later this morning as to which funeral home to take the bodies." The doctor turned to Ken and Chris, wiping his own eyes. "Come on, boys, let's get you back to your families." He handed the rings to Ken.

The family gathered at *Booker-Gilbert Funeral Home* on West Cedar Street just before noon. Due to the condition of the bodies, it was agreed by all the siblings, their parents should be cremated together, with their ashes combined in a single urn.

The urn should be buried at Greenlawn Cemetery near other family and friends. The funeral parlor would handle the cremation and other details.

The family agreed that the funeral service should be held at the cemetery. There would not have been room in the funeral parlor to hold all the people the family expected would attend. Christopher and Jerilyn were loved and respected around the country, and by many people around the world.

The Nashville news stations were on the scene by noon, and provided camera footage for their station and affiliates. The noon radio report was updated. "Last night our beloved Christmas Hotel at 100 N. Main Street on the square, burned beyond recognition. It is now confirmed that former owners Christopher and Jerilyn Wright perished in the fire. The fire fighters discovered burned hearing aids on the nightstand in room number seven, and their sons, Ken and Chris Wright identified their parents' wedding rings, and their mother's engagement ring. All other guests and staff survived with no serious injuries. The good people of Franklin have taken the Christmas Hotel guests into their homes or have driven them to a hotel or motel in Bowling Green and provided clothing for the day. All guests have chosen to remain for the funeral but the date has not yet been scheduled. The fire marshal still has not determined the cause of the fire. We'll keep you updated."

Chapter Twenty

Candlelight in the Square

"Keep me as the apple of the eye, hide me
under the shadow of thy wings..."
Psalm 17:8

Tuesday
December 29, 1998
The following morning's 6:00 radio report:

"A candlelight ceremony will be held tonight at
7:30 in the square in memory of Christopher and
Jerilyn Wright. The burial of Christopher and
Jerilyn Wright will take place at 11:00 a.m.
tomorrow at Greenlawn Cemetery. The bodies
were cremated and the ashes will be placed in the
same urn and buried together.

Update from fire marshal: 'It's been determined
the fire started in room number seven. The glass in
an antique kerosene lamp likely broke, causing

flames to shoot, and set the drapes and furniture on fire. The water supply to the hotel was shut off several hours before the fire started due to water leakage from burst pipes in the basement. The sprinklers did not operate because there was no water supply to the rooms. Smoke alarms sounded, so all guests made it out of the burning building. The family of Christopher and Jerilyn Wright reported their parents would not have heard the alarms. They were legally deaf without their hearing aids, which they removed every night. Remains of the destroyed hearing aids were discovered on the room's nightstand."'

Before heading to the candlelight ceremony, the five siblings and their spouses first stopped at the burned-out Christmas Hotel. On the Main Street side of the square and down West Cedar and East Cedar Street, bouquets of flowers, crosses, assorted wreaths, some Christmas designs and many black ones, were left beside the destroyed hotel. Attached to some of the crosses, bouquets, and wreaths were notes containing words of love for the Wrights.

Chris stooped and picked up one of the notes and read it aloud. "Attributed to the German poet Ludwig Jacobowski is the phrase from his 1899 poem: Don't cry because it's over, smile because it happened. I say: Don't cry because they're gone, smile because you and I will see them again—Nettie Sue Harris McLemore – devoted friend of Christopher and Jerilyn."

Lily dabbed at her eyes again. "Wow, that's so beautiful and so fitting. Remember Nettie Sue was Mom's first friend when she arrived in Franklin."

Lydia Grace picked up another note attached to a small piano ornament hanging from one of the bouquets, and she read aloud: "Most of us go to our graves with our music still inside us – Author-Oliver Wendell Holmes. I'll add: Not Christopher and Jerilyn. They were a symphony while on earth – Barbara Beasley Smith – family friend." Lydia Grace paused and dabbed at the tears in her eyes. "Oh my, that's so descriptive of our parents."

Lori Anna picked up a note and read: "...to give unto them beauty for ashes, the oil of joy for mourning, the garment of praise for the spirit of heaviness" ... Isaiah 61:3.

Carrie Emeline dabbed at her eyes, too. "We must come back and gather all these notes. There must be over a hundred remembrances. They should have a place of honor."

Ken nodded. "I agree."

Inside the square, a stage was erected for those who would sing, speak, or offer prayer at the candlelight ceremony. On a table near the stage, candles sat, ready to be lit.

The five Wright children, their spouses, children, and grandchildren greeted all who arrived. People from around Simpson County attended, and the reunion guests stayed to support the Wright family on this night and for the funeral in the morning.

Jonathan and Marianne, who sang in the square the first Sunday of the reunion, sang on the stage for the crowd. While Jonathan strummed the guitar, his wife Marianne sang, "When the Roll is Called up Yonder."

"When the trumpet of the Lord shall sound, and time shall be no more,
And the morning breaks, eternal, bright and fair;
When the saved of earth shall gather over on the other shore,
And the roll is called up yonder, I'll be there.
When the roll is called up yonder, I'll be there.

On that bright and cloudless morning when the dead in Christ shall rise,
And the glory of His resurrection share;
When His chosen ones shall gather to their home beyond the skies,
And the roll is called up yonder, I'll be there.

Let us labor for the Master from the dawn till setting sun,
Let us talk of all His wondrous love and care;
Then when all of life is over, and our work on earth is done,
And the roll is called up yonder, I'll be there."

Jonathan and Marianne took their seats on the stage, and Dr. Beasley sat on a stool at the microphone. His daughter Barbara stood beside him. "When the Wright family asked me to speak tonight, the first question I asked was, how long?"

The comment received a chuckle from the audience. Everyone knew the well-loved town doctor could speak for a long time on a subject he enjoyed.

"I have known Christopher longer than anyone in Franklin ... still living of course. The family requested I not be melancholy. They wanted tonight, and tomorrow morning at the funeral, to be a celebration of the life of Christopher and Jerilyn Wright. I understood completely. The hymn Jonathan and Marianne just sang, 'When the Roll is called up Yonder,' is fitting for Christopher and Jerilyn, because I know they are with the Lord Jesus tonight."

He paused to allow the murmurs of agreement to die down.

"They are both in a better place. Jerilyn no longer suffers from Alzheimer's, and Christopher will never have another heart attack. We here on earth will miss them, but I for one will see them again, and probably sooner than most of you, and I pray all of you will see them again, too."

He paused, cleared his throat, and took a sip of the water his daughter provided for him.

"As many of you know, Christopher and I go way back. I met him a year or so after I began my practice here in Simpson County in 1934. Christopher was born in 1913, raised here in Franklin, and he had been a chaplain in the United States Army Air Corps. When he was honorably discharged, he preached here in Simpson County. In 1936, I had the privilege of delivering his daughter Lily. You, who know me, also know I delivered more than a few babies in this county, and many of *you* out there, too before I retired in 1975."

Another chuckle erupted from the crowd.

"It was deemed both a happy and a sad day for Christopher. Lily was born, but his beloved first wife Ellie died. Christopher mourned his young wife for a time, but he soon realized Ellie was with the Lord, and he had a baby girl to nurture.

"Christopher handled the challenge well. Although, he temporarily stopped preaching, he did take a position as the Christmas Hotel manager for Captain and Mrs. Bazell, the second owners of Christmas Hotel. He was their hotel manager for five years and completely devoted to the hotel – but most of all to his daughter, Lily. Then he met the young World War Two widow, Jerilyn Marlene Seifert."

Dr. Beasley chuckled. "I think if the whole truth be known, Christopher was smitten with Jerilyn when he first laid eyes on her, but he was very professional in her presence."

There was a slight murmuring in the crowd, heads nodding, and some chuckles.

"However, five-year-old Lily kept bringing them together." Dr. Beasley paused and smiled at Lily. She returned the smile and gave him the thumbs up. "Young Lily could cause anyone to fall in love with her; she was such a delightful and precocious little girl. I think Jerilyn loved Lily before she loved Christopher. Lily wanted a mommy, Jerilyn needed God and a family, Christopher needed a loving wife, and to find his way back to God and preaching again. He had not preached since Ellie died. He'd become bitter following Ellie's death."

He paused again for a sip of water. "You'll have to excuse me. I think a slight cold is coming on." He cleared his throat. "Back to Christopher and Jerilyn. The miracle happened for all three of them their first Christmas together at Christmas Hotel. Christopher and Jerilyn wed on New Year's Eve 1941, only sixteen days after they met. Knowing they could not afford rings, Captain and Mrs. Bazell gave them their own rings – along with Christmas Hotel for a wedding gift.

"On May 15, 1942, I had the privilege of delivering Jerilyn's twins Kenneth Elliott and Carrie Emeline. Although their biological father had been killed in the war, and Lily's mom perished in childbirth, two more devoted parents could not be found than Christopher and Jerilyn. They loved those three children and raised them to love the Lord.

"Yes, they had their difficulties. Even devoted Christians like those two will have problems, but they put God first, even when their next child Lydia Grace was kidnapped at birth. Jerilyn later miscarried two boys, before I delivered Christopher Joseph Wright, Jr. in 1955, whom we all know simply as Chris."

He paused a few seconds and smiled at Chris. "By then, Lydia Grace had been returned to them and their family was complete." He paused to offer another smile and a nod toward Lydia Grace, who in turn returned the smile of encouragement.

"As of this date, Christopher and Jerilyn's union created forty-seven people out here with us tonight.

However, if my eyes don't deceive me, and I suspect they do not, I know these things; I see at least two more of their granddaughters in this crowd who are pregnant. They are the two older daughters of Ken and his wife Loretta."

The crowd laughed again, turned to look at Jenna and Rebecca, who in turn, smiled and rubbed their very pregnant tummies.

"Following Christopher's heart attack a couple years back, I visited Christopher in Vanderbilt Hospital. I asked him if he had a fear of dying. He had no hesitation with his answer and said enthusiastically, 'No! I welcome it with joy and excitement. We, as believers, know we will receive new bodies; no more sickness and no more pain.' I saw the wheels turn in his brain. His next statement was so soft, almost a whisper. 'Jerilyn won't have Alzheimer's. We'll walk with Christ on the Golden Shore.'"

He paused again and looked around the crowd.

"I'm not a preacher; I'm a doctor, but I want to leave you with a Bible verse and a poem: 'Keep me as the apple of the eye, hide me under the shadow of thy wings,' Psalm seventeen, verse five. It was a verse my long-time friend Christopher loved. Christopher trusted in his Lord Jesus, and so did Jerilyn.

"Christopher's deceased, dear friend Willard

Thomas from Georgia wrote this poem titled 'My Christian Faith.' This poem says a great deal about Christopher and Jerilyn. My daughter Barbara standing beside me will read it."

Barbara placed her arm around her father. In a clear voice she read:

"'I have a heavenly Father above,
Who makes me the object of His infinite love;
I am the apple of His eye,
He Who lives beyond the starry sky.

I have a Brother-Saviour Who died for me
On a rugged Roman tree;
I trust none other but Jesus' blood,
Washed by Calvary's crimson flood.

I have the Holy Ghost to lead and guide,
There I learn to trust and abide;
To follow His lead, I undertake,
For in His wisdom, He makes no mistake.

I have a home awaiting me,
So says John fourteen and three;
Just over the hill and down the way,
With our Saviour and loved ones ever to stay!'

Barbara stepped behind her father on the stage,

and Dr. Beasley took a sip of water and continued.

"Christopher admired and respected the poetry of his friend Willard Thomas. Christopher and Jerilyn's feelings could not have been said more beautifully. They knew where they were headed when they died. They knew the Lord loved them. They knew the family and friends who awaited them. They knew their family remaining on earth would be okay. Let's remember this amazing couple in love. I leave you with another song from Jonathan and Marianne, and one of Christopher and Jerilyn's favorite hymns: 'I Serve a Risen Savior.' Please listen carefully to the words."

Jonathan and Marianne stood. Jonathan strummed his guitar while Marianne's clear, sweet voice rang out in the candlelit night.

"I serve a risen Savior
He's in the world today.
I know that He is living,
Whatever men may say.
I see His hand of mercy;
I hear His voice of cheer;
And just the time I need Him
He's always near.

He lives, He lives,
Christ Jesus lives today!

He walks with me and talks with me
Along life's narrow way.
He lives, He lives, salvation to impart!
You ask me how I know He lives?
He lives within my heart.

In all the world around me
I see His loving care,
And though my heart grows weary,
I never will despair;
I know that He is leading,
Through all the stormy blast;
The day of His appearing
Will come at last.

As Marianne repeated the chorus, a hush fell over the crowd. No more words needed to be spoken.

Chapter Twenty-One

The Funeral

"For our conversation is in heaven; from whence also we look for the Saviour, the Lord Jesus Christ: Who shall change our vile body, that it may be fashioned like unto his glorious body, according to the working whereby he is able even to subdue all things unto himself."
Philippians 3:20-21

Wednesday Morning 11:00
December 30, 1998
Chris looked upon the cemetery where he would preach his parents' funeral. Lori Anna and their children walked with him, wrapping their scarves around their necks, while snow flurries whipped around the tombstones at Greenlawn Cemetery. Cars lined for miles, snaking their way to the cemetery, arriving from every direction in Simpson County, several other counties in Kentucky, and from down in Tennessee.

Not one reunion guest had gone home, but remained for the funeral. Folding chairs were set up around the stage for the elderly and those who had difficulty standing. Also, several of Franklin's businesses called stores in Nashville, Bowling Green, and Louisville to send a total of fifty chimineas and set them up in all directions from around the platform to knock some of the chill from the air.

The family knew the turnout would be far greater than the candlelight service, and they made certain everyone would be able to see and hear. Therefore, no tent canopy, normally provided for the family of the deceased was set up, and in its place the stage that had been used in the square the previous night was disassembled and erected at the grave site. Those who created the previous night's sound system did the same for today's funeral.

The large urn with the combined ashes of Christopher and Jerilyn sat upon the platform above the area of ground for the burial. Several local preachers offered to preach the funeral, but Chris wanted to speak out of love and respect for his parents. The siblings' desired to continue the celebration of their parents' life. In fact, the three Wright sisters requested to sing the hymns, and Lydia Grace would strum her guitar, the only instrument for the service. They chose not to wear black, the traditional color of mourning.

The three sisters all dressed in ankle-length winter white wool coats, stepped to the microphone to sing the first hymn. Lydia Grace spoke first for the trio.

"'Suppertime' was one of many favorite hymns of our parents. Please pay careful attention to the words as my sisters and I sing the hymn."

"Many years ago in days of childhood
I used to play till evenin' shadows come
Then windin' down an old familiar pathway
I heard my mother call at set of sun.

In visions now I see her standin' yonder,
her familiar voice I hear once more.
She said the banquet table's ready up in Heaven
It's suppertime upon the golden shore.

Come home, come home, it's suppertime.
The shadows lengthen fast.
Come home, come home, it's suppertime
We're going home at last.
Child, you're going home at last."

At the end of the hymn, Lily addressed the group, "When I hear this hymn, I do hear my mother's voice telling me to come home for supper.

However, I think my parents are now hearing the voices of their own mothers in Heaven. It's time for Mom and Dad to join those who went before them for the Heavenly supper."

Lily glanced around at the people who loved her parents. Women and men tried their best not to shed tears, but most of them failed. "The shadows do lengthen fast. We think our days on earth are long, and before we know it, we understand we are in the winter of our lives. When I turned sixty, I realized my time was drawing nearer, too. It's okay, because I know I will be with my family for eternity."

Carrie Emeline spoke next. "If my parents had known they were going home on the same day, they both would have rejoiced. Their love was a timeless love, and I know they are in a better place, and they are home. They are healed of their human infirmities and wrapped in new bodies. They are with the Savior Jesus Christ."

The sisters returned to their chairs, and Chris, also choosing not to wear black, stepped up to the microphone wearing a full-length beige wool coat over a beige suit. "Thank you for coming to celebrate the life of our parents Christopher and Jerilyn Wright. I thank my sisters for choosing this lovely hymn to sing, and they sang it so beautifully."

Chris paused to clear his throat. "My parents loved each other and their children, but they always knew the best was yet to come. They instilled the message within their five children. How great their Heavenly reunion with their loved ones must be. I look out at the tombstones and granite markers surrounding the final resting place for the ashes of our parents and I smile. Here at Greenlawn Cemetery are the graves of my father's parents. They were killed in a car wreck down in Tennessee when my dad was only seventeen."

Chris stopped a moment and pointed. "See the large gray granite tombstone over there? It's the grave of the woman who finished raising Dad; Lydia Grace Evans. Dad respected and loved her so much he wanted a daughter named for her: my sister Lydia Grace Wright Carlisle.

"Our parents have reunited with their first spouses: Mom's first husband, Pharmacists Mate First Class United States Navy Kenneth Seifert was killed when his ship was bombed at Pearl Harbor back in 1941. His earthly body was never recovered. When my brother and sister were born, the twins, my parents agreed my brother Ken should be named for his biological dad. His middle name is Elliott, the masculine for Dad's first wife. Ellie was my sister Lily's biological mother, and Ellie Wright is buried on the other side of Mrs. Evans."

Chris stopped again to clear his throat, and he wrapped his scarf tighter around his neck. Lori Anna smiled up at him, giving him the added encouragement he needed.

"Also, buried here are Thomas and Lucy Goodnight Hoy, the prominent Franklin couple who originally built Christmas Hotel in 1850." Chris pointed again. "If you look over there, you'll see a tall obelisk monument. Thomas Hoy is buried on one side, and Lucy Goodnight Hoy is on the other side."

Chris pointed in another direction. "The second owners of Christmas Hotel are buried over there: Captain Jacob Barnabas Bazell and his wife Mary Eve Winters Bazell. Carrie Emeline Bazell, their daughter, is buried beside them. Yes, as many of you know, my sister was named after their daughter. My mother found and read a diary Carrie Emeline Bazell penned many years before my mother arrived at Christmas Hotel. Those words were instrumental in leading my mother back to the Lord. My mother was so grateful, she wanted Carrie Emeline named after her. Of course, I was named for my father. I think you could figure that name out."

The crowd chuckled.

Chris smiled and winked at Lily. "Since I mentioned for whom we were named, I can't leave out my oldest sister, Lily. She was named for her biological mother Ellie's favorite flower, the Easter Lily. Lily was born on Easter Sunday, but I'll keep the year secret – as least for now." He winked at his oldest sister again. She smiled and nodded.

"Back to family and close friends buried here. Staff Sergeant Andrew McConnaughey was a remarkable and fine Christian man. He served honorably in the United States Army, and he was the beloved first husband of my sister Carrie Emeline. His son Drew was born shortly after Andrew McConnaughey was killed in battle in Vietnam. Andrew is buried two graves down from the platform from where I'm standing.

"Also, at this Heavenly reunion are our mother's parents buried at Memorial Park Cemetery in Dayton, Ohio. Others buried at Memorial Park Cemetery are the parents of Andrew McConnaughey, and Jerry Staats, an army buddy. Jerry was killed in the same battle with Andrew. They were all from Dayton; the city where my mother was born and raised." Chris moved to the other side of the stage, partially for warmth and partially to dispel some nervousness. He'd never preached a funeral of people so close to him; a funeral of family.

"Imagine all the people our parents met at Christmas Hotel through the years; people who have already gone home to their glory. My parents are having a Heavenly reunion with them, too. I sincerely believe they will meet the two boys Mom miscarried between 1948 and 1953. We don't know, but maybe those two boys, the brothers of my siblings and me, may have grown up in Heaven. A mystery we'll all have answered one day.

"If my dad had one fear, it was the fear he'd die before Mom. Even though he knew his five children would care for his wife, he didn't want her separated from him. I think the Lord, in His divine wisdom, took care of the issue. My father has no more worries.

"My parents, Christopher and Jerilyn, knew they had received God's amazing gift of eternal life. They both had nailed down their salvation many years ago, and raised all their children to know the Lord Jesus. Another of their favorite hymns was 'In the Garden'. Listen to the words as my sisters sing this inspirational hymn."

The three women stepped up to the microphone and Chris sat in one of their chairs. Their voices rang out:

"I come to the garden alone
While the dew is still on the roses
And the voice I hear falling on my ear
The Son of God discloses.

He speaks, and the sound of His voice,
Is so sweet the birds hush their singing,
And the melody that He gave to me
Within my heart is ringing.

And He walks with me, and He talks with me,
And He tells me I am His own;
And the joy we share as we tarry there,
None other has ever known."

Chris and his sisters changed places. Chris stood in silence for a moment before speaking. "My parents would take long walks together, in the garden at home, in the square, the cemetery, and in the country. They held hands and they lived for Jesus Christ. My parents walked with God. Dad rarely lost his temper with his children, but when he did, I think he hurt more than we did. When we had disappointed him, it was more painful for us. None of Dad's children ever wanted to disappoint him.

"Christopher and Jerilyn prayed daily for all their family and friends to be saved. Their greatest desire was to spend eternity, praising God, with every last one of their family and friends. Revelation chapter twenty four, verse four says 'And God shall wipe away all tears from their eyes;

and there shall be no more death, neither sorrow, nor crying, neither shall there be any more pain: for the former things are passed away.' Our parents knew it was possible that all their friends would not spend eternity with them, but they knew the Lord would wipe away their tears if that happened. If there's anyone out there today who hasn't chosen Christ as his or her Savior and you are under conviction to do so, please allow me to help you. I promise you, my parents and all your loved ones will rejoice in Heaven." He paused a moment to survey the crowd.

"My sisters have chosen another hymn. 'Take Your Burden to the Lord and Leave It There.' This old hymn was another favorite of my parents. They believed one should not carry burdens, but give them over to the Lord."

The sisters replaced Chris at the microphone, and they looked out upon the huge crowd. Lydia Grace strummed her guitar.

"If the world from you withhold of its silver and its gold,
And you have to get along with meager fare,
Just remember, in His Word, how He feeds the little bird –
Take your burden to the Lord and leave it there.

*If your body suffers pain and your health you
can't regain,
And your soul is almost sinking in despair;
Jesus knows the pain you feel, He can save and
He can heal –
Take your burden to the Lord and leave it there.*

*When your youthful days are gone and old age
is stealing on,
And your body bends beneath the weight of
care;
He will never leave you then, He'll go with you
to the end –
Take your burden to the Lord and leave it
there."*

Chris joined his sisters. "With this hymn, we conclude the gravesite celebration of the lives of Christopher and Jerilyn Wright."

He dropped his head, and Lily placed her arm around him. With a slight quiver in his voice he blinked back tears, and his voice shook. "I loved my parents, as did my siblings, our family, and all of you. We will miss them, but we who know the Savior will see them again. Christopher and Jerilyn Wright are in a better place. Remember them in the way they lived. They loved all of us, but most of all they loved their Lord Jesus. It's what my siblings and I will remember, and the memories are wonderful. Don't ask the Lord why He took them. Leave the question here ... in this cemetery and walk away."

He had to pause before he could continue. Clearing his throat he continued. "Know our Lord made the best decision for Christopher and Jerilyn Wright. My sisters will sing one last hymn as you head to your cars. 'Farther Along,' another favorite hymn of my parents. Helping to make sense of a senseless world, in the words of my late mother, 'There's One who knows.' Go with God, and know you are loved."

The three sisters remained at the microphone, and Chris stepped down from the platform and stood beside Lori Anna. She rose up on her tiptoes, kissed Chris's cheek, and wiped his tear. "It was a lovely service, Chris. Your parents would be so proud."

Chris hugged his wife to him and together they listened to the words of the hymn, while the crowd walked to their cars.

Tempted and tried, we're oft made to wonder
Why it should be thus all the day long;
While there are others living about us,
Never molested, though in the wrong.

Farther along we'll know more about it,
Farther along we'll understand why;
Cheer up, my brother, live in the sunshine,
We'll understand it all by and by.

"Faithful till death," saith our loving Master;
Short is our time to labor and wait;
Then will our toiling seem to be nothing,
When we shall pass the heavenly gate.

Soon we will see our dear, loving Savior,
Hear the last trumpet sound through the sky;
Then we will meet those gone on before us,
Then we shall know and understand why.

Chapter Twenty-Two

A Rebuilding Committee Forms

"Where no counsel is, the people fall: but in the multitude of counsellors there is safety."
Proverbs 11:14

Tuesday
January 05, 1999
Later that day, Carrie Emeline and Ken would be leaving to return to their respective homes in Bellingham, Washington and Lexington, Kentucky. They stood shoulder-to-shoulder one last time in front of what was left of Christmas Hotel with Chris, Lily and Lydia Grace.

The siblings slowly walked around the premises from East Cedar Street to the front of the building on North Main Street; still finding it difficult to believe this hotel in which they all grew up was lost. The fire department had blocked off the ruins with barricades the morning after the fire.

The three sisters cried again, and the brothers wrapped their arms around them. Lily reached in her purse, pulled out a packet of Kleenex, and shared them with her sisters. "I never dreamed something like this would ever happen. Christmas Hotel has been such a part of my life for sixty-two years." She looked at her siblings. "I'm sorry ... that statement was selfish of me. I realize a huge part of all your lives, too. For the first time, I'm happy Mom and Dad aren't here to see this." She dabbed at her eyes and blew her nose.

The smoke stench was still powerful. Ken looked up at what had been the rooftop. It had collapsed into several of the floors. "Do you think any part of Christmas Hotel is salvageable?"

"I met with the insurance adjustors yesterday morning." Chris shuffled back and forth on his feet. He wasn't sure if he was trying to stay warm or just nervous. "It's not good. They can't give us all the money we need to rebuild Christmas Hotel to the magnificent structure it was. They suggested we cut some corners."

Carrie Emeline closed her eyes a second before responding. With all she'd been through in her life, she was determined and a fighter. "What do you say, Chris?"

He didn't say anything for a moment. He shook his head and puckered his lips. "It's not at all what I want. I want to rebuild it right. I just don't know how. I don't have a set of the original blueprints. I checked the courthouse, but when the old courthouse burned in 1882, all documents on file were destroyed. There are no known copies."

Always the positive influence on those around her, Lydia Grace smiled through her tears. "Cheer up, Chris. We have numerous pictures and recorded descriptions of every area of Christmas Hotel. We can provide this information to an architect to create new blueprints."

"Very true. However, I met with an architect yesterday afternoon in Nashville. I had no idea an architect would be so expensive. Just the retainer fee was completely out of my tentative budget."

Lily, the pragmatic sibling, and always the big sister, watched her siblings and spoke up. "We can't do this alone. We're going to need help, and the good people of Franklin are the ones to ask. They will want Christmas Hotel rebuilt, too and as spectacular as ever. We can start by calling for a meeting with some of the movers and shakers in town. We're going to need a lawyer. There are women in Franklin who know how to raise funds. We need donations. Christmas Hotel was declared historical years ago, so there's a strong possibility we could receive grants with very low interest. We'll just need to know how to cut through all the red tape. John and I are retired. We'll do some research at the Goodnight Memorial Library today and see what we can find out about grants."

Lydia Grace beamed and turned to her younger brother. "Jacob and I can help, too. We'll get our agent to book some extra concerts, and the proceeds can be applied to the Christmas Hotel rebuilding project. We can all pitch in and do this. I don't want to cut corners either. We're just going to need legal advice and a lot of workers. Christmas Hotel has friends all around the world."

Ken, the older and wise brother to Chris, cheered him on, too. As Chris grew up, he constantly looked to Ken, his only brother and thirteen years his senior, for advice. "I agree, Lydia Grace. We can all get this done ... together. You won't be alone, Chris. You have your family and a lot of friends in Franklin."

Chris was humbled by the inspiring words he received from his four siblings. "I thank you, and I love you all. I guess I was having a little pity-party after yesterday's meetings with the insurance adjustor and the architect. You four give me hope."

The three women hugged Chris, and Ken hugged and slapped Chris's back. All five turned, and together they again stood shoulder-to-shoulder and viewed the ruins.

"Baby steps," Lily nodded. "Baby steps."

Chris called his friend and Simpson County attorney, Sid Broderson around noon and explained the situation. Sid requested an emergency meeting with Mayor Jim Arnold and City Manager Tom Gordon to be held in the courthouse at 7:00. He also invited several Franklin business owners, and his wife Jill invited women she knew who were known in Franklin as successful fundraisers. Dr. Beasley arrived with all six of his children, and Lily and Lydia Grace, along with their spouses, were present, too.

Chris explained the situation. The invitees were especially pleased to be part of this meeting, and all desired for Christmas Hotel to be rebuilt in all its glory. The mayor and city manager had plenty of contacts for construction crews to begin clearing the unsalvageable debris. They also knew reconstruction crews who would be on hand to excavate and store any architectural pieces of the interior and exterior which should be restored.

Sid Broderson offered to represent as the attorney for the Christmas Hotel rebuilding project, and gratis. Jill Broderson, an interior decorator by trade, offered to design fifty-nine of the sixty rooms, and also free of charge. The only cost encumbered would be in the furnishings.

Barbara Beasley Smith offered to head up a team to restore room number seven with period furnishings of circa 1850. Her five siblings offered to work on her team, and their service would also remain complimentary, only costs for the furnishings and any travel expenses they might incur would be paid from the insurance monies.

Mary, Mabel, and Harriet, the women invited to the meeting, who excelled at church fundraising, said they'd set a reasonable fundraising goal and send out donation invitations to the people of Simpson County, several surrounding counties, and the reunion guests. They also knew some prominent people in Simpson County and surrounding counties who might match all gifts donated. They would keep a goal chart at the courthouse, and update it as the funds arrived.

Dr. Beasley stroked his chin. "I'm a retired medical doctor, as you know, but I have met a great deal of people over the years. Many times, in the first few decades of my practice some of my patients didn't have the money to pay me, so they gave me fruits, vegetables, chickens or whatever they had on hand." He laughed. "I was a typical country doctor. They always said someday they'd find a way to pay me back. I have a few favors I can call in from children or grandchildren of those patients who are now in the construction business. I think all of us here tonight can get Christmas Hotel rebuilt in all its grandeur – and in budget."

Chris looked around the room at his life-long friends, and at his sisters Lily and Lydia Grace who dabbed tears with their handkerchiefs. "Thank you all so much," he said. "My family and I couldn't do this without your help. I can't tell you what your support means to our family ... and Christmas Hotel."

Mayor Arnold shook Chris's hand. "You're welcome, Chris. We're all happy to help. Franklin has benefited economically from Christmas Hotel, so it's our turn to give back."

Chapter Twenty-Three

Dr. Beasley and Captain Bazell

*"Peace I leave with you, my peace I give unto you:
not as the world giveth, give I unto you. Let not
your heart be troubled, neither let it be afraid."*
John 14:27

Wednesday Morning
January 06, 1999
Chris sat at his kitchen table. He sipped his
morning coffee, drummed his fingers on the table,
and read the architect's projected proposal. The
children were back at school, and Lori Anna
worked in the family office to patch together Mom's
last manuscript. Lori Anna announced on New
Year's Eve, the day his parents married fifty-seven
years ago, she would finish it and dedicate it to his
parents. All royalties would go toward money
needed to rebuild Christmas Hotel.

Chris would have to settle on an architect soon.
He wasn't certain who to choose, and realized that
last night he should have asked the Christmas

Hotel Rebuilding Committee – as they'd chosen to call the project. The most expensive architect was not always the right one. This proposal was giving him a major headache.

All was quiet in the Wright home – until the doorbell rang. Chris walked to the door, and Bobby looked up from his resting spot on his over-sized doggy bed. With rheumy eyes he stared at Chris, and dropped his head back down and groaned. The dog probably hoped his master or mistress had returned. Bobby had been quiet and mourned his parents' absence. Chris petted the old dog's head. "I know, Bobby. It's hard, isn't it, fella?"

Chris opened the door to a smiling Dr. Beasley. "Hi, Dr. Beasley, come on in and have a seat."

Lori Anna must have heard the voice of their old friend, because within five minutes she joined them in the living room with a pot of coffee, three mugs, cream, sugar, and some leftover breakfast croissants she'd baked earlier.

"I heard about the cost of the architect," Dr. Beasley stroked his chin and nodded his head. Chris's eyebrows knit together, as he was truly puzzled. The meeting he'd had with the architect on Monday had only provided him an estimate. He didn't have the exact cost until the courier brought the proposal this morning. Dr. Beasley chuckled. "It's a small town ... remember? I also personally know your tentative architect."

Chris knowingly nodded and laughed. "Oh, yes, I'm aware how quickly information travels, sir."

Dr. Beasley reached in his pocket and pulled out a folded, yellowed piece of paper and handed it to Chris. Chris opened it and read aloud. "Right-3 (3 times) Left-20 (2 times) Right-21 (1 time)." He looked up at Dr. Beasley. "It looks like the numbers on a combination lock."

"You are correct, Chris." Dr. Beasley grinned, took a sip of his coffee, and settled comfortably in the chair. "I remembered this last night after the meeting, and I shuffled through old documents until I found it. I have a story for you and Lori Anna."

Raring back in the recliner, he began. "Back in 1934, when I was a young man, fresh out of medical school in Tennessee, I looked for a town to practice medicine. I heard about Franklin, Kentucky, needing a doctor, so I came to visit. I fell in love with this town and its people, like so many others before me. Like your mother, Chris. I decided Franklin was where I'd set up my practice.

"Well, I was lonely back then; no wife and children. I didn't marry Jane until 1948, and I didn't even know her until after the war. Therefore, when I wasn't working, I spent a great deal of time at Christmas Hotel. Your dad was in the United

States Army Air Corps, and he had not yet become the manager of Christmas Hotel, so I had not met him. I visited Captain and Mrs. Bazell at Christmas Hotel."

Dr. Beasley paused, took a sip of his coffee, and he smiled at Lori Anna. "Good coffee."

"Thank you, Dr. Beasley."

"Well, the Bazells kind of took me under their wings. I spent many evenings with them having dinner at their table, and later enjoying interesting and companionable conversation in the Christmas Hotel lobby. One evening, Captain Bazell was very serious. He pulled out the piece of paper you're holding and said, 'I trust you, Dr. Beasley. You're a good, young man. When Thomas Hoy built Christmas Hotel, an architect from Nashville drew up the plans. The drawings were on file at the courthouse. However, as everyone around here knows, our original courthouse burned in 1882, and all documents were lost in the fire.

"'Mr. Hoy was a smart man,' Captain Bazell continued, and he winked at me with a slight smile and a mysterious look in his eye. 'Mr. Hoy had an extra copy made, and he kept it in his office behind the front desk at Christmas Hotel. However, I got to thinking the designs were not safe there either.'"

Dr. Beasley stopped, took another sip of coffee, a bite of his croissant, and nodded to Lori Anna.

"The croissant is delicious, Lori Anna. Thank you."

She smiled. "You're very welcome, sir."

Dr. Beasley cleared his throat and began again. "So where was I? Oh, yes ... the story of Captain Bazell and the Christmas Hotel blueprints." Dr. Beasley continued, and said in his Captain Bazell deepened voice, "'After the Great War ended, some new safes were developed and claimed to be fire and waterproof. I bought one. I hoped to store a few of Carrie Emeline's precious items in it, and the original hotel blueprints and purchase orders. The safe is down in the Christmas Hotel basement where we have all of Carrie Emeline's things stored. All her belongings are in crates marked CEB, and the safe is nearby.

"'So why am I telling you this, Dr. Beasley?' he said. 'Well, Mrs. Bazell and I have no living heirs. Someday, the Lord is going to take us home, and when He does, *and* if Christmas Hotel is ever damaged, I want someone to know where the architect's designs are stored, *if* they are ever needed. Those numbers you are holding are the safe's combination. They represent the date my daughter died on March the twentieth, and her age ... twenty-one at the time of her death.'"

Dr. Beasley took another sip of his coffee and a bite of the croissant, nodding his pleasure again to Lori Anna along with a smile lighting up his old eyes. "Chris, the conversation took place about a year or two after I arrived in Franklin. If you don't know about the safe's contents, possibly your dad never did either."

Chris laid the yellowed and frayed slip of paper on the coffee table, sat forward on the sofa, and with his elbows on his knees, clasped his hands together under his chin and shook his head no. "I don't believe my dad knew about the contents. He probably thought, as I did, everything in the sequestered area belonged to Carrie Emeline Bazell. Everything around the safe was in crates and marked CEB ... at least up to the day of the fire."

"Chris, do you know if the safe was pulled out of the ruins?"

"I'm not sure, but everything salvageable is stored over at the old warehouse. The fire marshal has closed off Christmas Hotel, so we can't go traipsing around in the burned out building."

"You know, Chris, when Captain Bazell told me the story, and gave me the numbers, he did say it would take a fire or a flood at Christmas Hotel to see if the safe would hold up."

Chris smiled. "I suppose we may find out today, Dr. Beasley. I know every bit of the hotel was drenched from the fire hoses and/or burned. If you'll remember, there was also the water heater leak. It flooded the entire basement back in '75. So

... would you like to take a drive with Lori Anna and me to the old warehouse and see if the safe was moved there? The fire marshal gave me the warehouse key yesterday, but I've not felt up to looking everything over until now."

Dr. Beasley smiled and let down the recliner. "I'm ready when you two are ready!"

The fire marshal had informed Chris that anything salvaged, so far, was catalogued as to the description of the item and where it was found in Christmas Hotel. Chris turned the key in the lock, removed the lock, and the oversized door creaked on its hinges. He pushed open both doors, and the three stepped into the dark building. Chris had brought a flashlight, and he located the light switch. The old warehouse lighting was dim, and the huge building stretched before them. They spotted the Christmas Hotel items corded off to their right.

Lori Anna wrinkled her nose. "It's musty smelling in here, and mixed with the awful burnt odor." She walked closer and picked up the edge of one of the lobby rugs. "Most of the hotel stuff is still soaked. I suppose it's too cold and damp in here to dry it out. Maybe we should bring in some large blowers, so the items don't develop mold and mildew."

"Good suggestion." Chris turned the flashlight on the area.

The three of them spread out looking for the old safe. "When the fire marshal gave me the key to the warehouse, I wish I'd asked for a copy of the catalogued list," muttered Chris to his wife and the doctor.

They located recovered items from the kitchen, dining room, front desk, basement, and the chapel, all heavily water-logged along with much smoke damage. Chris shook his head. "This is so sad. I suppose all the artwork is destroyed. Some things can be replaced but not portraits of the Hoy and Bazell families. It appears no items in the sixty rooms and the ballroom were salvaged."

Lori Anna was the first to spy the old safe. "I found it!"

The two men hurried to her side, and Chris pulled out the paper with the safe's combination. "Well, here we go." He handed his wife the flashlight. "Lori Anna, please direct the beam onto the lock."

Chris knelt and settled back on his heels. He said a quick prayer, and rotated the numbers in the appropriate directions and number of times, listening to each click. The old safe opened on the first try.

He looked up at Lori Anna and Dr. Beasley. They were smiling down at him. He asked Lori Anna for the flashlight, and he shined it into the safe. Holding the flashlight with one hand, he reached in, and picked up a handful of papers. Looking up to his wife and Dr. Beasley, he let out a shout. "Yes! Everything appears dry and not burnt." He gently pulled out everything in the safe.

Handing a very old Bible to Lori Anna, she carefully opened it to the first page. "Chris, there are Bazell family birth and wedding dates recorded in here, beginning back in 1750."

Chris grinned. "It's too bad there are no Bazell heirs, but we can place it on display at the new Christmas Hotel."

Dr. Beasley gave him a thumbs up. "Good, positive thinking, Chris."

Next he pulled out a porcelain doll and handed it up to Lori Anna. "I wonder if this was Carrie Emeline Bazell's doll," mused Lori Anna softly. "If so, it's probably at least a hundred and thirty years old. Another item to go on display at the new Christmas Hotel."

Chris pulled out several more documents, including the bill of sale for Christmas Hotel from Thomas Hoy to Captain Bazell, and an 1848 to 1850 ledger listing all original items purchased for the interior of the hotel, and the costs. Then he pulled out the coveted blueprints. He nodded and flashed a smile up at the other two.

"Here they are! They're undamaged and just a

bit yellowed after all these years."

He handed the blueprints to Dr. Beasley. "Thank you, Dr. Beasley, for your excellent memory and for being such a good friend to Captain Bazell. Because he trusted you with the combination to his safe over sixty years ago, we will save a great deal of money toward the rebuilding of the hotel. We won't need to hire an expensive architect to make new drawings, and Christmas Hotel will be reconstructed exactly as it should be."

"You are very welcome, Chris. I'm glad I could be of help," the old doctor responded in his typical kind and humble manner.

Chapter Twenty-Four

Demolition Bids and Sorting Clothes

"Every good gift and every perfect gift is from above, and cometh down from the Father of lights, with whom is no variableness, neither shadow of turning."
James 1:17

Thursday
January 07, 1999
As always, Chris and Lori Anna were up by 4:00. Together they took a quick run on the two newly purchased treadmills in their home's finished basement before getting the children up for school. None of the treadmills from the Christmas Hotel's basement could be repaired. They finished their run and both rushed upstairs for a quick shower and to dress for the day.

"What's on the agenda for the rebuilding project this morning, Chris?"

"Mayor Arnold and City Manager Tom Gordon chose two companies which would have the time to begin the demolition and the preservation of any salvageable parts of Christmas Hotel's structure. The burned-out building is such an eye-sore. I'd like to have the debris removed as soon as possible, so we can begin reconstruction. Both companies are coming today to bid on the project – one this morning and one this afternoon."

He sat on the edge of the bed, sighed, hung his head, and rubbed his temples. "This is when I miss Dad and Mom the most. I have big decisions to make. Even though we've owned Christmas Hotel for over ten years, I could always go to them, especially Dad to discuss the major issues. Right now, even with all our help from the Christmas Hotel Rebuilding Committee, I wish I could sit down and discuss everything with Dad. I just miss my parents so much, Lori Anna." He blinked back the tears.

Lori Anna sat on the bed beside him, wrapped her arms around him, kissed him on the cheek, placed her head on his shoulder, and sighed. "I miss them too, Chris. I can't go into their room to dust without being torn apart ... crying. I need to start packing their clothes. I think the homeless shelter in Bowling Green where your sisters volunteer would appreciate anything we can donate."

She cupped his cheeks in her hands. "Your

parents left a big hole in our hearts, the family, and for many in Franklin. People are still placing flowers and wreaths around the ruins of Christmas Hotel and leaving cards of sympathy and remembrance. You need to pray about these decisions, Chris. You must stop carrying this burden and turn it over to the Lord." She kissed him again and stood. "If you'll get the children up and dressed for school, I'll start breakfast."

Two hours later, Chris watched Lori Anna open the door to his parents' bedroom, and he walked to the burned-out hotel to meet with the owner of the first demolition company.

*****

At 11:30, Lori Anna took a much-needed break from the packing in Christopher and Jerilyn's bedroom. Chris would be home at noon for lunch. She mixed up batter for cornbread, poured it into the iron skillet, and lifted it into the oven to bake. Chris walked into the kitchen and found her stirring the beef stew she had prepared before the packing began. He walked up behind her, placed his arms around her, pushed her long hair aside, and kissed the nape of her neck.

"Smells good in here, honey. What's for lunch?"

She tapped the wooden spoon on the side of the large iron kettle, set the spoon on a plate by the stove, and turned to give her husband a passionate kiss.

"Beef stew, my love." The timer on the stove sounded. "If you'll pour us each a glass of milk, set the table with butter, napkins, and silverware, I'll get the cornbread out of the oven, and then you can give thanks to the Lord."

She grabbed two pot holders, set the iron skillet on the range top, and dipped up two bowls of beef stew. She cut three slices of the hot cornbread, placed the slices on a small plate, and set the bowls of stew and bread on the table.

He gave thanks and took the first spoonful. "Yum. Delicious as always." He smacked his lips and smiled in satisfaction.

She grinned. Chris always seemed pleased with whatever she prepared, and she was happy to cook for her handsome husband. He hadn't changed much from the day they married: tall, an athletic build, short, brown hair, no premature gray, and striking blue eyes. "Glad you like it. How did the meeting go with the owner of the first demolition company?"

"I suppose it was okay. I won't know the complete bid until Saturday. He promised to put a rush on it. He said if his company got the job, he'd have a twenty-man team ready to go Tuesday, and be finished by the end of the week."

"What's the name of this company?"

"*Lewis and Sons Demolition and Salvage.* They're located out of Nashville. I must say, Mr. Lewis, the owner, appeared thorough as he tramped through the ruins. I told him loose interior items have been removed and stored at the warehouse. I wanted him to save as much of the façade as possible, including the roof. It appears both stone carvings reading CHRISTMAS HOTEL and WHERE JESUS' BIRTH IS A DAILY CELEBRATION are intact, but in need of some patching and a good cleaning. Also, the two angels, and the brass plaque which says 1850, appear to be salvageable."

Lori Anna set down her spoon and dabbed her mouth with her napkin. "Oh, Chris ... that's such good news. Those items are such an integral part of the exterior of the original hotel."

"I said the same thing, too. The glass in the double glass front doors is shattered, and the doors are bent from when the firemen stormed the building, but maybe the right preservation company can restore them. There's just so much we won't know until the reconstruction begins."

Lori Anna stared at the plaque on the kitchen wall above the back door. Lily brought it yesterday just for Chris. On the plaque was a picture of Chris as a baby when he took his first step. The caption read "Baby Steps." Lori Anna pointed to the plaque. "Remember what Lily said to you ... baby steps,

Chris. Everything will work out. The Christmas Hotel Rebuilding Committee will handle much of this. I know Jill Broderson has already started on the designs of the fifty-nine rooms, and Barbara Beasley and her siblings have put out the word about the correct furniture from circa 1850 for room number seven. Barbara has spread the word through our reunion guests and newspaper ads around the country. She's provided pictures of what the room looked like, so people can respond."

Chris finished his second slice of cornbread. "Enough talk about Christmas Hotel. What did you work on this morning?"

"I went down to the basement and brought up every empty cardboard box I could locate. I also called the *Piggly Wiggly* and asked the store manager to put some boxes aside for me. I picked up about twenty boxes from him. From their bedroom closet, I've packed all of your dad's and your mom's clothes, but I still need to sort clothing in the drawers. If I can finish packing other items, except very personal things of course, such as their Bibles, devotionals, and journals. I'll take the clothes to the shelter today after the children are out of school. They can go with me. I'll call Lily and Lydia Grace to see if they'd like to join us."

Chris nodded and stood. "Sounds good. Honey, I hate to eat and run, but the next appointment is at two." He checked the slip of paper in his pocket. "I'm meeting with Mr. Haggarty of *Haggarty's Demolition and Salvation Company, Inc.*"

Chris rinsed his dirty dishes and set them in the sink. "The Christmas Hotel Rebuilding Committee is gathering at 4:00, but I should be home no later than 6:00 for dinner. Good luck with your packing. I wish I could help you."

"Thanks, Chris, but I think you have enough on your plate at this time. I can handle things here at home. I love you."

"I love you, too." He planted a quick kiss on her lips and was out the door.

*****

Lori Anna sorted and packed the remaining clothes, carefully picking up each item and scrutinizing for wear and tear. She didn't want to send something to the shelter that needed mending. After about an hour, she sat in the old rocker to rest and view the room. *So many wonderful memories.*

Her eyes landed on the Bible on the night stand. In her mind's eye, she could see Christopher and Jerilyn in the living room, praying together, holding hands, and reading from their Bible. Chris once told her it was their daily ritual every morning of their life together. She focused on the picture above their bed. Chris had taken this photograph when he still lived at home. His parents knelt in prayer, holding hands.

This scene was not unusual, but she remembered when Chris told her how the inspiration for the picture had crossed his mind. When he saw them in the living room praying, he returned to his bedroom, grabbed his camera, and snapped a quick picture of his parents. He had waited until they each said Amen, but their heads were still bowed. They looked up, a surprised expression on each of their faces and then smiled. He captured their smiles with a second picture.

He offered the explanation before they could say anything. "I love you both so much, and when I saw you in prayer, a verse crossed my mind in Joshua chapter twenty-four verse fifteen ... 'but as for me and my house, we will serve the Lord.' When you two were in prayer, a vision of you two and these words crossed my mind. Would you object if I had the words framed with your picture? I'll use the smiling picture or the picture with your heads bowed. You can choose."

Lori Anna smiled in memory of when Chris told her how this picture came about. The answer had been yes, because the picture and words were framed above their bed. The picture with their heads bowed was chosen. *This picture will be rehung in the living room here at home. I want all family and friends to see it when they visit. I will not send it to the shelter.*

Lori Anna once again sorted and packed, and she was almost finished when the children arrived home. "There's a plate of oatmeal cookies on the counter and fresh milk in the fridge," she called down to them. "Don't forget to hang up your coats and wash your hands."

Twenty minutes later, Olivia, Abigail, and Michael stood on the threshold of their grandparents' bedroom. Olivia's face was scrunched, her brows knit together, and her lower lip trembled. "Wha ... what are you doing, Mom?"

Lori Anna had finished the closet and was working on items in the chest and dresser. She patted the bed. "Come here and sit with Mommy ... all three of you."

"What are you doing with Grandma and Grandpa's clothes?" A tear escaped down Olivia's face.

Lori Anna wiped the tear away with her thumb, hugged her daughter, and kissed the top of her head. Lori Anna paused before she answered, and took a deep breath. "I'm doing what Grandma and Grandpa would want. They're in Heaven and no longer need these clothes. There are poor people who do. Remember the time we visited the homeless shelter?"

"Y-e-s," Olivia answered, drawing the word into

three syllables with a quiver in her voice.

"Well, I remember you saying there were some people who could use some new clothes and coats. I thought the four of us, and Aunt Lily and Aunt Lydia Grace, could go the shelter and distribute clothing. In fact, your aunts are on their way now to help us."

Lori Anna watched the realization take place on Olivia's face. Olivia hugged her mom. "You're right, Mom. There are a lot of people who can use these clothes."

Lori Anna smiled and kissed her daughter's forehead. "Thank you for understanding, Olivia."

Abigail added, "There were children at the shelter, too. What if we bring some toys we don't play with anymore? In fact, I have clothes I've outgrown. I can give them away, too."

Abigail sat on the other side of Olivia. "Come here, Abigail." She pulled Abigail down on her lap and hugged her. "Your suggestion is wonderful, sweetheart," she kissed Abigail's cheek.

Michael was sitting beside her and he added to the conversation. "I got a new twenty-inch bike for Christmas. What if I give them my old tricycle? It's still shiny. I don't need it anymore, because I can ride a big boy's bike – *and* I've got clothes too small for me."

Michael sounded so excited. *What amazing*

children you gave us, Lord. Lori Anna hugged and kissed Michael, too. "I'm so proud of all three of you. Go and make piles of everything you're giving away." She handed each of them a box. "You can use this box for your clothes and smaller toys. Please make sure the toys aren't broken or dirty. The clothes and toys will make wonderful gifts for many children."

As Olivia, Abigail, and Michael hurried off to gather the items, Lori Anna sat back on the bed, looked up, and said aloud, "Thank you, Lord, for these beautiful children with such big hearts."

Chapter Twenty-Five

A Date for Chris and Lori Anna

"Beloved, let us love one another: for love is of God; and every one that loveth is born of God, and knoweth God."
1 John 4:7

Saturday
January 09, 1999
The two bids to clear the site arrived Saturday morning by a courier service. Chris sat at the kitchen table while Lori Anna bustled around preparing their lunch. He read the gist of the bids to her.

"The pricing on each bid is similar. However, Mr. Lewis has a large crew ready who can complete the demolition this coming week. Mr. Haggarty won't be available for three weeks. I think we should go with Mr. Lewis. I really hate for the townspeople to spend another three weeks looking at the rubble."

"I agree, Chris. I know our friends are grieving

the loss of Mom and Dad as we are. Everyone will have something to look forward to once we begin rebuilding Christmas Hotel. Will you need to meet again with the Christmas Hotel Rebuilding Committee before making the final decision?"

"No, just with Sid Broderson. He's keeping track of the expenditures, along with all monies brought in, so there's a check and balance to the financial situation. I'll meet with him later today and go over the two proposals."

Lori Anna leaned down to Chris where he sat and wrapped her arms around him. "I said this will come together, Chris. We just need to keep the faith God will work it all out. Hopefully, by December we will have the joy of seeing the rebuilding of Christmas Hotel completed."

He turned his face up to her, they kissed, and he pulled her down on his lap. "I love you, Mrs. Wright. You are my best cheerleader. You keep me encouraged – and focused."

"I aim to please, Mr. Wright."

"How about a dinner date all alone with me tonight?"

"You mean *sans* children?" She smiled at him and smoothed his hair with her fingers.

"Yes, just us. We'll have dinner in Bowling Green at the *Bistro*. Maybe the children can spend the night with Lydia Grace and Jacob at the farm, and they can bring them into town for church in the morning."

"I'll call them right after lunch." She planted a kiss on his lips.

*****

They placed their order for the house special: Mediterranean tilapia with roasted asparagus and wild rice, relaxed, and enjoyed the ambience of the restaurant. The *Bistro,* an 1890s converted home, located in historic downtown Bowling Green, and just two blocks from Fountain Square, was a popular place to eat for their many guests. The Wrights ate here on most trips to Bowling Green.

Tonight, just like when they were courting. Chris had placed the reservations, and requested a table next to the stone fireplace. Crisp linen tablecloths graced each table along with centerpieces with fresh-cut flowers. Waiters served their guests in starched black and white matching uniforms. The original oak floors were sanded smooth with a light stain, but not glossy.

Lori Anna had twisted her long black hair up on her head in a chic and timeless style. Her dark brown eyes sparkled from the firelight and Chris found himself staring into them. He placed his hand over hers. "This is like *déjà vu,* Lori Anna. You're just as beautiful as you were on our first date."

Lori Anna blushed. "Thank you, Chris. You're pretty handsome yourself."

"We should make time more often, just for us. I'm so sorry I haven't been there lately for you and our children, especially while you packed my parents' clothes, and then took everything to the shelter."

She placed her other hand on top of his. "Chris, I think you've had a full plate with your Christmas Hotel duties, and the children and I understand. In fact, the children and I had a wonderful talk when they arrived home from school Thursday." She explained in detail what happened.

He sat back in his chair, withdrew his hand from her hands, and closed his eyes for a few seconds. When he opened them, Lori Anna was looking at him with concern on her face.

He smiled. "I was just thinking what exceptional children we've been blessed with. Yes, at first I was saddened we wouldn't be having any more biological children after Olivia was born, but Abigail and Michael ... I couldn't love them any more than I do, even if they were our own blood-children."

He sat up straight again and took her hand once more. "In fact, I've been meaning to ask you. The house seems empty without babies. What do you think about adopting another baby? I mean, after

Christmas Hotel is rebuilt."

Lori Anna didn't hesitate. "I'd say yes. I know your parents would be happy knowing their room had been filled with a baby."

"Oh, speaking of a baby, which is what Mom called each book she wrote, I've been meaning to ask you: how is the manuscript coming along?"

"Actually, very well. I've been writing and editing while the children are in school and you're off to meetings. Mom did complete the majority of the book before she started to ramble and repeat herself, and she left excellent notes in her outline before she quit writing altogether. So I know where the story is going and, importantly, how it ends. I'm doing my best to remain faithful to the way she wanted it. I should have the first draft together by early February."

"Is it another story about Christmas Hotel?"

"Yes. I'm going to find a way to add in our reunion guests and some of the Franklin community who we've been privileged in knowing."

"Speaking of reunion, if Christmas Hotel can be finished in December, what do you think about another reunion? We can invite all the guests back for the ribbon-cutting ceremony. Of course, everyone in Franklin and the media would have to be invited to the event too. Thoughts?"

"I like it, Chris. Maybe I'll have Mom's book

published by then. Her original publisher is interested, and with a sizable offer. I'll need to respond very soon with the outline and the work already completed, and hopefully the book can be released by December."

"Sounds like a plan."

The food arrived, and they bowed their heads and said a prayer of thanks.

"By the way, what did Lydia Grace say when you asked her to watch the children tonight?"

"She was very happy to do so, and she reminded me to have them wear their work clothes and work shoes, because Jacob would have them doing chores in the barn. She also stressed *twice* for me to pack their church clothes and shoes for the morning." Lori Anna laughed and shook her head. "Lydia Grace is an efficiency expert, Chris. I suppose she needed to be: attentive wife, running a household, raising Anthony, and helping to plan all the concert dates over the years.

"She also said, and I quote, 'I'm happy to be of assistance while my little brother courts you again, Lori Anna. In fact, any time Chris wants a date with you, just ask. Jacob and I will be happy to take care of our nieces and nephew. You two could use a night alone together.'"

Chris grinned. "I love my sister. She's one-of-a-kind."

After dinner, Chris suggested they walk over to Fountain Square Park and enjoy the remainder of the evening.

"Yes, let's do."

She snuggled closer to Chris while they walked.

Other couples meandered around the three-tiered fountain or stopped and read from the many historical plaques regarding events and battles of the Civil War. Trees and shrubs surrounded the fountain, along with five statues representing the mythological figures of Ceres, goddess of grain, Pomona, goddess of fruit, Melpomene, goddess of tragedy, and Flora, goddess of flowers. Hebe, the fifth and final goddess sat atop the fountain, keeping a watchful eye across the sky, the goddess of youth and life.

"I love this magnificent and unique fountain, Chris."

"Let's have a seat on *that* bench." He pointed toward the bench and steered her in the direction. "Do you remember this particular bench?" he asked, as they cuddled together.

"Chris, I will never forget the only other time, more than a decade ago, that we came alone to this restaurant and we sat on this bench after dinner. You are such a romantic; one of the many reasons I love you."

"Lori Anna, before that date I had already

begun falling in love with you. Your sweetness, your enchanting dimples, your long, glorious hair – and your big brown eyes I could get lost in."

"I was already in love with you, Chris, because I fell in love with you when I was a little girl, but you knew that." She settled even closer to him, and he draped his arm around her. "I propose we take the time to have a date night at least once a month. I know we've been busy with the Christmas Hotel rebuilding project, the manuscript, and our children, but we need some *us* time."

They gazed into the spectacular fountain. Chris took a deep breath and slowly released it. "Lori Anna, I miss my parents so much, but I thank God He gave me you. I don't know how I could have gotten through their funeral without you by my side. I love you so much, and I need you so much. I know how my parents felt about each other ... a love for all time. I feel the same about you. I never want to be separated from you." He kissed her lips.

An elderly couple, holding hands, walked by, smiled at them, and walked on.

"Oh, Chris, aren't they lovely? They look to be in their late eighties. They remind me of your mom and dad. I want us to be in love in our old age, too."

"We will be, Lori Anna. You can count on it." He kissed her again, and she sighed.

A young twenty-something couple walked by

and smiled at them.

"Chris, we may be putting on a show."

"Let them eat their hearts out." He kissed her again.

Chapter Twenty-Six

Christmas Hotel Rebuilding Committee News

"And let us not be weary in well doing: for in due season we shall reap, if we faint not."
Galatians 6:9

Monday
January 18, 1999
With the demolition complete, and the reusable pieces of the building structure catalogued and stored in the warehouse, the Christmas Hotel Rebuilding Committee met at the courthouse at 6:30 p.m. The meetings would now be scheduled every Monday evening in the community room at the courthouse to share news.

Barbara Beasley Smith offered to record the minutes, and shared a report on furnishings for room number seven. "A man in a Seattle, Washington antique store may have an identical desk from the same era to the one in room number seven. He sent me the picture." She showed it around the conference table. "I'm flying there tomorrow morning to check it out, and its authenticity. I need to make certain it's not a reproduction."

Chris stared at the picture. "Wonderful news, Barbara. It does look like the original." He chuckled. "Wouldn't it be amazing if it contained the secret drawer?"

Heads nodded in agreement. Dr. Beasley added, "I second that thought. If Jerilyn hadn't found that diary in the secret drawer, she may never have stayed in Franklin. You would not have been born, Chris. That would have been detrimental to the future of Christmas Hotel."

Chris then turned to Dr. Beasley. "Dr. Beasley, thank you. You've meant a great deal to the Wright family. I can't thank you enough for not only doctoring our family through the years, but for being a family friend, and for saving us a great deal of money on an architect. I really appreciate you and your children for helping on this project."

"Chris, my daughters, son, and I would not have missed it for anything," answered Dr. Beasley.

"I have news, too," Chris smiled. "The reconstruction crew, *Command Commercial Building and Restoration* out of Hendersonville, Tennessee will begin their work one week from today. Sid and I have already approved their bid.

They won out among four other bids. The company comes highly recommended, and they proposed having the job complete by the first week of November."

Chris turned to address Jill Broderson. "Jill, will it give you enough time to have the fifty-nine rooms painted, furnished, and completed by the second week of December for a ribbon-cutting ceremony?"

"Perfect, Chris. I should have my design of the fifty-nine rooms and the furnishings presented for approval by our first meeting in March. There are the costs, of course, for my husband to approve, also," she added, and smiled at Sid.

Chris nodded. "Jill, I want you to know your family has been extremely important to the Wright family through the years. Your grandfather Judge James handled the paperwork back in '41 to pass the ownership of Christmas Hotel from Captain and Mrs. Bazell to my parents. *And* in later years, your uncle, Judge Joe Moss James handled the paperwork for my wife's adoption before she was born. I have been meaning to say this for some time and it just seems appropriate now. The Wright family is indebted to your family."

"Thank you, Chris. My family has been happy to help your family through the years. Christmas Hotel means a great deal to us, also." Jill then chuckled, "Don't forget, you're providing me with tremendous advertising for my decorating business."

Chris laughed and turned to Sid. "If you ever decide to run for judge in Simpson County, Sid, you've got my vote."

"Thank you, Chris."

The church fundraising ladies reported next. Mary spoke for herself, Mabel, and Harriet. "We have sent out letters to all of your reunion guests, run the fundraising ad in nationwide newspapers of major cities, and notified the churches in the five-county area. I requested the gifts mailed to the Christmas Hotel Rebuilding Committee at the courthouse address. The courthouse has set up a lock box to collect the envelopes as they arrive. We will keep a goal chart at the courthouse and update it weekly for the locals, as donations are counted, and keep the out-of-town contributors updated by a monthly newsletter."

"We can save a great deal of postage by gathering email addresses," added Barbara. "Email has become popular and it's free. I'd be happy to handle the updates by email on my home computer, unless of course one of you three ladies has access to a computer."

Mary thought about the suggestion. "I can use the computer at the library to send the email updates. I'll ask the contributors for an email address in their first update letter. I think you have enough to do, Barbara, flying around the country to find furniture." She patted Barbara's hand across the table. "I may even buy my own computer." Her eyes twinkled. "After all, I'm only seventy-two."

The others around the table smiled at Mary and shook their heads. "Yes, I believe you can handle a personal computer," Barbara stated as matter-of-fact.

"Harriet and I came up with a fundraising suggestion, too," said Mabel. "The Hospice Center in Nashville has memory paver blocks on their walkway. People have been donating money for the pavers in memory of a loved one. The pavers are different sizes depending on the amount donated. We thought since most people appreciate seeing their name on something, let's offer walkway pavers around the new hotel on the East Cedar and the North Main Street sides. For example, a full square paver block could be $5,000, a half square $2,500, a quarter ... $1,250, and an eighth $750. We could even add a wall in the new lobby or behind the check-in desk with a family name engraved at $250, and a list of those who purchased pavers. The name on the block or the wall can be their own name or in memory of someone. What do you think?"

Chris smiled and nodded his head at the

wonderful suggestions. "Excellent idea, ladies. I'll speak with the reconstruction company to see how this can be accomplished." He looked around the room at the committee. "I could not have done all of this without your help. I can't tell you how much I appreciate all of you."

Dr. Beasley nodded. "Chris, we all loved your parents, you, and Christmas Hotel. Now let's get to work. Can we adjourn this meeting, Sid?"

The committee chuckled at the practical doctor.

"Yes," said Sid. "Meeting for the Christmas Hotel Rebuilding Committee this week is officially adjourned."

Chapter Twenty-Seven

Faith and Joy

"And the peace of God, which passeth all understanding, shall keep your hearts and minds through Christ Jesus."
Philippians 4:7

February 1999
Dr. Beasley was correct about Jenna and Rebecca's pregnancies. Born a day apart in February, Jenna named her baby Faith, and Rebecca named her baby Joy. All the Wright siblings visited the new mothers and their husbands at the hospital in Lexington. Jenna and Rebecca had chosen the names soon after their grandparents' funeral.

Jenna smiled holding her bundled baby. "We wanted the family to know we had faith and joy in our Lord and Savior Jesus Christ ... no matter what trials befall us."

"We knew we were having daughters, so we thought what better way to express to our family we'd all be okay. This will be a year of peace and happiness," added Rebecca.

Chris hugged his nieces, both women tall like Ken, but straight black hair like Loretta. "You two chose the names well."

Lily nodded. "I concur." Ken looked on as the proud grandpa. Chris slapped Ken on the back and laughed. "Are you feeling old, brother?"

"Every day, Chris, but I couldn't be happier." He paused and with glistening eyes, he blinked. "I only wish Mom and Dad could have met their newest great-grandchildren."

"I know, brother ... I know."

Lydia Grace, always the optimist stopped the melancholy moods. "We have Faith and Joy, our next generation to dote on."

Carrie Emeline chimed in. "Now my twin will know the joys of being a grandparent. I have five grandchildren, so you're way behind, Ken."

"You had five *children* and I only had three, *and* you had a huge head start," Ken bantered back.

Carrie Emeline raised her eyebrows and smiled.

Lily finished the conversation. "Okay, technicalities, you two. Let's pray for this next generation as it prevails, and life continues in the Wright family. Chris, will you lead us in prayer?"

"Happily, sis. Dear Heavenly Father...."

Later in the day, the Wright siblings and their spouses gathered at Ken and Loretta's lovely historic 1875 home in Lexington. "Chris, while we're all together, do you have an update for all of us on Christmas Hotel?"

"Yes, I do. The restoration is coming along nicely. The framing should be complete in a couple of weeks. Barbara Beasley Smith has headed up a huge project, recreating the furniture for room number seven. The desk she found up in Seattle, Washington was authentic and it even had the secret compartment." He laughed. "Unfortunately, it was empty. No mysterious diaries hidden away. The man who owned it agreed to hold it until early November, and then he'll ship it. She also found a lady's vanity identical to the one in the room, in Salt Lake City, Utah. It's purchased and being held, too."

Loretta brought coffee on a tray. "I heard that. Too bad there's nothing hidden in the secret drawer."

Chris stopped a moment to pick up a cup of coffee and take a sip before he continued. "Good coffee, Loretta."

She nodded and smiled.

"Jill Broderson is still working on the designs for the other fifty-nine rooms and will have them to the committee for approval by the first meeting in March. The three fundraising ladies are doing a phenomenal job. They've already received almost

$50,000 in donations, *not* including the paver blocks they have pre-sold: so far, twenty-four in various sizes. Currently they have over $300,000 in pending pledges. Therefore, with what we received from the insurance company, what we have collected in donations and sold pavers, and the pending donations and paver requests, we should be able to restore Christmas Hotel in all its splendor."

"Wow, great news!" said Ken. "I didn't expect so much money, so soon!"

Carrie Emeline's jaw dropped. "Wow! Especially as it's only February,"

Chris nodded his agreement. "Lori Anna and I have already shared this next piece of information with Lily and Lydia Grace and their husbands. We are planning another Christmas Hotel reunion, to be held over fewer days, beginning at the ribbon-cutting ceremony. We hope to have the ceremony on Monday, December thirteenth. We'll invite the same reunion guests and the townspeople for the event. And then on Christmas, following the morning service, I'd like all our family to gather for a private reunion. Hopefully, we can get all our children and you who have grandchildren together for a private reunion."

Carrie Emeline hugged him. "Splendid idea, Chris! I'm sure all my children and grandchildren will want to come. We can let them know now, and they'll have plenty of time to plan on attending the family reunion."

The others echoed the same sentiments.

Chapter Twenty-Eight

With God All Things are Possible

"But Jesus beheld them, and said unto them, With men this is impossible; but with God all things are possible."
Matthew 19:26

May 1999

After putting the children to bed, Chris and Lori Anna prepared for a casual evening at home.

"Lori Anna, I've decided to build the Nativity scene for the lobby," Chris said, as they grabbed sodas from the fridge and popped corn for a movie together. "I learned so much about woodworking from Dad all these past many years. All the tools are in the workshop out back. I can do this. Besides, I'm tired of not going to work each day."

Lori Anna smiled. "I know you miss work."

"I do. Rebuilding Christmas Hotel is coming along nicely, Jill's room designs are complete, and she's begun purchasing furniture, drapes, et cetera for the fifty-nine rooms. Sid oversees the finances. Barbara has nearly found all the furniture for room number seven. I'm barely needed at this point."

Lori Anna chose a couple of lap quilts, followed Chris into the living room, and curled up beside him on the sofa. Chris placed his arm around her shoulders.

"I'm fine with everything you said, Chris, except the last statement. How can you possibly say you're barely needed? If anything, the children and I need you. But regarding the Christmas Hotel Rebuilding Committee, none of this would have come together without your leadership. They chose projects they specialized in, but you're keeping everything in order. You, my husband, are a terrific leader."

Dear Lord, how I love this woman You gave me. "You, my dear wife, as I've always said, are my best cheerleader. I don't know what I'd do without you. I love you so much, Lori Anna." He kissed her on the lips.

"I love you, too, Chris. You are my cheerleader, too – and my best friend. You complete me. In my opinion, I'd say we're a match made in Heaven."

"I second your opinion, Lori Anna." He kissed her again.

*****

The next morning, Chris and Lori Anna took their early morning run on the treadmills. About five minutes into their run, Lori Anna stopped, took a swig of her water, and hung her head over the treadmill control panel, leaning on both arms.

Chris stopped, too. "What's wrong, Lori Anna? Did you pull a muscle?"

She said nothing, but jumped off and ran to their basement bathroom with Chris at her heels. He offered a cold cloth when she finished retching. The toilet flushed as she pulled the handle, and she closed the lid. Sitting on the commode, she wiped her face with the cold cloth.

He knelt in front of her. "Do you think you ate something bad, or picked up a spring cold?"

She shook her head. "I think it's just my allergies kicking in. Grass and pollen are growing again."

"How long has this been going on?"

"Just yesterday morning, and now today. I think the bacon I had for breakfast yesterday didn't agree with me, either."

"You've only eaten a cup of plain yogurt this morning. Do you feel any better now?"

"I'd like to go lie down until it's time to get the kids up."

"You lie down, and I'll get the kids up, dressed, and fed."

"Chris, I don't want to put you to all the extra trouble. I know you want to work on the Nativity this morning."

"I can work on it when the kids are off to school. Go get some rest, honey."

"Okay, I'm not going to argue."

At 8:00 the children stepped off the last of the front steps, and Chris called out to Olivia, "Olivia, don't forget to hold Abigail's and Michael's hands on the way to school."

Olivia turned back to him. "I won't, Daddy."

Chris checked on Lori Anna, who still slept. He felt her forehead, but she didn't appear to have a temperature. *Please, Lord, she's in remission. She beat it, and she's a survivor. Please don't let the leukemia return. It was the worst time in our lives. We have three children who need her. I need her.*

He recovered Lori Anna with the quilt, headed to the kitchen, washed the dishes, wiped down the range top and counters, and walked out back to the workshop to draw the plans for the Nativity scene.

When he finished drawing the Nativity design, he thought he should check on Lori Anna. He walked in the kitchen's back door and she sat at the kitchen table drinking tea and nibbling on crackers.

"No better?" he asked.

"I'm sure it's nothing, Chris." Her voice trembled.

He pulled up a chair and with his right hand he took her hand in his. "I'm worried about you. We've been through this before." He ran the fingers of his left hand through his hair.

Lori Anna smiled. "Do you know you finger your hair whenever you're nervous?"

He chuckled. "My dad did the same thing. I guess I picked up the silly habit from him." Then he sobered. "All jesting aside, Lori Anna, I'm *very* worried. We were told eleven years ago the leukemia could return. You're in remission. There are no guarantees. I don't want to take any chances."

He released her hand and stood. "I'm calling Dr. Gentry's office. I want you to go in today for a check-up and blood work."

She frowned. "We may be jumping the gun, Chris. It's only been a couple of days. Why not see how I feel tomorrow?"

He stared down at her. He knew he needed to be firm or she wouldn't go. "Two days is long enough. Please go take your shower, if you're able, while I call Dr. Gentry's office. I won't take no for an answer. You're too important to me and our children."

He helped her to her feet. "Do you feel steady?"

"Yes. I can walk upstairs."

"You may want to take a bath instead of a shower. I don't want you falling in the shower."

"Okay, worry-wart, but good advice, Chris."

He kissed her cheek as she held the handrail, then she slowly walked upstairs.

Chris completed the phone call with the doctor's office and made the appointment. Lori Anna was sitting at her vanity table in her bathrobe brushing her hair when he walked in. "You doing okay, sweetheart?"

"I just got dizzy again, and I thought I'd sit a minute before I dressed."

Chris took her hairbrush and brushed the long black tresses.

"You don't have to brush my hair, but I won't stop you. It feels good, and I'm tired."

"I know you're tired, but I'm here to help. We're a team ... right?" He smiled at her in her vanity mirror. She looked haggard to him.

She returned the smile and reached up to grasp his arm. "I love you, Chris."

He bent down to kiss her. "I love you more than life, Lori Anna." He pulled her to her feet, held her in his arms, and kissed her again. "Let's get you dressed. Dr. Gentry wants you in his office in thirty minutes."

As soon as they arrived at the doctor's office, Nurse Parks took them straight to the back with no wait. "Dr. Gentry has ordered a urine sample and blood withdrawn."

She handed the urine sample cup to Lori Anna and sent her to the restroom.

"When you're finished, leave the cup on this counter top, and then head to room number eight, where I'll draw your blood." She pointed in the direction. "You can wait for your wife in room number eight, Mr. Wright." The efficient Nurse Parks smiled to soften her direct orders.

Before entering the examining room, Chris waited and watched Lori Anna head into the restroom. He walked into the designated room, closed the door, and sat on one of the chairs provided. The room was small with only two side-by-side chairs, a supply cabinet, and a table large enough to rest an arm for blood withdrawal. The wall held a framed certificate of Dr. Gentry's medical license. It was crooked. Chris rested his elbows on his knees, his hands dangling between his legs, and bowed his head.

Dear Lord, we've been through this before. I asked You to heal Lori Anna over ten years ago, and I pray once again her leukemia has not returned. He sighed, sniffed, and wiped a tear. *I love her, Lord, and our children love and need her. Whatever is Your decision, please give our children strength ... and me.*

He looked up when the door opened. Lori Anna entered, closed the door, and sat beside Chris in the second chair beside the table. Chris noted the anxious expression on her face, smiled at her, and squeezed her hand.

Nurse Parks returned, tied off Lori Anna's arm, withdrew several vials of blood, and marked information on each vial.

Chris asked, "How soon will Dr. Gentry know the blood results?"

"Less than thirty minutes. The lab is across the street, and Dr. Gentry has already requested the lab to put a rush on it."

She finished drawing the blood, and another nurse grabbed the samples and headed out the back door, directly across from their room's open doorway. "In the meantime, I'll get you situated in room number four. Just follow me."

Chris and Lori Anna heard undecipherable whispering in the hallway, and then Nurse Parks joined them in room four. "Dr. Gentry has requested you get undressed, and here's a gown to put on and a sheet to cover yourself. He'll do a thorough examination."

Chris was a bit puzzled, and Lori Anna frowned, but she complied with the orders.

Dr. Gentry appeared. "Hello, Lori Anna. Chris tells me you haven't been feeling well. You want to tell me about it?"

She explained the last two days. "I actually

wanted to wait one more day, but my fussbudget hubby here insisted I come in. I'm sure it's just my allergies."

Dr. Gentry gently scolded her. "Chris is right to worry about you. With your leukemia history, it's best to take precautions. As Nurse Parks told you, while we wait on the blood and urine results, I'm going to do a thorough examination. I'll need to do a vaginal exam first, so feet in the stirrups, young lady. Chris can hold your hand."

Lori Anna obeyed, giving Chris a rather downcast look.

"Lay back and try to relax," Dr. Gentry added while washing his hands and arms.

Lori Anna lay flat on the table, her feet in the stirrups, but she could not relax. She looked at Chris again, and he squeezed her hand.

"This exam will also check for any abnormalities of the uterus, ovaries, or fallopian tubes. I'll check your abdomen too." He held up his hands, Nurse Parks dried them, and placed the rubber gloves onto them.

Both of Lori Anna's fists clinched, and she bit her lips.

"Have you had any pain or soreness?"

"No, Dr. Gentry."

The internal exam only lasted a few minutes, but Chris, worried about Lori Anna, felt like an hour must have gone by. Dr. Gentry pulled the sheet back down, completely covering Lori Anna, removed the gloves with a snap, and threw them into the disposable can. He grabbed his stethoscope.

"Please sit up, so I can check your heart and lungs." He placed the stethoscope on her heart and then on her back while she took deep breaths. Next he placed the stethoscope in several places on her abdomen.

"Okay, Lori Anna, get dressed, and the two of you can meet me in my private office in fifteen minutes. The lab results should be ready by then."

Nurse Parks escorted them into the doctor's office, where Dr. Gentry was seated in front of his computer monitor. He turned to them and gestured for them to have a seat across from him in the low-back brown leather chairs. He didn't speak for a minute but leaned back in his high-back brown leather chair. He laced his fingers together and rocked a few times.

Chris ran his fingers through his hair. "Dr. Gentry, what's wrong with Lori Anna? Has the leukemia returned?"

Dr. Gentry smiled, and Chris relaxed. "Lori Anna is fine, and she will be completely cured of this ailment ... in about seven months."

Chris pondered this information, and a smile

spread across his face. He looked at Lori Anna and back at Dr. Gentry. "She's ... pregnant?" he stammered, and his mouth gaped open.

Dr. Gentry smiled at them. "Yes, she is. Lori Anna, haven't you missed a couple of monthly cycles?"

"Yes, but I just thought it was stress over Mom and Dad Wright dying, the Christmas Hotel fire, the rebuilding, writing the manuscript, and of course raising three children. Dr. Gentry, I thought I couldn't conceive because of the leukemia – I'd probably be infertile. Didn't you say my chances would be less than two percent? How is this possible?"

He shook his head and smiled again. "I didn't say *im*possible, but likely *not* possible. However, the longer you're in remission, the better the chances. You've been in remission for over ten years. I won't sugar-coat this. You'll be treated as a high-risk pregnancy, but I will keep a close watch on you and your diet and exercise."

He paused again, sat back in his chair, and clasped his hands together. "I have more news." He paused for several seconds, worrying the two of them. "I heard two fetal heartbeats." He stopped, allowing this new information to sink in.

Chris and Lori Anna stared at each other. Together they said, "*Two*?"

"Yes, two," Dr. Gentry acknowledged with a wide grin. "This should be common in your family, Chris. Your mother had twins and so did Carrie Emeline."

"Twins run on my side of the family, too," added Lori Anna as she wiped a few tears and bit her lower lip. "My biological father and his wife had twins, and their second oldest daughter, too."

"It sounds as though you two will have plenty of advice coming from both sides." He stood. "Congratulations. This couldn't happen to a more deserving couple." He held his hand out to each of them.

Chris and Lori Anna stood and returned the handshake. "Thank you, Dr. Gentry," mumbled Chris. "I prepared myself for the worst news, and you gave me the best possible news!"

"You're both quite welcome. It's my pleasure. I enjoy delivering pleasant news. Nurse Parks will see you out and schedule the next appointment."

On their way to the car they were both still in awe. "Twins," they stopped and said in unison.

Chris chuckled. "We thought our pregnancy days ended with Olivia. A baby ... I mean two babies."

She smiled and touched Chris's cheek. "You're the one who keeps reminding me, 'With God All Things are Possible,' which I know happens to be one of your favorite quotes in Scripture."

He kissed her. "It surely is, honey, it surely is. Always keep reminding me. Twins. I'm completely stunned and somewhat in shock. I can't wait to tell our family."

Chapter Twenty-Nine

Blessings and Thanksgiving

"The LORD bless thee, and keep thee: The LORD make his face shine upon thee, and be gracious unto thee: The LORD lift up his countenance upon thee, and give thee peace."
Numbers 6:24-26

Thursday
November 25, 1999
Thanksgiving Day
Six months later, Chris remained in wonder over the revelation of twins coming next month. Today was a day to give thanks for all the Lord had done this past year. Christmas Hotel was now structurally complete. Barbara Beasley Smith had accomplished the purchases for all the antique furnishings of room number seven. Jill Broderson had concluded the painting along with tasteful, Christmas themed decorative wallpapering in fifty-nine of the rooms. When the furniture delivery arrived on Monday, December sixth, the new

Christmas Hotel would be complete; a good feeling for Chris, Lori Anna, and the rebuilding committee.

Chris scheduled the ribbon-cutting ceremony on Monday, December thirteenth, and all the reunion guests were invited for a free three-day stay. Some had already booked to stay on through Christmas or New Year's Day. All RSVP'd they appreciated the free offer, but they were paying this time, and they couldn't wait to see Christmas Hotel and the Wright family again.

On the Wednesday before Thanksgiving, a twenty-foot live Douglas fir tree arrived for the Christmas Hotel lobby. One of their reunion guests, Daniel Clement, owned a Christmas tree farm in upstate New York. He offered to donate a live tree at the beginning of every month indefinitely to Christmas Hotel. At first Chris wasn't sure. In the past, Christmas Hotel had used an artificial but life-like twenty-foot tree.

However, in the old safe, where he received the blueprints for Christmas Hotel, he also found paperwork for the purchase of a live twenty-foot tree. Therefore, the new Christmas Hotel would receive the same.

Chris met Daniel Clement and the men who would be setting up the new tree. He shook Mr. Clement's hand. "Thank you so much for this wonderful gift, Mr. Clement. My family and I never expected this fresh Douglas fir delivered and set up each month, *and* the pick-up of the old tree."

"Please call me, Daniel. My wife Ruth and I are happy to do this, Chris. It also provides an excuse for my wife and me to visit Christmas Hotel each month. I'd say a free gratis weekend stay is more than a sufficient trade-off. Ruth has been after me for years to slow down."

All the Wright siblings, their spouses, children, and grandchildren had assembled at the Wright family home for the Thanksgiving holiday.

The family gathered around four tables for their Thanksgiving dinner. New high chairs had been purchased for the arrival of Chris and Lori Anna's twins, so today nine-month-old first cousins Faith and Joy would use them. Heather, one of Carrie Emeline and Marcus's daughters, announced she and her husband were expecting a baby girl and arriving in five months. They planned to name her Hope, for the renewed hope of her family's future. These were exciting times for the Wright family.

The women spread the food out buffet style on three tables. The family stood in a circle around the tables and held hands in preparation for Chris to ask the blessing.

"Dear Heavenly Father, we thank You that all

the members of the Wright family are able to meet this Thanksgiving. It's been a long year since we congregated for the last Thanksgiving, and with so many ups-and-downs since. We can't help from missing our parents; however, we know they are having their own special Thanksgiving reunion with their friends and loved ones with You in Heaven, which we'll all experience someday."

Chris paused, cleared his throat and took a couple of breaths. "Without the union of our parents, Lydia Grace and I, and our children would not be here today, and Lily, Ken and Carrie Emeline and their children and grandchildren might not be the same fine persons they grew to be. Our parents were our rock for so many years. Help us continue to be faithful in our gathering together for many years to come. Keep our family strong, Lord. We thank You for the healthy birth of two babies this year: Faith and Joy, the coming of the twins in December, and the birth of at least one more baby in the new millennium. We thank You for all this wonderful food for the nourishment of our bodies and for the many hands who prepared it. In the name of Your Son Jesus Christ we pray ... Amen."

The others echoed their amens.

"Let's eat," shouted Ken, and several others responded with hollers and whistles.

*****

With the meal completed, Chris asked the family to bundle up and follow him to the woodworking shed. He entered first and flipped on the lights. There in the center of the shed sat the life-size model of the newly built Nativity scene. Everything had been recreated as before: the stable, the life size figures of Mary, Joseph, baby Jesus in the manger, the wise men, shepherds, barn animals, and camels. The family stood in awe.

Finally, Ken spoke almost in a whisper, "You did all this by yourself, little brother?"

"I did all the wood carving, but Lori Anna helped me with some of the painting ... when she wasn't finishing Mom's manuscript."

Lori Anna smiled. "Chris is being quite humble. You have no idea how many hours he spent building this Nativity scene. I did very little painting – just the expressions on the faces. Chris did ninety-nine percent. I must say this was a huge labor of love." She hugged her husband. "Chris, your dad would be so proud of you." She stood on tiptoes, kissed his cheek, and wiped the tear drop under one of his eyes.

"Thank you, Lori Anna."

Ken stepped forward and shook his brother's hand. "Well done, Chris. Lori Anna's right. Dad would be so proud of you. You certainly learned a lot about woodworking from him. This Nativity display is incredible."

Lily, Carrie Emeline, and Lydia Grace all hugged Chris, and wiped some of their own tears. All the family members congratulated him.

Chris thanked them all. "In the morning, I'll need help from all of you to wrap everything and transport the Nativity figures to Christmas Hotel."

"We can use my farm truck," offered Jacob.

"I brought my truck, too," added Ken. "Using your truck too, Chris, we should be able to get it all in one trip."

"In the meantime," said Lori Anna, "let's all head back into the house. We've got plenty of pies to savor: pumpkin, mincemeat, apple, cherry, and three cheesecakes. I'll put on some coffee, and I suspect there are a bunch of children who'd like ... *hot chocolate!*"

"Yes," yelled the children in unison. Chris and Lori Anna were the last to leave the workshop. Before turning out the light, they turned around for another look at the Nativity. Chris hugged his very pregnant wife to him and kissed her passionately. "I love you so much, Lori Anna. Thank you for what you said. A man likes being appreciated by his wife."

"I meant every word, Chris. Both of your parents would be so proud of what you've accomplished this past year – and not just this

Nativity. Christmas Hotel will live into the next millennium because of you."

Chris flipped off the lights, closed the door, and walked back to the house with his arm around Lori Anna.

Chapter Thirty

Ribbon-Cutting and New Beginnings

*"It is a good thing to give thanks unto the LORD,
and to sing praises unto thy name, O Most
High: To shew forth thy lovingkindness in the
morning, and thy faithfulness every night,"*
Psalms 92: 1-2

Monday

December 13, 1999

Chris opened the double brass doors into Christmas Hotel. Reminiscent of a year earlier, a light snow fell onto the two inches already on the ground. Couples and families walked toward the hotel through the Christmas decorated square or on the sidewalks. Some pushed baby carriages or strollers, some used canes or walkers. Several pushed family in wheelchairs on the freshly shoveled and salted sidewalks.

Chris smiled. *I love it.* He turned to Lori Anna, his siblings, and their spouses seated on stools at the front desk, and the Christmas Hotel Rebuilding Committee seated in the lobby. "They're coming.

Everyone ready?" He heard a resounding "yes" from all. "Then let's go!"

At 9 o'clock in the morning, all forty-nine members of the Wright family, and the Christmas Hotel Rebuilding Committee stood outside in front of Christmas Hotel. A red ribbon wrapped around a pole on East Cedar Street, across the front of Christmas Hotel, and around a pole on North Main Street. The crowd filled the square over a hundred feet deep on the other side of North Main Street.

A microphone was set up on the street corner for Chris's welcoming speech. All businesses around the square halted as the proprietors stood outside their doors. The press and television station crews arrived to record one of the biggest events in the little town of Franklin, Kentucky's history.

The new Christmas Hotel was as identical to the original as possible It stood five stories tall, built in the Italianate style architecture. A massive stone block near the top of the fifth story bore the deep carving CHRISTMAS HOTEL. Another carving, also in stone bore the words of the hotel's mission: WHERE JESUS' BIRTH IS A DAILY CELEBRATION. These two blocks were salvaged from the old structure with every single letter of the wording intact; just a few cracks needed to be patched.

The restored massive double brass and glass doors, two stories high, were recessed about twenty inches into the building. Two angels, carved into the façade adjacent to each brass-trimmed door were also salvaged from the original structure. Below the right-hand angel, the brass plaque inscribed with the date 1850 had been replaced, and the gas coach lights shining in welcome above both angels were new.

The clock in the square rooftop cupola facing the park had to be replaced. Chris, the Wright family, and the Christmas Hotel Rebuilding Committee watched the smiling, happy faces of the reunion guests and commented their pleasure down the receiving line from one to the other.

Tears were shed and everyone clapped or whistled when Chris stepped up to the microphone. The audience quieted.

"Welcome, reunion guests, people of Franklin, and several surrounding counties. My name is Chris Wright, and this lovely lady by my side is my wife Lori Anna Wright. We are the owners of Christmas Hotel. Yes, we are *very* pregnant ... just in case you hadn't noticed."

Laughter sounded around the square.

"We thank all of you for coming on this snowy morning. All these people behind the red ribbon played a part in rebuilding the new Christmas Hotel. For those of you who do not know my siblings and their spouses, I'll introduce them, and ask them to step forward and wave as I call their names: Lily and John – Ken and Loretta – Carrie Emeline and Marcus – and Lydia Grace and Jacob.

"Others behind the ribbon are the Christmas Hotel Rebuilding Committee. I'll ask them to step forward, too, and wave as I call their names: Franklin Mayor Jim Arnold – Franklin City Manager Tom Gordon – County Attorney for Simpson County Sid Broderson and his wife Jill Broderson who decorated fifty-nine of the guest rooms – Dr. Beasley and his five daughters: Betty – Barbara – Susan – Beth Ann – Bonnie – and last but certainly not least, low and behold, Dr. Beasley finally received a son and named him John. Would you all please step forward?"

More applause and a few chuckles from the crowd broke out.

"We also have three of the best fundraisers in three counties: Mary Roberts ... Mabel Anderson ... and Harriet Tuttle. Please join my family and me in giving all these people on the Christmas Hotel Rebuilding Committee a hand."

A thunderous applause filled the air along with several more loud shouts and whistles.

"The remainder of the people standing here are Wright family children and grandchildren who also wanted to welcome you.

"When you walk around the outside of the new

Christmas Hotel you'll be walking on the pavers many of you donated in your name or in memory of someone. Please check them out during your reunion stay. As you enter the lobby, we will hand you a brochure describing the rebuilding process along with plenty of pictures of the progression. We included what's new about the building and what we salvaged from the original hotel. We managed to recover the blueprints from the original hotel, so the footprint is as identical as possible, adjusted where necessary to meet the current building regulations. You'll be assigned the room you were in last year of the fifty-nine rooms we reserve. The Wright family room, number seven, remains as the one room never let to guests, and you'll notice two new plaques on the wall outside the room. The room is dedicated in memory of the daughter of Christmas Hotel's second owners, Carrie Emeline Bazell, and also to our parents Christopher and Jerilyn Wright.

"Regarding the fundraising, as most of you know through the monthly updated newsletters, the insurance company did not provide all the monies needed to restore Christmas Hotel in all its glory. We thank those who donated to the cause, and your name is emblazoned on the granite donor wall inside the lobby. Or you may have chosen to purchase one of these sidewalk pavers ... or both.

For those who would still like to donate, Mary, Mabel, and Harriet have never been known to turn away money!"

Chris waited while another round of laughter and applause rippled through the crowd.

"My wife, Lori Anna, finished the manuscript my mother had been writing several years ago, and last May, she received a $100,000 advance from Mom's previous publishing company."

The crowd murmured, applauded, and smiled.

"Lori Anna has donated the money along with future royalties of the novel for additional upkeep of the new Christmas Hotel."

Another round of applause commenced.

"*There's more.* You'll all go home with a free, signed and personalized advance copy."

A rousing applause broke out.

"After you are checked in, the noon meal will be held in the dining room, and a tour from top to bottom of the new Christmas Hotel will commence at 1:30 following your meal. So let's hold hands and pray.

"Dear Heavenly Father, all of us standing here in Your presence thank You Christmas Hotel has been completed, and all these wonderful friends are here today to celebrate with the Wright family the grand reopening of Christmas Hotel. The original Christmas Hotel stood for nearly one hundred and fifty years, and we ask Your blessing upon the new hotel and to see it safely into and throughout many decades of the new millennium. May those who come here find their Christmas miracle, and realize the miracle is in Your Son Jesus Christ. We pray this in the name of Jesus Christ ... Amen."

The crowd echoed their Amens.

"Now, without further ado, let's cut this ribbon!" Lori Anna handed Chris the scissors and together they cut the ribbon. Another round of applause, whistles, and shouts were heard from the crowd, along with flashes from the cameras of the reporters and guests.

For the next couple of hours, Chris, his four assistants, and Lori Anna checked in the guests. The guests paused as they walked into the lobby and viewed the angel atop the tree. Like the original angel. it looked down on those in the lobby and at any angle, seeming to watch and follow everyone.

Lily informed the guests, "My sister Lydia Grace and I were wandering in some antiques stores in Nashville and we came upon this angel. She looks like the original angel with the same sweet smile. We even wondered if they had been made at the same time by the same company. There's nothing written on her to provide information. It's as though she was meant to adorn this tree. Anyway, we have her to watch over our guests in the new Christmas Hotel lobby, just like the original."

However, the real show stopper was when the guests saw the new life-size Nativity. "Beautiful, marvelous," the people commented. "It looks just like the original. Who created this?" the question from most of the guests.

Ken addressed each group. "My brother Chris learned woodworking from our dad. He took it upon himself to create this Nativity over the course of this past year. I must say, it's very close to the original."

The guests nodded in agreement. They'd look next to the fireplace. Carrie Emeline gestured to the fireplace and stockings. "Regarding this beautiful fireplace, all the stones were salvaged from the original, but we did have to construct a new wooden mantel. Chris built the new mantel, also.

"My two sisters, my two sisters-in-law, and I sewed, crocheted, or knitted the forty-nine stockings with names embroidered on each for the current Wright family." She chuckled. "With three more babies on the way, we're going to need to get busy again making more stockings. My daughter Heather is expecting, and she and her husband have already named their upcoming baby girl Hope. As you heard, Chris and Lori Anna are due any day with twins, but we don't know the sex. They want to be surprised."

Following the noon meal, all the siblings and their spouses conducted the tour of the new hotel, beginning in the ballroom on the fifth floor and working their way down to the second floor of the hotel.

Chris pointed to the new wall pictures and shadowboxes. "View the twelve extra-large framed pictures on these walls. In these frames, you'll see all the notes of love shared on the two sidewalks around Christmas Hotel after it burned. My siblings and I wanted to preserve these notes, and there was no better way than to frame them to share with all the visitors to the new Christmas Hotel. You'll also see the framed pictures of our new Christmas Hotel in various stages while under construction."

Lily pointed to the two plaques outside room number seven and read each one aloud. "In memory of Carrie Emeline Bazell: March 20, 1884, and the second plaque for our parents: Christopher and Jerilyn Wright: December 28, 1998. The dates on each plaque were the dates they died in this room.

"I know most of you have heard the story of when our mother first arrived at Christmas Hotel back in 1941. There was no room available in the inn, one could say, except room number seven. The

Bazells never reserved room seven because it's where their beloved daughter passed away from pneumonia. However, the Bazells were a couple with big hearts. They offered this special room to our mother, and it remained only for our family's use when our parents married. If the Bazells had not given this room to my mother back in 1941, she and my dad may never have met. We'll never know what would have happened," she mused.

She cocked her head. "As you know, Mom had suffered from Alzheimer's for several years, but she became amazingly aware the last day our parents' were alive. My siblings and I don't know for sure, but maybe they wanted to spend that fateful night together where their relationship began, while Mother experienced a day of lucidity."

Chris held up an old-fashioned key. "If you'll remember, this room remained unchanged from when the hotel was built 150 years ago. When Christmas Hotel was restored, we decided to keep this room in circa 1850 appearance. Barbara Beasley Smith led the search with the help of her four sisters and one brother. They found the furnishings nationwide - even down to the antique lock and key."

With the old-fashioned key in his hand, Chris turned the old lock and stepped into the room. "The only two furnishings not from the 19th century are the two kerosene lamps. They are electric and just look old. We agreed the kerosene lamps were too dangerous to add back into this room. We certainly didn't want to chance another fire. Please enter in groups of twenty if you'd like to see the newly restored room."

After the final group had toured the room, Chris locked the door and the guests headed down the stairs. Lori Anna grabbed Chris's hand, grimaced, and held her stomach. "Chris, I think I'm in labor. I've been having contractions for the last hour, but they're getting much stronger."

"Dr. Gentry is probably still here. I'll get him."

Lori Anna doubled over in another contraction and cried out. Lily, Carrie Emeline, and Lydia Grace had not gone down the steps yet and they turned when they heard Lori Anna.

"Hurry, Chris. I think the babies are coming," Lori Anna said in a much louder voice.

Then her water broke.

Quick-thinking Lily took charge. "Chris, get her back in room number seven. Carrie Emeline, go find Dr. Gentry. Lydia Grace, help me spread towels on the bed."

Chris opened the door and picked up his wife. Lydia Grace grabbed the towels from the bathroom, Lily threw back the bed covers and the two sisters spread layers of towels over the sheets. Chris placed

Lori Anna on the bed.

Carrie Emeline returned. "Dr. Gentry left thirty minutes ago with Dr. Evans for a meeting in Nashville at Vanderbilt Hospital. Mr. Hanover is calling Dr. Gentry's office to page him."

Lori Anna cried out again. Her breathing was labored, and her face contorted in pain. She grabbed Chris's arm and struggled with her words while she dug her nails into him, "The babies ... won't wait very long, Chris."

Lily turned to Carrie Emeline. "Go to the hotel speaker and ask if there's a doctor or a paramedic in the house. Surely one of these many guests can deliver the babies."

Lily coached Lori Anna's breathing while Chris timed the contractions, held his wife's hand, and offered encouragement. They heard Carrie Emeline's announcement for a doctor or paramedic over the speaker. Three minutes later, the ding of the elevator bell sounded and the elevator doors opened and closed. Dr. Beasley appeared in the doorway with Carrie Emeline. Lori Anna was in another contraction, and screamed.

"Sorry I took so long, but at almost ninety-two I no longer do stairs. Barbara is on her way to my house and will be back shortly with my medical bag. How far apart are the contractions?"

Chris checked his watch. "About four minutes,

Dr. Beasley. She's only experienced the contractions for about an hour. Can labor really come on so quickly, sir?"

"Every delivery is different, Chris. But to answer your question, yes. With all the babies this Wright family keeps having, you need another midwife, since Jerilyn's no longer with us." He looked around the room. "Lily, I choose you. Let's get washed up. You're going to deliver these babies while I instruct."

Lily's eyes grew big and rounded and her mouth gaped open, but she obeyed when he took her hand and dragged her toward the bathroom.

Dr. Beasley turned back to Carrie Emeline and Lydia Grace and barked orders. "I need boiling water, plenty of towels, four clamps, tongs, a pair of scissors, and a type of tub to bathe the babies. Bring some ice chips for Lori Anna. *Stat!*"

The women hurried out the door and returned within seconds of each other with the items. Carrie Emeline entered first. "The cooks had been boiling water for an evening soup, and one of them set a huge pot of water outside of our door with two pot holders. I've brought two roasting pans, ice chips, and here comes Lydia Grace with towels, clamps, tongs, and kitchen scissors."

The sisters set everything on the desk and vanity; and per Dr. Beasley, Chris grabbed the two pot holders and dumped some of the boiling water into the two roasting pans to begin cooling.

Obeying the doctor's continued instructions, using the tongs, Carrie Emeline doused the scissors and clamps in the hot water and set them on another clean towel. Lydia Grace and Chris pulled Lori Anna's dress over her head and removed it from her body. They draped a sheet over her to ready Lori Anna for Lily and the doctor.

"Move her down to the bottom of the bed, and prop her head with pillows," instructed Dr. Beasley. "Lydia Grace, climb upon the bed, kneel behind Lori Anna, place the pillows between the two of you. She'll need your help when it's time to push."

Chris pulled up a chair for the efficient old doctor. Lily followed Dr. Beasley's explicit instructions.

He showed Lily how to use finger widths to determine centimeters. Lydia Grace continued the breathing exercises with her sister-in-law, and Lori Anna screamed with each contraction, now three minutes apart.

"I don't remember ... it being so bad ... with Olivia," she managed to say.

"You were in a hospital room with a saddle block," Chris reminded his wife soothingly and patted her hand. Lori Anna grabbed his arm and dug her nails into him with each contraction.

Dr. Beasley gauged the labor. "Okay, she's now at ten centimeters, and Lily, notice how soft and thin her cervix is?"

"Yes," answered his pupil.

All the while Lydia Grace coached Lori Anna's breathing, and Chris encouraged. Carrie Emeline rubbed Lori Anna's eager lips with ice chips, and washed her face with cold water.

"I feel a burning ... down there and I feel like ... I need to push," Lori Anna struggled to say between breaths.

"It's time to push, Lori Anna," ordered Dr. Beasley. "The babies are ready to be born."

Carrie Emeline elevated Lori Anna's upper body using the pillows and three pushes later a baby boy was born. He immediately began crying.

"Lily," Dr. Beasley said quickly, "place the baby across Lori Anna's stomach so mother and baby can begin bonding skin-to-skin, and someone get a towel and cover him."

Lori Anna cried along with her little boy, stroked his body when Lily draped him across her bare stomach, and Carrie Emeline covered his body with the towel.

"Okay, Lori Anna, I need another push," coached Dr. Beasley.

A baby girl slid into Lily's hands. She wasn't breathing.

"Okay, hold her upside down and give her two firm whacks on the bottom."

The baby sputtered, coughed, and began breathing, hesitantly at first, then normally. Lily placed her beside her brother, draped across her mother's belly, and Carrie Emeline quickly covered the baby girl with another towel.

After several minutes, Dr. Beasley said it was time to clamp and cut the cords. "Let's swab their mouths while the babies lie on Lori Anna's skin." He showed Lily how. "In the future, you'll need to keep necessary items in a bag in your car. You'll never know when you're asked to deliver a baby or assist. Jerilyn kept all the birthing items in a leather bag, so you'll probably come across them somewhere in her belongings."

Chris reminded the doctor about saving the umbilical cords because of Lori Anna's leukemia.

"Right," he agreed. "I need someone to go to the kitchen and get two large freezer bags. Label one bag 'Wright baby boy' and the other bag 'Wright baby girl,' and make sure they go into the hotel freezer and soon. Date each bag."

Carrie Emeline headed down to do as instructed.

Barbara opened the door and handed Chris her dad's old dilapidated bag and closed the door. The doctor took the bag from Chris, removed the bulb syringe, and instructed Lily how to use it on each baby's nose and mouth. He then pulled out his stethoscope, listened to their heart and lungs, and showed Lily how to listen.

Lily smiled. "The hearts and lungs sound just as you described."

Dr. Beasley sat back and relaxed for the first time. "I'd say we have two healthy babies here." He acknowledged Chris for the first time. "Congratulations, Dad." He then smiled at Lori Anna. "Good work, Mom."

"Thank you, Dr. Beasley," she murmured while stroking her babies.

When Dr. Beasley said it was time, Lydia Grace picked up each baby and washed them one at a time, in the now tepid water in the roasting pans. Carrie Emeline returned and Lily placed the cords in the proper bags, handed the bags to Lydia Grace, and she labeled them and carried them down to the hotel's freezer.

Dr. Beasley continued to instruct with his orders. "Carrie Emeline, get on the speaker again and tell these reunion guests you need two baby gowns, some newborn diapers, baby blankets, socks, mittens, and two knit hats. We need to keep them warm." The doctor then turned back to Lily to show her what to do in tending to Lori Anna.

Chris pulled up another chair by his wife's head

and washed her face with a damp cloth and her belly where the babies had lain. At the knock on the door, Mr. Hanover handed Chris the requested baby items, and looked at Chris, wide eyed and eye brows raised in question.

Chris beamed in response. "Yes, Mr. Hanover, you can announce we have two healthy babies: a boy and a girl."

"Congratulations, Chris ... oh ... and you too, Lori Anna." Mr. Hanover smiled and closed the door behind him.

Within minutes the births were announced on the hotel's speakers, and a thunderous round of applause echoed around the walls of Christmas Hotel.

The now clean and dressed babies nursed at each of Lori Anna's breasts. Tears rolled down Lori Anna's face. "Thank you all so much."

Dr. Beasley smiled and patted her hand. "You're welcome, Lori Anna. I suggest you stay in this room with Chris for the night. Lily, Carrie Emeline, and Lydia Grace can bring you and Chris any items you'll need, such as more diapers." He winked at Lori Anna. "You won't have to worry about formula, since you're nursing the babies."

Chris shook Dr. Beasley's hand and pulled him into a hug. "Dr. Beasley, you've been here for this family so many times and over many decades. I

can't tell you how much I thank you, once again."
"You're very welcome, Chris." He turned to Lily.
"Lily did the delivery, though, and a great job she
did. You'll make a wonderful midwife for this
family and for others in your area who may need
you, just like Jerilyn."

"Thank you, Dr. Beasley."

"I think I'll drag my old bones home now. My
five daughters and son await me. They're cooking at
my place for dinner, along with their spouses and
my grandchildren. Oh, before we all forget,
someone should call Dr. Gentry's office, cancel the
page, and schedule an appointment for Lori Anna
and the babies for tomorrow."

Lily spoke next. "We're going to leave you two
now with our nephew and niece. They're beautiful."

"One more request," said Chris. "I have a
camera here in my office. Will all of you stay a
moment while pictures are made? You, too, Dr.
Beasley. Mr. Hanover can photograph pictures of
all of us."

The family took turns taking pictures with Lori
Anna and the babies: one with Chris seated on the
bed and his arm around his wife; one with Dr.
Beasley and Lily, both standing beside the bed and
bending over Lori Anna; one with Lily, Carrie
Emeline, and Lydia Grace all seated on the bed
around Lori Anna and the babies. Mr. Hanover

took a picture of all the family involved in the birth, and Dr. Beasley in one group picture bending over Lori Anna around the bed.

Lydia Grace offered to take Olivia, Abigail, and Michael home with her. All three children had remained in the hotel's office with Mr. Hanover during the deliveries. "I'll tell them about the babies, and I'll bring them here in the morning."

"Thanks, sis. You're wonderful. Lori Anna and I may have our hands full tonight. Oh, and if you don't mind, before you go, please leave two dresser drawers on the floor beside our bed and line them with blankets. The drawers will become their makeshift cribs for tonight."

When they were alone, Lori Anna and Chris continued to stroke their bundled sleeping babies. "I wanted to nurse Olivia, but I couldn't, because of the leukemia." She caressed each baby, and Chris bent down to kiss his wife. She frowned and stared when she saw the marks on his arm and hand. "Did I leave those marks?"

Chris looked to see what her eyes were viewing. He chuckled. "I suppose I needed to have a little skin in the game, too. After all, you did all the work. It's okay, Lori Anna. Don't be alarmed. I know, sweetheart, you wanted to nurse Olivia, but now you have a second chance." He touched his son and daughter. "They're beautiful, aren't they?"

"They certainly are, Chris. We have undoubtedly been blessed ... again. We never dreamed of having more biological children. How very special to have these babies born in the Wright family room number seven on ribbon-cutting day, *and* delivered by Lily with the aid of Dr. Beasley, *and* assisted by Carrie Emeline and Lydia Grace. The miracles at Christmas Hotel continue."

"They certainly do. Uh, we have a decision to make. We haven't discussed names, since we didn't ask their sex in advance. What are your thoughts?"

"Well, before Olivia was born – and wow, sometimes it's hard to believe it was eleven years ago – you said you didn't think you wanted a third Christopher. 'Confusion with three Christophers in the family,' you said, and I agreed. However, we didn't have to worry then, because we had a girl. Now I really would like our son named Christopher Joseph Wright. He'll be Junior, since you're now senior."

Chris nodded and smiled. "I'm fine with it now. We'll call him Christopher, as his grandpa was always called." He paused. "What about our daughter?"

Lori Anna smiled back at him and looked around. "This room ... there can be no other name but Jerilyn Marlene Wright."

"Thank you, Lori Anna. I completely agree. I

was hoping you'd suggest it." He kissed her, and they burrowed in their own bed and watched their babies now sleeping in their makeshift cribs.

Chapter Thirty-One

Love of Family, Friends, Legacy, and Looking to the Future

"Brethren, I count not myself to have apprehended: but this one thing I do, forgetting those things which are behind, and reaching forth unto those things which are before, I press toward the mark for the prize of the high calling of God in Christ Jesus."
Philippians 3:13-14

Saturday
December 25, 1999
Christmas Morning
Many of the reunion guests stayed over to celebrate Christmas with the Wright family. At 6:00 Christmas morning, all fifty-one current members of the Wright family gathered in the dining room at ten tables pulled together to accommodate the growing family. The dining room was full with many of the townspeople and hotel guests.

Although Chris was the youngest of the siblings,

as the owner of Christmas Hotel, the others in respect offered Chris their father's seat at the head of the table, and Lori Anna took Jerilyn's seat at his right side. The babies slept in their infant seats at Chris and Lori Anna's feet. Their waiter, Steven poured coffee and water, leaving several pots on the tables. Chris glanced around at all his family members and friends in the dining room. "Family, friends, and love are what's important."

The others nodded in agreement.

Ken responded. "You're right, brother. It's what our parents were about, and they passed their love for family and friends down to us."

Lily nodded and smiled. "I can't think of a better legacy."

"I know we all tend to say this a great deal, but we've truly been blessed," added Carrie Emeline.

"'The Wright family will be okay,' is what Mr. Gabe told Carrie Emeline and me a year ago," said Lydia Grace. "I agree. We *will* be okay. The legacy of the Wright family and the mission of Christmas Hotel will live on!"

Chris took a sip of his coffee, smiled, and nodded. "I wish I could have met Mr. Gabe like you two did. I'm sure every encounter was special."

Lydia Grace nodded. "It was."

Carrie Emeline nodded in agreement.

"I'll attest to that," added Marcus. "He played a

big part in straightening me out back in '74." He smiled as he took Carrie Emeline's hand and kissed her fingers.

Steven returned and set some crackers and apple juice in sippy cups on ten-month-old Faith and Joy's high chairs, who fussed. Their mothers, Jenna and Rebecca thanked him for his assistance.

"What omelets can the chefs prepare for the Wright family this morning?" asked Steven.

The family turned to Chris first.

"I'll take my usual, Steven – the ham, cheese, and diced tomato omelet with a dash of hot sauce, please."

Around the table, they all placed their orders. When the food arrived, the family held hands and bowed their heads for Chris to ask the blessing.

"Dear Heavenly Father, I thank You for this second reunion, the reopening of Christmas Hotel, and the opportunity for all the members of our family to gather together on this Christmas Day in celebration of the birth of Your Son Jesus Christ. We thank You for this wonderful food You have provided for the nourishment of our bodies, and cooked by the amazing Christmas Hotel chefs."

Baby Faith interrupted the prayer with an excited scream at Joy, and baby Joy screamed back; both babies laughed and banged their sippy cups on their high chair trays.

Chris chuckled, too. "We thank You, Lord, for the four new and healthy babies this year at our table, and the newest baby arriving after the millennium ... baby Hope. God bless our growing family. In the name of Your Son Jesus we pray ... Amen."

The family added their amens.

Chris watched from his chair behind the pulpit as the people entered the Christmas Hotel chapel for the Christmas message. His brother-in-law, Jacob, sat at the highly polished new baby grand piano. Lydia Grace arranged for her harp to be moved from her home into the chapel, and Lily and Carrie Emeline stood beside them. The three sisters were singing, "O Little Town of Bethlehem," – Lily's all-time favorite hymn.

Chris smiled to himself and looked up to the ceiling. *Thank you, Lord. Some things will not change, and it's good. I love the fact Lily still leads off the family Christmas service with her favorite hymn.*

The three sisters and Jacob were just finishing up the final stanza when the last guests were seated in the chapel and the overflow into the lobby.

O holy Child of Bethlehem,
Descend to us, we pray;

Cast out our sin and enter in,
Be born in us today.
We hear the Christmas angels
The great glad tidings tell:
Oh, come to us, abide with us,
Our Lord Emmanuel!

Chris rose and took his place behind the pulpit. "Emmanuel, or God, with us. Yes, He is; yesterday, today and forever. Last night on Christmas Eve we read the Christmas story in Matthew, and today we will read the account of Christ's birth in Luke, as is the continuing tradition at Christmas Hotel. Please stand in honor of the Lord's Word and turn in your Bibles to the Gospel of Luke, chapter two verses one to fourteen."

When he finished reading the verses, Chris asked the crowd to be seated. "In Luke chapter two verses eight and nine, I repeat, 'And there were in the same country shepherds abiding in the field, keeping watch over their flock by night. And, lo, the angel of the Lord came upon them, and the glory of the Lord shone round about them: and they were sore afraid.'

"The angel was speaking to the shepherds. When the shepherds dropped to their knees, they were terribly afraid. Naturally, the shepherds were afraid, and you'd most likely be afraid, too. This was huge news, and the amazing news was delivered by angels. Have you ever been visited by angels? Two of my sisters, Carrie Emeline and Lydia Grace, and Carrie Emeline's husband, Marcus, were all talking about this at breakfast. The three of them have been visited by one particular angel on different occasions in their lives. Each time was during a traumatic period of time.

"Lydia Grace was only eight, Carrie Emeline was visited several times in the early seventies, and Marcus was visited when the Lord knocked to ask him to accept His gift of salvation. My sisters were visited again the night of the Christmas Hotel fire. I always wished I could have had the experience, but if I had, would I have been like the shepherds and cowered in fear?"

He paused a few seconds and gazed around the congregation.

"I hope not. I'd like to think I'd be in awe that the Lord sent an angel to speak to me. These angels told the shepherds not to be afraid, because they wanted to share with them the Good News. In Bethlehem, on that very day, was born the long-awaited Christ, the Savior. Whenever God arrives, things always change. Joy comes with the change. Yes, there are times, even as Christians, when we will have sadness, disappointment, pain, suffering, or anxiety. If we know the Lord Jesus as our Savior, these feelings will not last forever."

Again Chris paused as emotions swept over him; he took a deep breath and exhaled. "What about grief? How does grief fit into the equation? Last year, all of you were here when Christmas Hotel burned down just over two days after Christmas. We all grieved together when my parents perished in the fire. I thank God our guests were spared. It was a difficult time for all of us. I still miss my parents."

His voice grew hoarse. He paused a moment to clear his throat. "However, at their funeral, *and* today, I celebrate their lives. My siblings and I spoke at breakfast about the legacy our parents passed on to us. They passed on their love for family and friends. I think about the last day my parents dwelled on this earth.

"As all of you know, my mother was afflicted with Alzheimer's, but on the last day of her life she was coherent. Our family was given the gift of spending one more day with our real mother – a woman who knew all of us, and she was able to show her love for us, and us for her. What a miraculous gift from our Lord."

He paused a moment to blink back tears and sniff.

"God sent His only Son into the world to save us from our sins. We who accept His free gift will have eternal life with Him. What an astounding gift of love from our Heavenly Father. Someday, all our bodies will be lying in the grave, like my parents. However, the souls of those who know the Lord Jesus as our Lord and Savior will not remain in the grave. The Bible says in second Corinthians, chapter five verse eight, 'We are confident, I say, and willing rather to be absent from the body, and to be present with the Lord.' Yes, we will be clothed in a new body."

Chris paused again, and took two deep breaths and exhaled. He cleared his throat and continued. "What a blessing for my family to know for certain, when our parents passed from this life, they went to their new life with the Lord Jesus. They both are whole again in their temporal bodies. We don't know, but wouldn't it be wonderful if they were young again? I find it comforting, and I hope you do, too. C.S. Lewis said, and I quote, 'There are better things ahead than any we leave behind.' I agree."

He waited as a murmur of shared agreement passed around the folk gathered, with a few Amens thrown in.

"If you don't know Jesus as your Lord and Savior, this can be the day to do so. Let us celebrate His birthday and accept His gift of salvation. I was nine years old when I invited Jesus into my heart. I didn't know a great deal about sin at such a young age, but I knew when I disobeyed my parents that I was sinning. If I lied, it was a sin. If I stole anything, like a cookie, it was a sin. If there is anyone in this chapel or in the lobby hearing this message today, and you don't know the Lord Jesus, I pray you will step out now and kneel at this old-fashioned altar. My family and I will take a Bible and show you in the Bible how to be saved."

Five people prayed with Chris and his four siblings for the gift of salvation. Chris stood with them, and the congregation applauded their new brothers and sisters.

"If you didn't come forward and would like to receive His gift of salvation, you can do so from your room here at Christmas Hotel or at your home ... or anywhere. Christ will meet you where you are. Sit down in a quiet spot and pray. You must recognize you're a sinner and you're under God's judgment. Realize the Lord God sent His only Son to die in your place, paying your sin debt. Realize you must repent and ask His forgiveness for your sins. Understand being a so-called good person won't get you saved and give you the reward of eternal life. More questions? You can come and speak with me anytime. My door is always open.

"Now, if my sisters and brother-in-law will return to the piano and the harp, I'd like the congregation to sing 'Joy to the World,' because it's what I feel right now – *joy*."

"Joy to the World, the Lord has come!
Let earth receive her King;
Let every heart prepare Him room,
And Heaven and nature sing,
And Heaven and nature sing,
And Heaven, and Heaven, and nature sing.

He rules the world with truth and grace,
And makes the nations prove
The glories of His righteousness,
And wonders of His love,
And wonders of His love,
And wonders, wonders, of His love."

Chris returned to the pulpit. "Isaiah chapter fifty-two and verse fifteen says, 'For ye shall not go out with haste, nor go by flight: for the LORD will go before you; and the God of Israel will be your reward'. I want you to know the Lord will go before you and be your rear guard.

"Thank you all for coming on this Christmas morning and celebrating His birth with my family and me. I love all of you. Go with God."

Chapter Thirty-Two

The Wright Family's Reunion
at Greenlawn Cemetery

*"That which hath been is now; and that
which is to be hath already been; and God
requireth that which is past."*
Ecclesiastes 3:15

Christmas Morning after Church
December 25, 1999
Chris, Lori Anna, the Wright siblings, their spouses, children and grandchildren shook hands with guests as they left the hotel, some for the day and some to leave Christmas Hotel and return home.

Dr. Beasley and his children were first at the door. "A wonderful service, Chris. Thank you."

"You're welcome, Dr. Beasley. I'm pleased you and your children and their spouses could join us."

Sid and Jill Broderson shook his hand next. "It's wonderful coming to a Christmas Hotel service again, Chris. Jill and I have missed it."

"Yes, it is wonderful," replied Chris. "I've missed preaching the sermons."

Chris shook the hand of the last guest, and Lily then hugged her brother. "It was a lovely Christmas service, Chris. Five people got saved on Christmas. How wonderful! Also, it was another spectacular reunion."

Chris hugged Lily back. "Yes, it was. It really felt like Christmas." He turned to all his family. "We have time before the noon meal to visit the cemetery, and I'd like us to visit as a family unit; and our own family reunion. Let's bundle up and walk over together. Carrie Emeline and Marcus haven't seen the sculptured fountain they personally ordered for the grave, or the memory monument we all ordered."

The family walked through the cemetery, visiting those who had gone on to be with the Lord, pausing to pay their respects. Lori Anna carried little Jerilyn, Chris carried baby Christopher, and Olivia played little mommy, holding Abigail and Michael's hands. Everyone stopped at the sculpture and fountain.

Lily turned to Carrie Emeline and Marcus. "The sculpture and fountain combination is beautiful and so fitting for Dad and Mom."

"You're right." Carrie Emeline nodded. "The

grounds of the hotel in Vancouver, where we stayed before the Alaskan cruise, were so beautiful, and the flowers were incredible. You should visit there someday. Mom saw the sculpture/fountain first. She thought the chiseled young couple who sat above the fountain looked so much like old pictures of her and Dad wearing the 1940s clothing, and the hairstyles were so like theirs. Mom pointed the young couple out to Dad and asked him if he remembered. I thought he would cry. Yes, Dad had remembered."

Carrie Emeline turned to Marcus and hugged him. "Thank you, Marcus, for finding the artist to sculpt the copy. As Lily said, it's so fitting on this ground near their gravesite. People who visit here can enjoy this fountain. Marcus, we need to visit in the summer when the fountain is running. I'd also like for all of us to plant a tree for Mom and Dad in the space behind the monument. I think a tree would be lovely."

"Planting a tree is a wonderful suggestion," murmured Lydia Grace. She cocked her head in closer examination of the marble couple who held hands, smiled at each other with the new-love look about their faces. "It does suit Mom and Dad."

"I like the marble monument all of you chose, too," added Carrie Emeline. "The words are appropriate for them." She read them aloud.

"Here lies:
Christopher Joseph Wright
April 14, 1913-December 28, 1998
Beloved Husband of Jerilyn Marlene Wright
Beloved Father of Lily Elaine, Kenneth Elliot,
Carrie Emeline, Lydia Grace, and
Christopher Joseph, Jr.

And

Jerilyn Marlene Wright
March 22, 1921-December 28, 1998
Beloved wife of Christopher Joseph Wright
Beloved Mother of Lily Elaine, Kenneth
Elliot, Carrie Emeline, Lydia Grace, and
Christopher Joseph, Jr.

Together in Life, Together In Death
'We know Our Redeemer Liveth'

Their souls are in Heaven and reunited in
eternity with family and friends.

"Perfect." Carrie Emeline dabbed at her eyes with her handkerchief. Other family members did the same.

"Why don't we all kneel and pray?" Chris asked his family.

Chris and Lori Anna, each holding a bundled

baby, knelt at the monument along with the rest of the family.

"Dear Heavenly Father," Chris prayed, "I can't tell my parents about these babies, so I ask You to tell them, Lord. Please tell our Mom and Dad we know their spirits are with You. We miss them, yet we are happy for them, too. We wish our parents could have met our son and daughter named for them: Christopher and Jerilyn, but they will someday. Jenna and Rebecca each birthed a baby girl this year, naming them Faith and Joy. Please tell our parents about all four babies. They'll all continue the legacy of the Wright family."

Chris lowered his head, cleared his hoarse throat, and then looked up to the Heavens. "We know Mom and Dad are reunited with family and friends, a Heavenly reunion. We know they are happy. Yes, we miss them, but we know we'll see them again. We have the promise in knowing Your Son, Jesus Christ. Thank You for loving and watching over this family, Lord. In Your name, Jesus, we pray ... Amen."

Together, the family added their Amens.

They looked up and saw a bearded old man in farmer's overalls several yards away, waving his old floppy hat toward them. Lydia Grace turned to Carrie Emeline, grabbed her arm, and said in amazement, loud enough for all the family to hear,

"It's Mr. Gabe!"

Mr. Gabe addressed the family. "The Lord offers His security for yesterday, today, and tomorrow. Leave the broken irreversible past in His hands, and step into the future with Him. The Wright family will be okay. He loves *all* of you," and Mr. Gabe vanished within seconds.

Epilogue

Eighteen Years Later

December 25, 2017

Lily Elaine Wright Demeter, now eighty-one years old, and her husband John Demeter still own their home in Russellville, Kentucky. They have four grown children, eighteen grandchildren, and eight great-grandchildren. Lily received her midwife license and to date has delivered or assisted in the delivery of fifty-one babies.

Kenneth Elliot Wright, now age seventy-five, and his wife Loretta have three grown daughters, nine grandchildren, and three great-grandchildren. They still reside in Lexington, Kentucky.

Carrie Emeline Wright McConnaughey Taylor, now age seventy-five, and her husband, Marcus Taylor, have five grown children, seventeen grandchildren, and five great-grandchildren. They still reside in Bellingham, Washington.

Lydia Grace Wright Carlisle, now age seventy-one, and her husband Jacob Carlisle still live on the Wright family farm on 31-W, and they still hold concerts around the world a couple times per year.

Their one grown son, Anthony, is now a world-renowned concert pianist like his parents. Anthony and his wife Julia reside in the Carlisle family luxury apartment home at 640 Park Avenue in New York, New York. Anthony and Julia have three school-age children at home.

Chris Wright, now age sixty-two, and his wife Lori Anna Stanley Wright, age forty-nine have five grown children, and they adopted two more children in 2005: a girl, Hannah, now age fifteen, and a boy, Nathan, now age thirteen; both full siblings. Chris and Lori Anna continue the ownership and management of Christmas Hotel and still reside in the Wright family home at 210 South College Street Franklin, Kentucky. Lori Anna has become a best-selling author.

Chris and Lori Anna's oldest child, Olivia, graduated college at the University of Louisville. She became a photo-journalist and travels the world, working for a world famous magazine. All those years working with her mother taking pictures of cancer patients at Vanderbilt Hospital in Nashville, Tennessee, spurred her interest in photography. Most of her photography assignments take place in underdeveloped countries, and many of her pictures are taken in rural hospitals and small villages. Olivia is married to Edmund Lowry, also a photo-journalist, and they have two children.

Abigail and Michael each graduated from the University of Kentucky, remained in Lexington near their Uncle Ken and Aunt Loretta and many cousins. Abigail married Jonathan Edward Spears, and they have two children. Michael married Elizabeth Anne Cunningham, and they have one child.

Christopher Joseph Wright, Jr., now age eighteen, attends college at Western Kentucky University in Bowling Green, Kentucky where his dad was graduated. His major is in business management, and he hopes one day to manage and later own Christmas Hotel. Christopher is dating Rachel Anderson, the young woman whom he hopes to marry after graduation. When Chris is seventy, he and Lori Anna intend to pass the baton for ownership of Christmas Hotel to Christopher, Jr. when Christopher, Jr. will be twenty-six.

Jerilyn Marlene Wright, now age eighteen, moved to Dayton, Ohio where her grandmother for whom she was named was born and raised. Young Jerilyn attends Wright State University Medical School and intends to become a doctor of geriatrics. She was awarded a scholarship at the renowned college and is working on campus for Dr. O'Brien in his study for Alzheimer's research. She lives near *Dayview Nursing Home* in New Carlisle, Ohio, where she works part time.

Her grandmother's life-long best friend, the widow Emma Showalter, now age ninety-six, resides at *Dayview Nursing Home*. It's at WSUMS where Jerilyn met Simon Atkins, now a pre-med student in pediatrics, and the man whom she hopes one day will propose marriage.

In May, 2000, the Wright siblings and their spouses planted the Red Maple memory tree in honor of Christopher and Jerilyn by their monument at Greenlawn Cemetery. The tree now stands twenty feet tall, and shades the monument and the sculpture/fountain. In 2006, Chris and Christopher built a bench that sits under the tree; a wonderful place for the family to reflect.

To appoint unto them that mourn in Zion, to give unto them beauty for ashes, the oil of joy for mourning, the garment of praise for the spirit of heaviness; that they might be called trees of righteousness, the planting of the LORD, that he might be glorified.
Isaiah 61:3

About Saundra Staats McLemore

Saundra Staats McLemore is a member of the American Christian Fiction Writers (ACFW) and the Ohio chapter of the ACFW. Saundra is also a member of Landmark Baptist Church in Dayton, Ohio. After thirty-three years, Saundra is recently retired as President/CEO of McLemore & Associates, Inc., a nationwide sales and marketing business she built in 1984.

Saundra's passion has always been history, and she enjoys reading historical Christian fiction. Saundra's novel *Abraham and Anna* was endorsed by two of her favorite authors: Richard Paul Evans (author of *The Christmas Box*) and Jeanette Oke (author of the *Love Comes Softly* series). Saundra has two series published: The two-book inspirational eighteenth century *Staats Family Chronicles* and the six-book inspirational *Christmas Hotel* series. Saundra is currently writing her ninth novel: *For the Love of Ali*.

Born and raised in the state of Ohio, Saundra is married to Robert, and Anthony is their only child. The other two members of the family are the cat

Charley, and the mixed-Treeing Walker Coonhound Sadie.

The new series: *The Bellingham Bay* series is still a work in progress. The first book in the series: *For the Love of Ali*, Saundra hopes to complete by the end of 2019, but it probably will not be in print before 2020 or 2021. Check her website or email her regarding new novels.

Website: **www.saundrastaatsmclemore.com**
Email: sstaatsmclemore@aol.com

Saundra Staats McLemore

Author's Notes:

It's always sad to end a series and say goodbye to characters you've grown to know and love. I first began writing the *Christmas Hotel* series in 2011. In six years, six different inspirational stories were written, but all contained the Wright family, and the family thread wove through all six books. I planned for all six books to stand alone, but if you jumped into the series in the middle, you might like to go back to the first book, *Christmas Hotel*, to see how it all began, when Jerilyn first met Christopher and his precocious five-year-old daughter Lily in December, 1941.

I'd like to review the inspiration for the first book *Christmas Hotel* and those "real people" from Franklin, Kentucky, who "visited" the six books.

Christmas Hotel was inspired by an article from January, 2008 in the *Franklin Favorite,* a newspaper in Franklin, KY. The article spoke about a diary left behind in the now razed Keystop Motel in Franklin, KY. The diary, dated 1873, possibly belonged to a young girl named C.E. Bazell from Rock Camp, Ohio. An Ohio assistant librarian traced the diary to a girl named Carrie E. Bazell who lived in Rock Camp with her parents until the late 1800s. Carrie Bazell died March 20, 1884 at the age of twenty-one, according to a brief obituary. It's amazing how a small newspaper article can stir one's heart, as this story did mine.

Regarding Dr. Beasley who "visited" all six books:
Dr. L.F. Beasley was a practicing physician in Simpson County, Kentucky from 1934 until he retired in April, 1975. He served in WWII beginning sometime in 1942. He made house calls until he retired. Dr. Beasley delivered many babies and conducted many surgeries. He died in 2011 at the age of 103. His mind was good; he drove his car until age ninety-nine and played golf into his late nineties! He did not like his given names, therefore he went by his initials L.F., and so I will not reveal his given names either. (Information provided by his daughter Barbara Beasley Smith Swearingen formerly of Franklin, Kentucky.)

Other "visitors" to *Christmas Hotel, Christmas for Lucy, Christmas Redemption,* and *Christmas Pact* were my husband Robert E. McLemore's parents, Nettie Sue Harris McLemore (currently resides in

Bowling Green, KY, and is ninety-four years old as of this writing) and James (Booker) E. McLemore (deceased). Nettie Sue's parents were Roy Harris and Josie (Mama) Harris.

In *Christmas Hotel, Christmas Pact,* and *Christmas Hotel Reunion:*
Mt. Vernon Church is an actual country church in Simpson County. My husband's great-grandfather, Bailey Peyton Harris, donated the land for Mt. Vernon Church around 1873 or 1874. Nettie Sue Harris McLemore, the granddaughter of Bailey Peyton Harris, is still a member.

In *Christmas for Lucy:*
Young Robert E. McLemore, a "visitor" to the series, grew up to be my wonderful husband of thirty-six years as of this writing. His collie, Tony, was the first dog in his memory which lived on the McLemore family farm; therefore, I decided to insert the collie in *Christmas for Lucy.* Robert was a 1970 graduate of Franklin-Simpson High School in Franklin, Kentucky, and attended the University of Kentucky and Western Kentucky University following high school. Jimmy McLemore, and my husband's late brother, was a U.S. Army veteran and he visited *Christmas for Lucy.* Jimmy has been deceased since 1990. Mr. Davidson on Morris

Street was my husband's step-grandfather on his father's side of the family. He was Franklin, Kentucky's butcher for many years.

In *Christmas Redemption:*
Judge Joe Moss James was a paratrooper in the Korean War from 1952-1955. He was the Simpson County Sheriff from 1962-1966 and later a Simpson County Judge from 1966-1977. He married Geraldine (Jerri). (Information provided by his daughter, Jan Murphree.)

Regarding Book Four, *Christmas Pact:*
I have never before written a book that portrays some events which happened in my own family, as I have done in *Christmas Pact.* My brother, Specialist Four Gerald Martin Staats, was killed in battle on the twenty-sixth of February, 1970. The events that took place in *Christmas Pact* on that day regarding Andrew and Jerry were the exact information provided for my family by the United States Army on the fateful day. Jerry was buried the day following my nineteenth birthday, and he was my only brother. March ninth was the date my father, mother, and I had been due to meet Jerry in Hawaii for R&R, so I included it in Andrew and Carrie Emeline's story. The Valentine's Day flowers were my brother's final gift to our mother. Like

Carrie Emeline, my mother refused to throw them out until the flowers were long dead.

If you are ever in the area, you can visit the grave of my brother, and many other military veterans, at Memorial Park Cemetery on North Dixie Drive in Dayton, Ohio. There is a military circle straight to the rear of the entrance of the cemetery, and Jerry's grave is on the North-West side of the military circle. God bless all our veterans.

I would also like to add that the United States Army uniform worn by the model on the cover of *Christmas Pact* is my brother's dress uniform from when he was stationed in Germany and later Vietnam. The uniform is now nearly fifty years old. My mother passed away five weeks before the release of *Christmas Pact*. Unfortunately, she did not have the opportunity to view the cover picture before she died.

Also, regarding *Christmas Pact:*
In 1922, a local Baptist church started a mission at the corner of thirty-eighth and Market Streets in Louisville, Kentucky. On March 29, 1923, the mission became known as Shawnee Baptist Church. Over the next forty-nine years, church attendance declined from four hundred to just sixty. As a last

effort, the deacons called Lonnie Mattingly, a young man from Bowling Green, Kentucky, to be their pastor. Energized with a renewed focus, Shawnee Baptist Church soon began to grow again.

In *Christmas Hotel Reunion*, we meet some more people of Franklin, Kentucky, who "visit" the story. Sid Broderson, was a County Attorney for Simpson County in 1999, which is when *Christmas Hotel Reunion* is set. (In 2017 -- the original story published by Desert Breeze Publishing) Sid Broderson is a Family Court Judge for Simpson and Allen Counties. His wife Jill Broderson is a business owner/interior decorator in Franklin, Kentucky. Also, as you learned in the other five stories, the Wright Family resides in the actual home of Sid and Jill at 210 South College Street Franklin, Kentucky. Franklin Mayor Jim Arnold and Franklin City Manager Tom Gordon visit the story.

Dr. Beasley's children all "visit" in *Christmas Hotel Reunion*: Betty, Barbara, Susan, Beth Ann, Bonnie, and John. Dr. Beasley's wife Jane "visited" in *Christmas Love and Mercy*, but she passed away in 1997. Beth Ann passed away in 2016, when *Christmas Hotel Reunion* was still an early work in progress.

Also, Chris and Liz Wright from England "visit" in *Christmas Hotel Reunion*. I have known Chris Wright since 2010, when I "met" him while he edited my first book *Abraham and Anna* and its sequel *Joy out of Ashes*. He is a Christian author of many years standing, and has since edited all eight of my books before they were sent to my publisher. I have never met him in person, as he lives in Bristol, England, and I have yet to cross the pond/Atlantic Ocean. It's on my "bucket list", though. I know him as an excellent editor and a kind and patient man. He'd have to be patient to work through my typos, errant commas, and absent or extra quotation marks!

His beloved wife Liz passed away in 2016 from Alzheimer's. They were married five weeks shy of fifty years. You might think my character Christopher Wright was named for this Chris Wright and you'd be partly correct. However, the name Christopher has always been one of my favorite male names, and the aviators and inventors of the airplane, Orville and Wilbur Wright, hail from Dayton, Ohio, my home town. Therefore, the name Christopher Wright came from a combination of both. I did ask Chris Wright from England in advance if I had his permission to name my character as such. His only comment was (and I paraphrase) "Only if he's a good sort of fellow!" Information about Liz Wright provided by Chris Wright, my editor.

The name Jerilyn Marlene Seifert was devised from three individuals. My brother's nickname was Jerry, my sister's middle name is Marlene, and a very good friend of my brother in high school was Kenny Seifert. Kenny was killed in a car crash in 1971. Now you know the history of Christopher and Jerilyn Wright's names.

It's taken me twenty years to write about the horrific disease, Alzheimer's. I dedicated *Christmas Hotel Reunion* in memory of my father William Warren Staats who developed complications from Alzheimer's, and he died July 21, 1997. I watched this man, who stood six foot one and weighed around 210 pounds, become a shell of the man he once was. It's so hard to watch a man who was a leader in his profession, and once revered by so many people, regress to infancy. While he was in the throes of Alzheimer's, I discovered one in four will have the disease by age sixty-five and one in two by age eighty-five. My sister and I suspect at least seven of our dad's nine siblings had Alzheimer's. Knowing the disease runs in families, these are chilling results for our Staats family members. Some of the events that took place with my dad and his Alzheimer's disease, especially on the Alaskan cruise, were provided by my step-mother Bertha Staats. I incorporated those events in Jerilyn's story during the cruise.

Reviews are always appreciated. If you so desire, please post an honest review at Amazon.com and Barnes and Noble for *Christmas Hotel Reunion* and the whole series. Thank you!

And the work of righteousness shall be peace; and the effect of righteousness quietness and assurance forever.
Isaiah 32:17

These things I have spoken unto you, that in me ye might have peace. In the world ye shall have tribulation: but be of good cheer; I have overcome the world.
John 16:33

Alzheimer's Information as of this Writing:

Alzheimer's Hotlines and Websites

24/7 Helpline | Alzheimer's Association
www.alz.org

24/7 Helpline: 1.800.272.3900.

24 Hour Alzheimer's Caregiver Line Alzheimer's Helpline |
https://alzheimerscareresourcecenter.com/alzhei mers-care-crisis-line/

Helpline - Alzheimer's Society
https://www.alzheimers.org.uk/helpline
Information about the Alzheimer's society dementia

Alzheimer's Foundation of America Toll-free Helpline
https://www.alzfdn.org/AFAServices/tollfreehelp line.html
www.alzscot.org/services_and_support/dementi a_helpline

Help with Alzheimer's | Caregiver Resources |
alzheimers.gov
*https://alzheimers.acl.gov/caregiver_resources.ht
ml*

All Scripture verses are taken from the KJV of the Holy Bible.

"Where Does She Go" – Poem by John E. Moss – Jamestown, KY.

Poems by Willard Thomas of Gainesville, Georgia – deceased: "My Emotions", "My Christian Faith", "Two Lives Together"

"I Know Why (and So Do You)" 1941- -performed by Glen Miller Band and singer Paula Kelly and the Modernaires – Also from the 1942 movie *Sun Valley Serenade*

"Farther Along" – Reverend W.A. Fletcher – 1911

"Precious Lord, Take My Hand" – Rev. Thomas A. Dorsey – 1932

"Silent Night" – Franz Xaver Gruber and Joseph Mohr – 1818

"Amazing Grace" – John Newton – 1779

"How Great Thou Art" – Carl Gustav Boberg – 1885

"Ave Maria" – Franz Schubert – 1825

"O Come All Ye Faithful" – Frederick Oakeley – 1841

"O Holy Night" – Aldolphe Adam – 1847

"Hark the Herald Angels Sing" – Felix Mendelssohn – 1739

"Count Your Blessings" – Johnson Oatman, Jr. – 1897

"He Touched Me" – Bill Gaither – 1963

"In the Garden" C. Austin Miles – 1912

"Suppertime" – Ira F. Stanphill – 1950

"When the Roll is Called up Yonder" – James Milton – 1893

"I Serve a Risen Savior" – Alfred Ackley – 1933

"Take Your Burden to the Lord and Leave it There" – Charles A.

Tindley – 1916

"Joy to the World" – Isaac Watts – 1719

"What a Day That Will Be" – Jim Hill – 1958

"Chattanooga Choo Choo" – Mack Gordon and Harry Warren – 1941

"In the Mood" – Tin Pan Alley Composers Joe Garland and Andy Razaf – 1938

"Sentimental Journey" – Les Brown, Ben Homer, Bud Green – 1944

"Boogie Woogie Bugle Boy" – Don Raye, and Hughie Prince – 1941

"Dancing Cheek to Cheek" – Irving Berlin – 1935

"O Little Town of Bethlehem" – Phillips Brooks – 1868

"Jesus, Keep Me Near the Cross" – Fanny Crosby – 1869

"A Long Line of Love" – Paul Overstreet and Thom Schuyler – 1986

The Lion, the Witch, and the Wardrobe – C.S. Lewis – 1950

Curious George — Hans Augusto Rey and Martha Rey – 1939

Christmas Hotel Reunion Discussions and Questions for Book Clubs

In the following questions, please either answer for yourself or try to see the situation through the eyes of a man or woman you know well.

1) What passages strike you as insightful, even profound? Is there a bit of dialogue you find funny or poignant that summarizes the Wright family?

2) Do Christopher, Jerilyn, and their children seem real or believable? Can you relate to their predicaments? To what extent do they remind you of yourself, or others, in the past or present?

3) Did certain parts of the book make you uncomfortable? Did this lead to a new understanding of awareness or an aspect of your life you had not thought of before?

4) What is the book's most important message? Why do you think the author wrote this book?

5) Is the plot engaging? Is this a plot-driven book: a fast-paced page turner? OR did the story unfold too slowly with a focus on character development? Did

you find the plot predictable? What are your thoughts about the plot development? How credible did the author make it? Was the ending satisfying? If not, why and how would you change it?

6) The fire at Christmas Hotel was unpredictable by family, friends, and guests. How well do you feel the children handled the death of their parents? If an unexpected death occurred in your family, how was it handled? Did you grieve for Christopher and Jerilyn?

7) Christopher took Jerilyn on the cruise to Alaska, knowing she suffered from dementia. Would you have taken such a trip with your spouse if he or she suffered from dementia?

8) Have you or a member of your family or a friend experienced the dreadful disease of Alzheimer's or dementia? Did you or this person turn toward or away from God?

9) Is there a particular comment by Christopher, Jerilyn, or their children which states the book's thematic concerns? Do you feel the Wright siblings and other friends and family grew and matured by the end of the story?

10) At Christopher and Jerilyn's funeral service the people sang the lyrics, "We'll understand it all by and by." Is this just meaningless comfort or a profound truth?

11) Discuss loneliness, fear, depression, trust, and other emotions felt by the Christopher, Jerilyn, the Wright siblings, and their children.

12) Do you regret the author allowed the deaths of Christopher and Jerilyn in the final story of the Christmas Hotel Series? Keep in mind that Christopher and Jerilyn were eighty-five and seventy-seven respectively in 1998. In the epilogue, in 2017, they most likely would no longer be alive on Earth. Do you think it was fitting for them to die together? Also, keep in mind, Christopher was extremely concerned he would die before Jerilyn.

13) If you've now read all six books in the Christmas Hotel Series, do you feel the author wrapped up the siblings' storylines adequately?

14) How are the struggles and events that the characters experience through their life spans, such as war (World War II and Vietnam), illness (cancer), death(due to illness or war), and loss(possessions, miscarriage, or kidnapping)

similar to the those we experience today?

15) What social, cultural, and spiritual differences and similarities do you see between the Wright family's world and our world?

> *"To appoint unto them that mourn in Zion, to give unto them beauty for ashes, the oil of joy for mourning, the garment of praise for the spirit of heaviness; that they might be called trees of righteousness, the planting of the LORD, that he might be glorified."*
> Isaiah 61:3